Finding Values

FINDING VALUES

Lyn Miller

Matador
Unit E2 Airfield Business Park,
Harrison Road, Market Harborough,
Leicestershire. LE16 7UL
Tel: 0116 279 2299
Email: books@troubador.co.uk
Web: www.troubador.co.uk/matador
Twitter: @matadorbooks

ISBN 978 1803130 309

Back cover photo by Michael at Click Photoshop, Morningside, Edinburgh
EH10 5HX.

Illustrated by Dave Hill
British Library Cataloguing in Publication Data.
A catalogue record for this book is available from the British Library.

Printed and bound in Great Britain by 4edge Limited
Typeset in 11pt Minion Pro by Troubador Publishing Ltd, Leicester, UK

Matador is an imprint of Troubador Publishing Ltd

This book is dedicated to the memory of my parents-in-law, Donald and Ida Miller.

I think that Ida would have enjoyed reading this story. Although Donald didn't regularly read fiction, he always asked about the progress of my writing. Unfortunately, my work didn't evolve quickly enough for either of them to be able to read any of the results. But I can still remember their interest and encouragement.

Part One

2007

Chapter 1

The whole story that I'm going to tell you came about as a consequence of two deaths, although I didn't know either of the deceased.

On a Friday morning in mid-March, I was struggling to concentrate on my usual office routine, typing up a valuation report for a client in Brighton. The sun was shining for the first time in days after a wet and windy spell, and I have to admit that the view from my office window was distracting me, drawing my attention away from the computer screen every few minutes. The Wedgwood-blue shade of the sky seemed to be a sign that spring had begun. The floating clouds were white, puffy and benign; a lovely change from the recent purple-and-grey variety.

My phone rang and I picked up. "Claire Ford here. Good morning."

"Claire, Anthony would like to see you. Are you free?"

"Of course. I'll be right there, Olivia."

I'll admit that I felt apprehensive. Anthony Greene, the director of Braithwaite, Crosshall & Greene, wasn't a scary character but I didn't come across him in my daily work, so a call to his office was unusual. I thought that I'd better pop into the ladies' en route. As I washed my hands after exiting the cubicle I studied myself in the mirror. Wispy tendrils of hair were escaping from the French roll I'd attempted earlier that morning. I tried to tame them back into shape, and applied a quick top-up of lipstick. Then I climbed the two flights of stairs to Anthony's suite of offices.

"Have a seat, Claire." Olivia greeted me. "He's on the phone right now but he won't be long. He was grateful that you were able to be so prompt."

I perched on the edge of a brown velvet armchair opposite Olivia's desk. The design was such that it would swallow me up and make it impossible to rise elegantly if I relaxed back into it, so I kept my knees pressed together and my feet planted on the floor.

"Any plans for the weekend?" Olivia was obviously trying to put me at ease.

"Well, I'm hoping to finally get along to the exhibition at the Hayward Gallery. I've been meaning to see it for ages; if I don't go soon it'll be over. How about you?"

"Oh, I'll be busy with a birthday party for my son. He's going to be six; you can imagine it'll be hard work amusing a group of noisy little boys."

I found it hard to envisage the immaculately turned-out PA with her soft, refined voice surrounded by a horde of grubby six-year-old boys. "Mm, I should think so. I hope it all goes well," I managed.

Then Olivia's phone buzzed and she gestured that I should go through to see Anthony.

Anthony's office was even closer to the sky than mine and, with the added height, I caught glimpses of the Thames through the south-facing windows, beyond and between the buildings opposite ours.

"Good morning, Claire. Thanks for coming up. Would you like a coffee?" Anthony guided me to an informal huddle of chairs around a low glass table.

"Yes – black with sugar, please," I requested as I chose the most upright of the seats available.

He poured coffee from a vacuum jug, handed me the cup and offered a bowl of sugar lumps and some tiny tongs. I picked out a lump and stirred it into my coffee. It looked dark and strong, as I liked it, and had a proper coffee aroma.

"You're probably wondering about the summons." Anthony smiled at me. He was a trim, silver-haired man; elegant in a dark suit with a white-and-pink striped shirt and a claret-coloured tie. My previous contact with him had been limited to polite small talk at office events. "I have a problem that I hope you can help me with. Miles White was scheduled to carry out an important valuation, but unfortunately his mother has died suddenly. His father has Alzheimer's and was totally dependent on her, so poor Miles will have to be on leave for some time, what with arranging the funeral and sorting out some care arrangements for the old man."

"Oh dear, that's tough for him. Where do his family come from?" I asked. I didn't know Miles well but was aware that he was single, and that he travelled extensively for the firm. He seemed to enjoy his foreign jaunts, and within the company he was famous for extravagantly woven stories about his experiences.

"Somewhere in Somerset, I think," Anthony replied. "Anyway, he was all set to value an important estate for me. You've been with us for a number of years now, and I know that you achieved your chartered status some time ago and have begun to carry out some independent jobs. So I feel that you're experienced enough to take over this project, and I'm sure that you won't mind a bit of travel."

"I'd be glad to help out," I replied, wondering where Anthony would send me. Miles had recounted tales from the French

Riviera and the Costa del Sol, and even as far afield as South Africa.

"Excellent. Well, here are the details." Anthony handed me a pale green cardboard-bound A4 file. "It's the estate of Murdoch Maclean. He was unmarried with no known direct descendants. His lawyers have been able to contact a great-nephew who lives in Australia, but he's not interested in taking on the house, so everything needs to be valued with a view to selling, although I'm not sure of the market for remote Scottish castles."

"Scottish?" I enquired. My dream of an exotic journey to a warm climate quickly withered.

"Yes, it's on a small island off the coast of Mull I believe."

Well, it would definitely be travel into the unknown – I wasn't sure that I'd ever heard of a place called Mull.

"Why don't you take the file and familiarise yourself with the details? I'm around all day so we can meet again later in the afternoon if you have any questions. Basically, we'll need a full inventory. Then you can value what you're able to and advise me of any specialists we'll need. For example, I think there's quite a collection of old weaponry. Also, have a chat with Olivia; she knows about the arrangements that Miles has already put in place for accommodation and travel, and can rearrange air tickets and the like." Anthony stood up and proffered his hand to be shaken; the sign of my dismissal.

I stopped by Olivia's desk on my way out. "Anthony said you'd help me with the travel and accommodation for this Mull trip," I said.

"Yes. Let me see." She manoeuvred her mouse and tapped a few keys. "OK, we should be able to transfer the car hire in Glasgow into your name, and the hotel in Oban and guest house in Mull will both be fine. All it needs is for me to book a flight for you. Miles wasn't sure how long the job would take, so he left the return flight open and the arrangement with Mrs McDonald in Tobermory is flexible."

"When am I expected?"

"You'll have to fly up on Sunday. The car is available from midday and the Oban hotel is booked for Sunday night. Miles made an appointment with the solicitor, a Mr Stewart, for Monday morning, and booked the two o'clock ferry over to Mull. Mrs McDonald will expect you from Monday night. I don't think Miles organised the boat over to the castle. I expect he was going to do that once he arrived. There's a phone number here for a Mr Archie MacTavish."

I listened to these details with increasing dismay. I'd always been a town-and-city person, and it seemed that my destination would be in the back of beyond. I needed to look at a map to assess just how bad it was going to be.

"Can you put it all together once you've booked the flight, and send it to me? I'd better have a look at this file and try to clear my desk if I'm to be away for a few days."

"Of course, Claire. I'll get straight on to it." Olivia smiled as I left her office, and I couldn't help imagining how lovely it would be to always have an Olivia in the background to arrange things and smooth one's path through the working day.

When I returned to my office I quickly brought up Google Maps and typed in 'Mull'. There was a choice of 'Isle of Mull' or 'Mull of Kintyre', so I clicked on the former. The map that appeared showed an island shaped something like a crab with its 'claws' pointing west. I could see Tobermory on the island and Oban across the water; both had been mentioned by Olivia, so this must be the place. I zoomed out and ascertained that it could have been worse; it wasn't the most distant island from Glasgow and Edinburgh, which I knew were reasonably sized cities. There were many other more remote islands to the north and west.

I decided that I should try to complete the Brighton file before lunch. Hopefully Olivia would have all of my arrangements finalised by then and I could dedicate the afternoon to researching 'Operation Mull'.

"So, you don't even know how long your exile to this *'Aylan Creegak'* will last?" Jessica asked.

I had a long-standing arrangement to meet up with my friend for Friday-night drinks in Gordon's wine bar, and I'd been explaining about my forthcoming trip as we demolished the contents of a shared cheese platter and worked our way through a bottle of Nero d'Avola. Jessica's intentional and exaggerated mispronunciation of the Gaelic name annoyed me and put me on the defensive. Not that I knew how to say 'Eilean Creagach' properly myself.

"I wouldn't call it an exile. It was a compliment to be asked to step in and take on such a complicated valuation. And I won't be living in the castle on that island; I'll be in Tobermory, the main town on Mull."

"Which is probably a small village on another island," Jessica pointed out. "Claire, I know you – you'll hate it. There will be nothing to do."

"Well, then I'll finish the job that much quicker and be home sooner."

"You'll have to wear wellington boots. Do you even own a pair?"

"No, but why will I need them?"

"Everyone knows that the Highlands are all peat bogs and heather and it rains a lot."

"Aren't the peat bogs in Ireland?"

"You'll hate it."

I had to agree that Jessica did know me well. We'd met at Oxford. Assigned to the same tutor, we'd quickly formed a habit of commiseration over various drinks once our torture by tutorial was completed. Some days it was a soothing cup of tea; other occasions required a glass of wine (sometimes several), or in the summer perhaps a refreshing glass of home-made lemonade would revive us. We'd become close friends and confidantes. After university we'd both headed to London, so it seemed natural to look for a flat together. Over the next ten years we'd shared various digs, until Jessica moved in with her now-fiancé Chris and I bought my own place.

I'd had enough of her opinions about my inability to cope in the countryside, and decided to change the subject. There was one topic that was guaranteed to distract Jessica.

"So, anyway, how are the wedding plans coming along?"

The next day I phoned my parents to let them know that I would be away on a business trip.

"Well, that sounds quite important, dear, but how will you manage out in the wilds?" Mum asked.

"I'm not going to be camping or roughing it, Mum. I'm booked into a very nice-looking guest house. It's got five stars on Tripadvisor." I'd looked it up.

"Yes, of course, but there won't be anything to do."

"I'll have the contents of a castle to log and value. I think I'll be quite busy."

My dad, a dealer in antiques, was much more interested in the job. Of course, in his imagination the castle would be full of treasures. "How old is the building?" he wanted to know.

"According to my information folder it's a common Scottish castle design; a tower house. It was built sometime in the early fifteenth century."

"And the old man was living in it until recently?"

"Yes, he seems to have been a bit of a hermit. No doubt I'll learn more about him from his lawyer and the locals once I get there."

"What an amazing opportunity. It's unfortunate that it's so remote, or I might have come to visit. You'd probably appreciate a bit of company, too; it could be lonely up there."

"I'm sure I'll have plenty of work to keep me occupied, and there will be other people living on Mull."

"Yes, but you have to admit that you're not a big fan of the countryside and the great outdoors. Theatres, restaurants, wine bars and galleries are more your preferred milieu."

I was getting a bit fed up of being so neatly pigeonholed by everyone. "Well, I'd better go and pack my wellington boots," I replied. "Jessica assures me that I'll need them." As I'd told Jessica, I didn't own a pair of wellingtons but my Chelsea boots were quite practical, and I'd take a pair of trainers. I should probably get down to packing as I'd need to be up early tomorrow. My flight was at 10.30 from Heathrow.

First I made myself a mug of coffee, then I hauled my suitcase out from the cloakroom and began to search my wardrobe and chest of drawers for attire suitable for the Highlands. I took a sip from my mug, enjoying the rich roast flavour, slightly offset by a hint of sweetness. I selected three jumpers, a few blouses and T-shirts, two pairs of jeans and two pairs of smart trousers. I removed a pile of underwear, a dozen pairs of socks and two pairs of pyjamas from my bottom drawer and put them into my case. All I needed now were some accessories and a jacket.

I tried to remember the last time I'd been in the countryside. When I still lived with my parents in my childhood home in Kent, I'd enjoyed riding my bike along the quiet country lanes and cycle paths. And I'd gone to Snowdonia on holiday with a group of friends after Oxford to celebrate our graduation. OK, that was more than ten years ago, and my holidays now tended to be city breaks, or resorts abroad in the sun. But I had a growing determination that I could enjoy the trip to Scotland. Maybe the idea excited me just because it sounded so unlike my usual habitat.

The deaths of Mrs White and Murdoch Maclean were the triggers for my journey. But my increasing sense of anticipation as I completed my packing was sparked partly by a feeling that this experience would be extraordinary, along with some satisfaction that Anthony had chosen me for the job. There was also a stubborn part of me which wanted to prove Jessica and my parents wrong. I would not only cope; I would positively embrace the adventure and enjoy living somewhere that promised to be so totally different.

Chapter 2

I sat, stationary, in the hire car for some time. First, I keyed the address of my hotel in Oban into the satnav. The journey time was estimated at just over two hours; not too bad. I studied the route and noticed that it took me along the shores of Loch Lomond. Even though I'd never been to Scotland I was familiar with the song 'The Bonnie Banks o' Loch Lomond'. I was amazed that I was going to pass somewhere famous, and partially recognised, so early in my journey. I was relieved that the airport was on the west side of Glasgow, so there would be no need to navigate through the busy city traffic. Although I'd passed my driving test in my late teens, I didn't drive frequently and wasn't terribly confident behind the wheel. I had no need for a car in London – it would be more bother than it was worth – so I'd never owned one. I relied on taxis, buses, the tube and trains, with a very occasional rental car if absolutely necessary. This was another reason for my delayed departure from the car park. I was taking a long time to study the dashboard and familiarise myself with the controls because I was nervous.

Eventually I started the engine, put the car in gear and set off without too much lurching and juddering. I was thankful that I didn't have a passenger, as my gear changes weren't exactly smooth. I followed the instructions of the mechanical voice and soon found myself crossing a major river via a long bridge. I consulted the map on my dashboard, which informed me that this was the River Clyde. Almost immediately, I left the urban surroundings behind and was immersed in deep countryside. The traffic was light and I was in no rush; I wasn't about to try and overtake anyone on the two-way road. I pottered along happily, leaving plenty of room ahead of me and giving myself space to glance at the scenery. I became aware that my knuckles were turning white, owing to the strength of my grip on the steering wheel. So, I took a moment to stretch out and wiggle my fingers, and made a conscious effort to relax my hands on the wheel.

Soon Loch Lomond was on my right. There were lots of different boats to see out on the water: canoes, yachts with sails, and speedboats. People were obviously taking advantage of a pleasant spring Sunday, although I hoped that they were well wrapped up, as according to my dashboard thermometer the outside temperature was only nine degrees, despite the sunshine. As I travelled north along the lochside the hills around me became noticeably steeper, and most had a covering of snow on their summits.

Leaving the loch behind, I was interested to see that the first town I approached had two names: Crianlarich and A' Chrìon Làraich. I knew that the name of the island I was heading for, Eilean Creagach, was Gaelic but I hadn't realised that ordinary towns would have separate Gaelic names and signage too. The road skirted Crianlarich and I began to feel the need for a break; maybe I'd find somewhere to stop in the next town. A little farther ahead I saw a sign advertising 'The Green Welly Stop'. That seemed to be a possibility, and a mile later I indicated right and pulled into a large car park by a shop, a petrol station and a restaurant.

Cold air hit me when I opened the car door, and the wind whipped my hair across my face. I was shivering as I hauled my jacket from the back seat. Thankfully I'd elected to bring my thick padded jacket, and I put it on, then walked briskly towards the shelter of the buildings. After a visit to the toilet and a cup of tea, accompanied by a sultana scone, I wandered into the gift shop. I'd realised that I wasn't fully prepared for the cold weather, but luckily there was a good stock of outdoor clothing. I browsed through the selection of hats and gloves and eventually chose a turquoise knitted beanie hat and some navy-and-turquoise gloves. I presented them at the till, paying with my credit card.

Back in the car, I turned on the ignition and checked the temperature. It was down to four degrees. I turned up the heater and shrugged off my jacket; the car would soon warm up. Deciding to put on some music to keep me company, I fished in my handbag for my mobile phone and its charger. I plugged it in and called up my stored music list. I hoped that the songs would be lively enough to keep me alert. Keane began to play as I turned out onto the road again.

Almost immediately the mechanical lady began to warn me, "Prepare to turn left." As I followed the instruction, I could see that this was a major junction. I was now heading west towards Oban, while the road straight ahead was signposted Fort William. My route wound across a moor and there was definitely less traffic now. The road descended steadily, and when I looked at the thermometer there was a resulting increase in the outside temperature. The sun was lower in the sky, blinding me at times despite the dropped visor. Luckily, the route twisted so that sometimes I was driving in the shadow of the hills, giving me respite from the glare, as sunglasses were another item that I'd neglected to pack. I got really excited when I spotted a herd of Highland cattle grazing in a field adjacent to an expanse of water which, with the help of the GPS, I identified as Loch Etive. I admired their shaggy coats and huge curved horns; I'd only ever seen them in pictures before.

At the village of Connel I reached the sea. The road turned to the south and there was another option to go to Fort William, but I kept straight on towards Oban. I was close now, and passed a large marina crowded with masts and overlooked by a stone castle. Heading down a final steep hill into the town, I held my breath as I took in the fantastic view. The town was built like an amphitheatre on the hillside around a curved bay. It had an outlook over green, hilly islands, still catching the late afternoon sun. In the town I had to follow a one-way system, almost completing a full circle to arrive at my hotel. Very thankful for the satnav directions, I steered the hired Golf into a parking space in front of the hotel, relieved to have arrived safely. It was in an amazing location, facing right onto the bay, and when I emerged from the car I was immediately hit by a distinctive and strong odour of seaweed. I stretched my back and rolled my shoulders before extracting my suitcase from the boot, then climbed the steps to the hotel entrance and reception.

"Good morning, Miss Ford. Do come in and have a seat." Mr Stewart, the lawyer, came forward to greet me and shook my hand with a firm grasp. He was a tall, thin man, and I reckoned that he was maybe around fifty. He had thinning blond hair and wore a navy pinstriped suit with a pale blue shirt. His tie was blue-and-green tartan, and I wondered if he wore it every day, or whether he'd put it on specially to meet the English visitor. "I hope you had a good journey. We're a bit out of the way here, but not quite so remote as your final destination at the castle, mind. Did you find a good hotel?"

"Yes, thank you. I was very comfortable and I had an amazing view from my room. I can't really take any credit for the booking, though, as Miles White had already chosen the accommodation. The Great Western?"

"Ah, yes. It's in a splendid location and there are plenty of big windows looking out onto the bay, allowing you to appreciate the scenery."

Because I'd arrived in the last of yesterday's daylight, I hadn't looked closely at the view until I'd opened my curtains in the morning. As I buttoned my blouse there'd been a low blast on a horn; so loud that it had made me jump. I'd parted the curtains to look out, and there was a ferry with smoke belching from its red funnel making its way past my window. It was really close, sailing between the foreshore and a green island opposite. I guessed that was the boat I'd be catching later in the day. Once dressed I'd made my way downstairs to the dining room. Despite the huge array of food on offer, I only had enough appetite for a small breakfast, as I was still feeling full after an amazing dinner of seafood the night before. As I settled my bill, I'd asked the receptionist for directions to the lawyer's office where I had my appointment. She'd advised me that it would be simplest to leave my car at the hotel and walk to Mr Stewart's office. "It'll take you about five minutes. Just follow the road round the shore into town; Argyll Street is the first one past the distillery. You can't miss it."

"Yes, I was sorry to hear of your colleague's bereavement," Mr Stewart said, bringing my attention back to the present. "But it means that we have the pleasure of your company instead."

I thought this comment bordered on the obsequious, and decided that we should move on from awkward small talk. "Well, maybe you can fill me in a little on the castle and the family," I suggested.

"Yes, we'll get down to business, then." He shuffled through a sheaf of papers on his desk, perched a pair of reading glasses on his nose and began a description of the life of Murdoch Maclean. "Murdoch was born in 1920 and initially brought up on the island of Eilean Creagach, which means 'Rocky Island' in English. There was a governess to teach him and his sister,

15

Isobel. Then at the age of ten he was sent to boarding school in Edinburgh. He served during the Second World War, and was involved in something pretty hush-hush. He never spoke about it much afterwards that I know of. Anyway, after the war he returned to live at the castle with his parents, and then took over the management of their estates on Mull when his father wasn't able to. After the old man died, Murdoch began to gradually sell off the land, and eventually all that was left of the estate was the island and Caisteal Glas – that means 'Grey Castle' in English. The proceeds of the land sales were put into a trust, with the income divided between Murdo and Isobel. That provided for his living going forward. Meanwhile, Isobel had married and emigrated to Australia after the war. It's her son, Angus, who will inherit the estate."

"Was Mr Maclean a recluse?" I asked.

"Well, some might say so. I'd say he was a quiet man who was content with his own company, but he certainly had friends on Mull, and he had visitors to the castle who came about the birds."

"Birds?"

"Aye, he was a great man for the birds. An ornithologist – quite respected, I believe. He had his own boat and often sailed to the Outer Hebrides to carry out his studies, and, as I say, other experts came to visit him. He produced a large number of sketches and paintings. I don't quite know how they'd be classified – I suppose that's up to you; whether they're art or natural history. For the last couple of years he had a live-in helper, or carer, as you'd maybe call it nowadays. He wasn't able to leave the island due to poor health and frailty, but his doctor insisted that he be admitted to the Community Hospital when he got a bout of pneumonia just after the New Year. They were beginning to look for a permanent place in a care home for him. But there's nothing on Mull, the nearest would be Oban, and Murdo was very resistant; he wanted to go home to the castle, and certainly not off the island. It was maybe kindest that he died before any further move was planned."

"So he didn't die in the castle?"

"No, ha ha, you'll not need to be looking out for his ghost there." Mr Stewart definitely giggled. I really did think that the man was a bit strange.

"Sure, and in terms of getting to the property?"

"Yes, well, we'll need to contact Archie. I've primed him to ferry you there and back daily, so we just need to let him know when you'll want to begin. Tomorrow, I'd guess?"

"Yes, I may as well get started. Will I need any keys for the property?"

"Yes. I have those here." Mr Stewart produced a very large padded envelope from a desk drawer. It made a thump as he laid it on his desk. I guessed that castle keys would be larger than your average Yale. "And Archie will help you with the generator if you need the electricity to be running."

I was speechless after this helpful comment as I'd never imagined that the castle wouldn't be attached to the grid. Was there running water? I'd better make an arrangement with my landlady to provide me with a packed lunch and a hot flask every day. There would certainly be no canteen, handy restaurants or sandwich shops to nip out to for lunch.

"Is there anything else I can help you with?" Mr Stewart enquired.

Having ascertained that I couldn't think of anything, we agreed that he would phone Archie and arrange for him to meet me at the castle's jetty at 9.30 the next morning. Mr Stewart was also keen that I should feel free to get back in touch with him if I required assistance. We shook hands again and I left his office, carrying the heavy keys in their envelope.

I checked my watch and, as I had three hours free before my ferry, decided that a cup of coffee was next on my agenda. I found a café just around the corner and ordered an Americano with an extra shot. Unable to resist my curiosity, I opened the padded envelope and tipped the contents out onto the table. There were around twenty keys. Some were dainty and intricate, and I thought would probably open a drawer or a cabinet. Others looked quite ordinary, like everyday house keys. But there was one giant. It was black with age, and I guessed it must be about twelve inches long. The handle was solid and in the shape of a thistle. The shaft was thicker than my index finger, and it had one large bit which was deeply notched. It looked just like you'd expect the front-door key to a castle to look. After I'd drunk my coffee I asked the barista where I could find a bookshop, as I thought that it might be useful to buy a map of Mull. It was easy to find the branch of WH Smith across from the harbour but they didn't seem to sell one map which represented the whole island. Three separate OS maps covered different bits of the island, and I opted for the one that included Tobermory, since that would be my base and I thought that the castle was quite nearby. I tucked my purchase into my bag with the keys and then set off back along the shore towards the hotel and my car.

The car clattered up the metal ramp onto the ferry and a man wearing a blue jumpsuit underneath a yellow safety jacket waved me forward. I manoeuvred the car closely in line with a grey minibus, as instructed. Once I'd parked, I squeezed out. There was only a small space for my door to open. I climbed the stairway up two decks, looking for a seat in the lounge next to a window. I settled down, intending to sit and enjoy the scenery, but I didn't stay there for long. Once we were under way the swell of the sea made the boat lurch and sway. This, combined with an odour of diesel and of frying food from the nearby café, brought on a sudden feeling of nausea. I quickly abandoned my sheltered seat and went to stand out on the deck. My eyes and nose began to stream in the cold air, and I was glad of my new hat and gloves. However, my stomach began to settle now that

I was out in the fresh air, so I continued to brave the elements. At least it was a dry day, and from outside I could watch the aerial acrobatics of the seagulls; squalling, airborne outriders accompanying the ship. They brought to mind Mr Stewart's description of Murdoch Maclean. He sounded interesting; different aspects of his character seemed to be quite contrasting. An outdoors man, a sailor, and active in the war; but also quiet and self-contained, an artist. I began to wonder what I'd discover at the castle. Murdoch's artwork sounded intriguing, and you never know, perhaps I'd find some explanation of his war work. Was he a spy? Behind enemy lines? I laughed to myself. If Jessica was here she'd certainly accuse me of becoming fanciful, letting my imagination run away with itself.

I noticed land approaching, the noise of the engines changed tone, and the boat seemed to alter its course slightly. A large grey-stone castle was perched on the hillside to our left; it had obviously been built originally to defend the bay. I knew it wasn't 'my castle' but seeing it sent a fizz of excitement through my veins. Tomorrow I'd open the door to Caisteal Glas; the key was in my possession. Then there came an announcement on the tannoy requesting drivers to return to their vehicles.

Chapter 3

At ten past nine the next morning I'd come to a standstill in my car, surrounded by sheep. I reckoned that I was still at least six miles from the jetty where I was due to meet Mr MacTavish. The sheep seemed to be spooked by the car and were bleating loudly. I could actually feel the vehicle swaying slightly as they barged into each other, trying to get past, bouncing the nearest member of the flock against the car. As they careered past my window their eyes met mine with what appeared to be a look of panic. It was raining; swathes of fine, misty droplets hung in the atmosphere. The sheep were wet and bedraggled, there was steam coming off them and they smelled bad, even with the window closed. Just as I thought that the flock would be never-ending, a pair of black-and-white collies came into view, rounding up the stragglers. A man walked behind them, wearing a dark green waxed jacket and a tweed cap. When he was level with the car he stopped by my door and crouched down at the window. It seemed that he wanted to speak to me, so I opened the door a crack; I'd switched the engine off and the windows were electric. When he raised his cap, I realised that he was a lot younger than I'd first imagined. He had wild, dark, curly hair and vivid blue eyes.

"Sorry to hold you up," he said.

"Yes, well, I'd better not hang about to chat; I'm late for my appointment at the jetty now. Do you move your sheep along here every morning?" I asked, thinking that I might need to set out earlier to avoid them.

I saw immediately that I'd amused him. His eyes lit up and he stifled a laugh, pretending that it was a cough. "Don't you worry; Archie will wait for you. And, no, we'll not be moving the sheep this way every day. We're bringing the ewes down off the hill to be nearer the farm for the lambing."

"Oh, I see. Anyway, I should be getting along." I wondered how he knew that it was Archie MacTavish that I was meeting. I hadn't said so.

He stuck his hand through the gap in the door for me to shake. "Grant Maclean."

"I'm Claire Ford," I responded, shaking his hand.

"Good day to you, then. I'd better not lose my flock." He straightened up, waved and carried on, catching up with the dogs.

I restarted the car and continued along the single-track road. I'd been shocked yesterday when, after driving about ten miles north from the ferry, the road had narrowed and become a single lane with passing places. I'd seen from my map that this was the case for most of the roads on Mull but I hadn't expected to have to adapt so quickly, on the way from the ferry to the island's main town! Gritting my teeth, I'd kept my eyes peeled for oncoming cars, while also trying to remember where the last passing place was. It had been a relief to arrive in Tobermory in one piece.

My instructions today were to look out for a road on my right, signposted to Croig, once I'd driven through Dervaig. From there it was a smaller road along to the jetty. So far, apart from the sheep, I'd met the school bus just as I was leaving Tobermory, luckily right beside a passing place. Farther along, a driver in a Land Rover had flashed, signalling for me to proceed, as they reversed back to the nearest passing place. I supposed that I would get used to this route if it was to become my daily commute. It hadn't only been the passing places and dodging oncoming traffic that had worried me; there were some crazy hairpin bends too.

At Dervaig I crossed a bridge between two lochs, the water flat and grey on either side. I drove on, and was beginning to worry that I'd missed my junction when I spotted the sign for Croig pointing to the right. After another few winding miles on this new road, I noticed the words 'Laimrig Glas' etched into a wooden plaque at the entrance to a small parking bay on the left. I drove the Golf into it and pulled up alongside a white Citroën Berlingo. Well, white must have been its original colour. Now it was mud-splattered and had a good scattering of rust to add to the brownish-grey hues.

The driver's door opened, releasing a waft of cigarette smoke. A burly man with slicked-back black hair and impressive sideburns, wearing a luminous orange waterproof jacket, unfolded himself from the driver's seat. If he'd been wearing different clothes I reckoned he could have passed for a 1970s Elvis Presley. He waved to me as he emerged. "Miss Ford? Archie MacTavish." He proffered his hand.

"Yes, I'm sorry I'm late. There were sheep on the road." I walked across to shake his hand.

"Oh, aye! A Highland traffic jam," he commented, laughing.

At the time I didn't understand the joke, which I later discovered referred to a humorous postcard widely sold in Scotland. But I was pleased that he didn't seem at all put out by my late arrival. I smiled.

"So, are you ready to set off, then?" he asked. "Any equipment you're taking?"

"Just this bag and my laptop," I replied. The bag contained measuring equipment (both a traditional tape measure and a laser device), dusting cloths and brushes, gloves, a set of magnifying lenses, a digital camera, and the envelope of keys from Mr Stewart. I'd also managed to squeeze in my packed lunch and thermos. I carried my laptop separately in a case that I could sling across my shoulders.

I retrieved the bags from the car, locked up and joined Archie at the top of a flight of stone steps. They led steeply down to a narrow stone jetty where a boat was berthed. I was glad to see that it wasn't too small; it had a cabin that would fit both Archie and me. It also looked clean and recently painted; in much better shape than Archie's van.

"Just be careful on these steps; they're a wee bit uneven and they can be slippy when it's wet," Archie advised, taking my equipment bag and leading the way down.

I took my time descending, holding on to the metal rail on the inside wall. At the waterside Archie waited in the boat to give me a steadying hand over the side. He stowed my bag, then began to untie the ropes tethering the boat to the pier.

"Now, do you want to wear a life jacket?" he asked.

"How long is the sail?"

"About fifteen minutes; the castle is just beyond the headland out there," he said, pointing.

I opted for the jacket at least for this, my first trip, and hoped he wouldn't be offended. He handed me a red, damp-smelling, horseshoe-shaped jacket which I put on over my head, securing the tapes at my waist while Archie gunned the engine. He neglected to wear a life jacket himself, but he did pull on a woolly green bobble hat before setting out.

"It'll be a wee bit bumpy," he warned. "The tide's coming in just now. Come in here to the wheelhouse to get some shelter."

Once we were moving, what had seemed like a gentle drizzle transformed into cold needles of rain driving into us, so I was grateful to share the wheelhouse with Archie. The boat bounced against the incoming waves as we left the shore.

"So, you'll no' ken yet how big a job this will be, how many days it will take. But dinna worry; I'm available for as long as you need me," Archie declared.

"Thank you. I might have a better idea after I've scoped things out today. I'm told you can fix up the electricity for me?"

"Aye, that shouldna be a problem."

"And is there running water?"

"Aye, once the generator is started there's a water pump attached. I've been carrying out a bit of maintenance for the old man for a while now. It's all weathertight and secure. There it is now, ahead of us."

I caught my first glimpse of the fortified tower house, perched on jagged grey rocks and surrounded by dark sea with white spray flying up from the breaking waves. The sky was leaden, adding to the gloom. I couldn't imagine why anyone would want to live in such austere surroundings.

As if he'd read my mind, Archie commented, "It doesna look that welcoming today. But sometimes it can be quite enchanting, you'll see."

I glanced at him. The word he'd used hinted at a romantic streak which seemed out of character for a seagoing handyman. Was he pulling my leg? But he looked perfectly serious as he steered the boat towards the sheltered side of the island, where I could see a small stone jetty similar to the one we'd just left.

After Archie made the boat fast we climbed up the steps, then followed a narrow, rocky path which brought us out at the side of the castle. Stopping by a thick wooden door with huge iron hinges painted black, he announced, "You'll have the keys."

"Don't we go in by the front door?" I asked, slightly disappointed not to be wielding the giant key. I began to rummage through the contents of the padded envelope.

"I've never been through it; always come in by the back door. That's the key we need, there." Archie identified one of the chunkier mortise keys, picked it out from the others and put it into the lock. It turned easily; the mechanism was obviously well oiled. "This is the ground floor. There's some storerooms and the kitchen. I'll go and get the generator running; it's in an outhouse round the back. Maybe you'll want to open the shutters to let in a bit of light."

Archie disappeared back outside. The corridor smelt musty and slightly of damp. I inched forward to where I could see a door ajar ahead of me. From the threshold I could make out a dim, rectangular halo of light at the far end of an enormous room. I guessed that this was coming in from around the edges of the shutters that Archie had mentioned, and I made my way in that direction, swearing as I bumped my hip on a bulky piece of furniture. Just as I got to the window and fumbled around for the catches on the shutter, the room was suddenly illuminated by a circlet of light bulbs hanging from the centre of the ceiling, and also several wall lights. This made my task much simpler, and I quickly unlatched the wooden shutters and folded them back into the window recess.

"If you like, I can stay to show you around, or you can explore by yourself at leisure." Archie gave me a choice as he strode into the kitchen.

I was tempted to retain his company for longer, but knew that I'd have to get used to being in the building on my own at some point, and it might be more fun to discover it for myself, at my own pace. So, I decided to go it alone. "That's kind of you, Mr MacTavish, but I think I'll manage on my own now that you've got the lights on. When will you be back for me?"

"Well, given that it's such a dreich day I reckon it'll be dark by about five, so I'd better come by at half four. Will that be all right? And it's Archie."

"Right, OK. I've got your number, Archie, so I can always phone you if I'd like you to come sooner."

"Oh, I don't think that the phone is connected any longer."

"But I've got my mobile."

"Aye, but is there a signal? A lot of the island isna covered."

Wow, I'd not considered that, and did he mean Mull or this island? It was all very well being on my own on a tiny island if I had my phone to connect me to civilisation, but I'd be truly isolated without a signal. And presumably I wouldn't have the internet either.

"Let me check." I dug the phone out from my pocket. The display showed plenty of battery, but no reception. "It might be the stone walls. Maybe it'll work outside." I was used to being cut off when travelling on the tube, where there was no reception until I came within range of a station or was above ground again.

"Perhaps." Archie sounded sceptical.

On exiting the back door I looked at the screen again – still no signal. "I'll come down to the jetty with you and try it from there." I left my bags in the kitchen and we retraced our steps to the jetty. I examined my phone again and was relieved to see two bars appear showing that I had a signal. "Yes, it's better here, so I can get in touch if I need to."

"Grand. Well, have a good day. I'll see you later."

He leapt into the boat, started the engine, unhitched the lines, and the boat moved off. I stood and watched as it dwindled in size, then disappeared into the mist. I shivered and, realising that I was getting soaked standing by the exposed pier, turned and climbed back up to the castle.

Re-entering the kitchen, I paused to take in my surroundings. It was a vast space dominated by two long wooden tables in the centre. I laid my hand on the nearest one; the wood was smooth from years of scrubbing and seemed warm to the touch. The room could have illustrated a history of cooking. The wall opposite me was dominated by a huge fireplace, and I could see a recess which would have housed a bread oven on one side of the inglenook. A massive black range occupied the space to my right. It had multiple doors, one would be for fuel, and the others varying sizes of ovens. It had six huge warming plates on the top. Next to it stood a more modern electric cooker. I remembered that my parents had owned a similar model before they renovated their kitchen to make everything sleek and built-in. The most up-to-date piece of cooking equipment was a microwave which stood on a shelf close to the window.

I felt slightly warmer now that I was indoors and sheltered from the elements. But no one had lived in the castle for three months now, so there would have been no heating on at all over the winter. The rooms would be chilly and my clothing wasn't warm enough for me to spend hours on end in an unheated castle. I strode over to inspect the fireplace, imagining that I could catch a scent of smoke. Maybe I could light a fire, then at least I'd have one warm room as a base. I peered up the chimney, wondering if it was clear of debris. But what would I use as fuel? Maybe Archie could help me with some wood, or didn't they burn peat in the Highlands? They must have had fuel in the past for the fire and the range. But unless someone had brought supplies over, there would be none on this island, which seemed to have scant vegetation growing on it. I went to examine the electric cooker. It was plugged in. I turned the knob for the front plate; a little light came on and I could feel heat rising when I held my hand above it. So, I could use the cooker as a heater in this room, and perhaps I would find a plug-in electric fire as I explored the castle.

I decided to start my reconnaissance. First, I needed to make a rough plan of the building with an estimate of the contents of each room. This would allow me to get some idea of the scale of my task and the time that it was likely to take me to compile a full inventory. I began by the back door, walking along the corridor which ran behind the kitchen. It contained a row of pegs from which many outdoor garments of various sizes hung, along with a pair of binoculars which looked powerful and expensive. Of course, they would be an important requirement for a keen birdwatcher. There were boots and shoes arranged along the wall under the coats, and hats and caps on a shelf above. Farther along I found an old-fashioned stand for umbrellas and walking sticks, which also contained a shotgun, barrel down. I didn't know much about guns; I just hoped that it wasn't loaded. The corridor led to a large room which seemed to be used for storage, mainly of cleaning and maintenance equipment: buckets, brushes, a vacuum cleaner, a stepladder, and shelves laden with old pots of paint, tins of polish, and dusters. In the centre of the floor I could see a hatch door which had an inlaid brass ring to pull it open. No doubt it would take me to a cellar; my imagination leapt to the idea of a dungeon, complete with large spiders. I decided to leave that investigation for another day. Retracing my steps to the back door, then turning in the other direction along the corridor, I found a modern toilet and washbasin. That would be useful. On my return to the kitchen I could see another door in the far corner. That opened into a spacious larder, tidy and empty apart from a row of old glass preserving jars on a shelf and a large stainless-steel American-style fridge, defrosted and bare, its door ajar. Such a modern appliance seemed out of place in a castle, but how sensible! If you lived on a tiny island a large fridge would be very practical. So, just because he lived in a castle, it didn't follow that Murdo Maclean had been completely immersed in the past. He had had good binoculars, modern plumbing and the kind of fridge that I'd love to own myself.

Next, I decided to venture upstairs. A narrow stone stairway brought me out into a corner of an oak-panelled hallway. It was extremely lofty as there was an open gallery on the floor above. Opposite me was an arched oak front door dotted with iron studs. This was obviously the main entrance which would require use of the giant key from my envelope. I resolved to try it out on another occasion. I could see a battery of switches on the wall beside the front door, so crossed the polished stone floor of the gloomy hallway and flicked the switches down. Immediately I was impressed by a bristling display of sharp objects all around the walls. There were ranks of stags' heads with magnificent antlers. The main light source was a stunning chandelier, its light reflected back from several display wheels constructed from swords and daggers. Opposite the front door was a grand staircase and behind this, underneath the gallery, were six creamy-coloured marble columns. I went to have a closer look. The marble was cool to touch and had beautiful olive-green markings. I would learn later that it came from Iona, another island off the coast of Mull. The columns guarded the twin doors to the great hall. Everything was dusty, but this room was obviously the showpiece of the castle, used for entertaining and to impress. It was also panelled in oak and had an imposing fireplace. Its decor was softer than that in the entrance hall, featuring mainly portraits and tapestries. There were also displays of silverware and china in ornamental cabinets. A magnificent dining table was placed at one end of the hall, and more comfortable chairs and sofas were grouped around the fireplace. There were jewel-coloured rugs on the floor, and velvet curtains hung by the windows. A baby grand piano was placed in a corner. I couldn't imagine how it had made its journey across to the island.

I decided to see what else was on this floor, then I'd have a break and eat my sandwiches. I found two more rooms on either side of the front door; one a cosy sitting room and the other a library-cum-study. I imagined that these were the rooms where Murdo had spent most of his time. The library was packed with volumes and there was a huge old-fashioned desk with drawers and cubbyholes. There were also display cabinets containing ornithological specimens: stuffed birds, eggs, even a couple of nests. It would take me a long time to catalogue all of the contents of this room. The living room looked quite conventional, and

I stepped in to look more closely at the paintings on display. They made a dense covering of the walls; watercolours, mainly depictions of birds. I peered, trying to decipher a signature. It was faint, an untidy scrawl, and I hadn't brought a magnifying glass up from the kitchen. But I was sure that it said, 'M. Maclean'. So, these must be Murdo's work. As I retreated from the room I was delighted to discover a portable electric fire against the wall; that would make my work in the castle much more bearable. I decided to take it with me, so picked it up and crossed the hall to the back stairs leading down to the kitchen.

As I crunched an apple, having finished off a round of tuna and cucumber sandwiches, all provided by Mrs McDonald, I began to type up my first impressions of the rooms that I'd explored before lunch. I'd take the camera when I went back up; it would be good to have some general views of the rooms to accompany my initial report.

Chapter 4

The next floor up, above the entrance hall, had five doors facing onto the gallery. Three of these opened into large bedrooms, each with a window and a fireplace. As soon as I entered, I knew that the room at the front of the castle must have been Murdo's. It contained a four-poster bed with a heavy canopy and curtains. But, although the wood and the style of the bed were traditional, the material looked modern. It was thick and heavy, a cream colour, and on it were depictions of hundreds of seabirds; some embroidered and others woven into the fabric. I didn't know much about birds, but I could tell that there were many different species represented. When the drapes were closed the person in the bed would be surrounded by wheeling and soaring birds. Adjacent to this room was a smaller dressing room which could be entered from the bedroom or the gallery. The fifth door opened into a bathroom which featured a toilet with a high wall-mounted cistern and a huge claw-footed enamel bath, but there was also a modern shower cabinet tucked neatly into a corner.

The top floor of the building was identical in its layout to the one below, with five rooms, but I discovered that each room was smaller than its counterpart beneath. Then, between the two front rooms I noticed a narrow corridor which led to a low doorway. Thankfully, I'd thought to bring the envelope containing the keys up with me. After trying a few keys, I was able to open the door and found myself on an outdoor walkway which encircled the building. This explained the smaller scale of the rooms on the third floor. The walkway was broad enough to allow two people to pass each other, its outer walls were crenelated and three feet in height. As I walked round, I noticed that the rain had stopped and the cloud was rising. I could see the whole of the island and a long way out to sea. No doubt this was the purpose of the battlements: to keep watch against possible attack, so that no surprise visitors were likely.

During the afternoon I took lots of photographs. I wanted a record of each room and the placement of its furnishings. At four o'clock I began to tidy up. I could leave most of my equipment behind but I'd need the camera and the laptop, and I decided that I'd better take the keys with me. Once I'd locked up I wandered down to the jetty, but there was no sign of Archie yet. Since the weather was now dry I was happy to wait for him there. I made a cushion by folding my waterproof jacket as protection against the cold and damp, then shuffled up to sit on the stone wall. I heard the sound of the boat's engine across the water long before I caught sight of its approach. Then I got a huge surprise when what I'd taken to be rounded rocks down by the tideline stirred and took to the water as the boat drew close. I hadn't realised that I'd been in the midst of a colony of seals. Their heads poked up out of the water as they watched Archie's approach. I pointed them out to him.

"Aye, they're inquisitive creatures," he commented as he tied the boat fast. "I'll just run up and turn the generator off, unless you've seen to it?"

I admitted that I hadn't thought about the generator and he set off up the path, leaving me to watch the watery acrobatics of the seals for another few minutes.

It was dark when I arrived back at the guest house, but there was a welcoming light on above the front door. The curtains hadn't been drawn across the lounge window yet, and lamplight spilled out over the gravelled area where I parked the Golf. On entering the front hall, I was greeted by a voice calling through from the back of the house.

"Is that you, Claire? How did you get on? Come away through to the kitchen and chat to me while I make our dinner. I'll put the kettle on for a cup of tea."

I went into the kitchen. "A cup of tea would be heavenly," I admitted.

When I'd met her on my arrival the day before, Isla McDonald had not been at all how I'd imagined a guest house landlady would be. The house was an impressive detached red-sandstone villa; its name was descriptive, Taigh Dearg meaning Red House. It sat well back from the road in a large garden surrounded by stone walls, on the outskirts of Tobermory. When I'd rung the front doorbell, I'd expected a middle-aged lady wearing a tweed skirt, pearls and a twinset to appear. Instead I'd been greeted by a tall woman dressed in denim dungarees over a thick red-and-black checked shirt. Her hair was blonde, voluminous and arranged in a sort of collapsing beehive. I thought that she was probably about the same age as me. Today she was still wearing the dungarees, but with a long-sleeved purple polo-neck jumper underneath.

"Sit down," she invited me. "Would you believe it? I've lived here all my life, but I've never been across to the castle. Tell me all about it."

So, I sat down at the kitchen table and described the layout of the castle, sipping tea from a mug as Isla chopped vegetables by the sink. "It's going to be a very big job. I hope you don't need my room back any time soon," I concluded.

"Not at all. It's yours for as long as you need it. We're still quiet for bookings; most years it gets busy from about May onwards."

"And I'll have to use the internet from here; I hope that's OK. There's none at the castle and I'll need to send a lot of information back to London on a regular basis: reports, the catalogue as it comes along, and photographs."

"Well now, I'm not sure that our bandwidth will be sufficient for that kind of thing. I'll check with Fraser when he comes back. But maybe you could ask at the library; their system might be better. Or... let me think... the estate office has a state-of-the-art computer. Grant might let you use it. I could ask him for you."

"I'd be very grateful. I can't really get my work done without a good connection."

"Don't you worry, we'll sort something out. Now, why don't you go and relax in your room or the lounge? I'm just about to pop this in the oven, so we'll eat in about an hour. I'm sure you'd like to put your feet up for a while."

I did feel tired as I climbed the stairs to my room. I suppose my day had contained a lot of new experiences. I had an urge to speak to my parents, so retrieved my mobile from my bag and plumped up the pillows against my headboard. As I sank back against them and stretched out my legs over the bed I thought about the four-poster bed that I'd discovered at the castle. Those magnificent hangings must have been specially commissioned for Murdo. I was already curious about the old man's character, and I was sure to learn a lot more about him as I studied the contents of his home in detail.

My phone had three bars of connectivity here, thank goodness. I brought up my parents' number and was soon telling my mum all about my experiences.

"So, how long do you think you'll be there?" she asked.

"Well, I'll talk to Anthony tomorrow to give him an idea of the size of the task. He might be able to spare someone else to come and help. If not, I reckon it'll take me about a month."

"A month?! You're joking."

"No, really. The castle's on four storeys, not including the cellar. There are twelve rooms, some of them huge and that's not even counting the storerooms and cupboards. It's a huge undertaking. But I was thinking, if I'm up here for longer maybe you and Dad could pay a visit. I know you'd both be intrigued by the place."

"Well, your dad's not home yet, but we'll think seriously about it and see if we can find a few free days."

"That would be great. And could you maybe pop up to my flat and water the plants? Next week would be soon enough; I turned the heating down so they shouldn't get too dried out."

"Yes, of course. One of us will see to that."

"Thanks, Mum. I'll phone again soon."

"OK, Claire. Love you."

"Love you too. Bye."

Once I'd finished talking to Mum I composed a text message to Jessica. I knew it was unlikely that she'd be home from work and free to talk right now. Once I'd sent the message I thought I should charge up my phone and my laptop. This led me to my suitcase to look for the chargers. I hadn't unpacked properly last night, so decided to do so now. My room had a chest of drawers, and lots of coat hangers in a wardrobe by the window. I managed to squeeze my empty suitcase in there too. Then I spent some time sorting out which toiletries and cosmetics I wanted in the bedroom and which were destined for the en suite. Once I'd finished I checked my watch and reckoned that dinner would soon be ready. Before I left I glanced round my room – it definitely looked much homelier now with my possessions spread about.

The previous evening, Isla had given me a choice. I could eat my meals in the dining room as a guest but would be on my own as I was the only one right now, or I could join her and Fraser in the kitchen. I elected for the kitchen and company, although I realised that I might be asked to move to the more formal arrangement if other visitors arrived. When I entered the room, Fraser was sitting at the kitchen table reading a newspaper and Isla was taking a dish of food out from the oven.

"Well timed. I was just going to call you," she said.

"Evening, Claire." Fraser folded the paper to make space for a steaming plate of lasagne.

"Hi."

"Help yourself to garlic bread, salad and Parmesan." Isla gestured to the dishes on the table. Once we'd all filled our plates and started to eat she asked Fraser about the internet.

"Aye, I think you'd find it a bit slow. It's fine for simple messages but photographs would be stretching it. I'll give Grant a ring after dinner and see if you could use his office. It would probably be OK in the evenings or at the weekend."

"Thanks, that would be great. This is delicious, Isla."

Next, Isla produced coffee and home-made shortbread. I felt I was being spoiled; I didn't really cook. At home I usually just heated up ready meals during the week. If anyone asked me, I'd say that I tried to do proper cooking at weekends. But the reality was that I was seldom at home; usually I'd be out on Friday and Saturday evenings, and then maybe have a brunch date on Sunday or lunch with my parents. Occasionally I held a dinner party but I hadn't got around to organising that yet this year. I took my coffee through to the lounge and switched on the TV. It seemed to be showing a news programme but the language was incomprehensible. I was hunting for a remote to try and change the channel when Fraser appeared.

"Oh aye, it's on Alba. I was watching the news earlier."

"Do you speak Gaelic?" I asked.

"I can do, but in practice I don't very often. I like to keep my ear in, though, so that's why the TV's on that channel. What would you like to watch?" He'd produced a remote from a shelf beside the fireplace.

"Oh, anything, really."

"I'll give you this, then, and you can look for something. Grant said he'd come by later for a dram, maybe in half an hour or so."

I must have looked blank.

"About the internet?"

"Oh yes, of course, thanks." I flipped through a few channels and settled down to watch *Mastermind*. I didn't expect to know many of the answers on the specialist subjects, but I liked to earn a respectable score on the general knowledge questions.

I was congratulating myself on beating the on-screen contestant when the door opened again. Fraser came in followed by another man. I recognised my shepherd acquaintance from that morning.

"Hello again," he greeted me as he entered the room.

I turned the television off.

"Oh, I didn't know that you'd been introduced." Fraser seemed puzzled.

"We introduced ourselves during a sheep jam this morning," I explained.

"Aye, after causing you a delay it will be good if I can redeem myself and help with the internet." Grant seemed to be teasing me again.

"You'll have a whisky, Grant. What can I offer you, Claire?"

I asked for a glass of white wine. When Fraser left to get our drinks, I explained the difficulty with sending my data to London.

"I don't see any problem with you coming by the office, especially if you bring a laptop. I'm not always there, though, so I'd have to get you a key."

"That's very good of you."

"Not at all. I was very fond of Murdo, and this will be helping him too, in a way."

"Yes, I suppose so."

"So, when would it suit you to come and see the set-up?"

"Really, as soon as possible. I've already got lots I could send and I'll be starting on the catalogue itself tomorrow."

"Well, how about first thing on Thursday morning before you cross over? I can have a key made tomorrow, show you the ropes on Thursday, and then you can come and go as you please."

"That should work. I'll just arrange to meet Archie later that day. I've already put back our time for tomorrow so that I can phone my boss from here first thing in the morning. The mobile reception on the island's not great."

"That's fine, then. Isla or Fraser can give you directions to the office. It's off the same road that you take to Dervaig. Ah, good man. I could murder a dram."

Fraser had reappeared with a tray of drinks, followed by Isla. My second evening on Mull turned out to be very sociable as we chatted together over our drinks.

"So, Claire, have you visited Scotland before?" Grant asked.

"No, never. I grew up in Kent, then went to Oxford to university, and I've been based in London ever since."

My companions asked a few questions about my background; enough to seem interested but not to a degree that became intrusive. They also told me a little about themselves and about the island. By the time I went to bed that night, although I still felt like a stranger, a real fish out of water, I had a warmer glow too that wasn't just from the wine I'd drunk. People here seemed to be genuinely friendly and helpful – maybe I wasn't going to be too lonely, even if I did have to stay for a month.

Chapter 5

My days on Mull soon began to fall into a pattern. After breakfast on Wednesday morning, I spoke to Anthony Greene before I left for the island. He didn't sound at all surprised by the length of time that I estimated I'd need for the job. He managed to convey a measure of sympathy, agreeing that I'd probably be away from London for at least a month, but was also quite clear that he couldn't spare anyone else to come and help. When I rang off I realised that I'd been naive. Anthony had always known the full extent of the project; he'd just been coy about giving me any timescale for the trip. But then again, I hadn't really asked.

I decided to tackle the castle from the top down. This was mainly because the rooms on the third floor were smaller and emptier. I felt that it would appear that I was making good progress when I could tick off five rooms and one completed floor quite quickly. I also thought that it would help me to develop a systematic way of working before I dealt with the more challenging rooms; hopefully by then I'd find a good rhythm and be more efficient. The drawback to this plan was the lure of the battlements. They seemed to beckon to me, and I'd find myself taking regular breaks 'for air'. The view never seemed to be the same twice, even in one day. The light and cloud formations were always changing, with a corresponding shift in the colours of the sea. The wave patterns altered with the wind and the tides, and I loved to watch the spray flying up when a larger wave hit the rocks. I kept a lookout for the seals, and even began to notice the seabirds wheeling around the tower house. There was bound to be a book in the study that would allow me to identify the different species. I was beginning to appreciate Archie's description of the castle and the island as 'enchanting'.

On Thursday morning I set off for Grant's office, following directions from Isla. I took my usual route towards Dervaig, then when I drew level with a little loch on my left, Loch Carnain an Amais, I saw an entrance on the opposite side of the road that I'd previously driven past. Turning right, I bumped over a cattle grid and immediately noticed that the sheep were roaming freely with no fences in sight, so they could easily wander onto the road. I continued cautiously and skirted slowly around a couple of animals grazing by the edge of the narrow track. They looked up and seemed to gaze at me suspiciously. I wondered if they were part of the flock that I'd encountered two days ago. I continued driving for a few minutes, then a drystone wall appeared on my right. A few hundred yards later I reached a gateway and a set of double wooden gates. There was a sign – 'Fearann Soirbheachail' – on one of the gateposts. I stopped and got out of the car to open the gates, drove though, then stopped again to go back and close them. As I was returning to the car I heard a shout and, looking ahead, saw Grant waving to me from the door of a small white bungalow just up the driveway on the left.

"Hi, Claire. Just drive up and park by my van," he called.

I could see the back of a silver-coloured Hilux beyond the building, and found a parking bay with plenty of space for my car alongside. I parked the Golf and walked back to the office. The door was ajar and I was met by an aroma of coffee wafting towards me.

"Would you like some coffee? Or has Isla filled you up sufficiently?" Grant held aloft a glass jug from a coffee machine.

"I have been well fed, but an extra dose of coffee at this time in the morning can't go wrong. Black with one sugar," I directed.

"Here you go. Have a seat."

I sat beside a large office desk and accepted the mug that he gave me. The room was square in shape. Most of one wall was taken up by a window which looked out over the moor towards a stretch of water, with mountains beyond receding into the distance. There was a detailed map, I presumed of the area, and several colourful graphs attached to a board hanging on the wall opposite the desk.

"So, this is the hub of the estate. It used to be a house for one of the workers, but he got married and moved away to the mainland, and I decided that I needed more space for an office than just a corner of my dining room."

I felt awkward; I'd assumed that this was Grant's house. I hoped I wasn't blushing, because unless he was a mind reader, he couldn't know my mistake.

"My house is farther on up the road." Maybe he was a mind reader. "This is just two rooms, with a bathroom and a kitchen. I turned the lounge into this office and I use the other room for storage. Now, somewhere I have your key." He rummaged around in a pile of papers on top of his desk and eventually produced a small white envelope which he handed over to me.

"Thanks."

"There's no security alarm to worry about and you can make yourself at home if I'm not here. The kitchen is through there for coffee, and the toilet is on the other side of the hall. Now, if you put your laptop on I'll give you the codes for the Wi-Fi and we can check that it all works OK."

I quickly connected and was able to demonstrate to Grant that I was up and running.

"That's grand. I was just thinking, I can bring through a wee table and a chair and set them up for you over there in that corner so you'll have your own space."

"That's very kind." I was beginning to feel awkward about creating extra work for Grant.

"Well, it's probably best if you're not sharing my desk and maybe upsetting my papers. I don't have much of a system, but I usually know where to put my hand on things."

With that explanation I realised that it actually suited him better to give me my own workspace, so I could relax again. "Well, thanks again, Grant. I'd better be on my way; don't want to keep Archie waiting for too long at the pier."

"I'll walk down and get the gate for you, save you hopping in and out of the car. My mother was keen on horticulture, and she made a garden in this area by the houses. That's why we have to keep the sheep out: otherwise they'd munch all the plants."

"Yes, of course they would. Well, thanks again and I'm sure I'll see you soon."

I went to my car and Grant walked ahead of me to see to the gate. He waved as I drove though. *He seems to be an affable sort*, I thought as I set off again across the moor, on the lookout for wandering sheep. I imagined that it would be pleasant working alongside him.

By the Friday evening I'd completed my inventory and photographs of the third floor of Caisteal Glas. Most of the furniture and objects were functional and of little value. But in one room I'd found a mahogany wall clock which I thought was Victorian. If it could be restored to working order it might be worth around five thousand pounds. My other big discovery was in the same room. It was an oil painting; a portrait of an elderly man wearing breeches, a high-collared shirt and a cravat.

From the condition of the painting and the clothing of the subject I guessed it was from the early nineteenth century, and its style and composition made me wonder if the artist might be Henry Raeburn. I couldn't find a signature, but perhaps after cleaning it would emerge. In his day Raeburn had been the 'must-have' portrait artist in Scotland, and many prominent families had given him patronage. As they owned estates and a castle, Murdo's family must have been wealthy and important, and so might well have commissioned a work from Raeburn. If I was correct the painting could be worth tens of thousands of pounds. But obviously it would need to be carefully studied, cleaned and restored, and have expert authentication.

When Archie tied up the boat by the car park on Friday evening I thanked him for the ferrying service that week. I'd already told him that he was likely to be helping me for quite a few weeks. He'd seemed relaxed about it.

"Aye, I reckoned as much. But that's no trouble to me, Claire. I can work around the boat trips and fit my other jobs into the time."

I asked him about his other work.

"I've been helping Fraser – you ken, Isla's man? We're refurbishing a cottage for holiday lets. He's mainly doing the joinery work: a new kitchen, windows, fitted wardrobes. I've been tiling this week, then I'll be on to the painting. So, as I said, I can fit that in around you."

I'd known that Fraser was a carpenter, but not that he and Archie worked together. And, although I hadn't met many people on the island yet, it seemed to me that everyone knew each other. I had hoped that I'd be able to persuade Archie to take me to the island on Saturdays too, but in contrast to his usual relaxed demeanour he was firm that that wouldn't suit him at all, even if Mr Stewart was willing to pay overtime for working at the weekend. I decided that I'd just have to spend the weekends at the estate office, sending all of my data back to London. I mentioned this plan at dinner on Friday evening.

"Oh, surely you'll not be working seven days a week? This isn't London, you know. You don't need to keep city hours around here," Isla chided me. "I'm going over to Oban on the ferry tomorrow. Why don't you take a break and come with me; have a look around the town?"

I was tempted.

"I can tell you why Archie won't work at the weekends," Fraser offered. "It would interfere with his fiddling."

I must have looked puzzled.

"He plays the fiddle – the violin. Most Friday and Saturday nights he'll be fiddling, sometimes locally, but farther afield too; other islands and on the mainland."

"Oh. At weddings and dances?"

"Aye, all kinds of occasions. Sometimes it's just him, but often he's with a band. Next time he's playing nearby we'll have to take you along. D'you ken if there's a local gig coming up soon, Isla?"

"I'm not sure, but you or Claire could always ask him, since you both see him on most days of the week."

"Yes, he was telling me that you're renovating a cottage together," I said to Fraser.

"Aye, it's coming on, and I've another contract after this one. It keeps me busy."

"But really, he prefers making furniture, if he could earn a steady income from it," Isla added.

"I imagine that people really love handcrafted pieces, but they're not affordable for most of us," I said.

"No – thank God for IKEA," Isla agreed. "Even though I love your stuff, Fraser."

"Do you have a workshop?" I asked.

"Aye, Isla and I share a studio down near the harbour and there's a workshop in behind."

"Do you make things too?" I asked Isla. I was certainly discovering a lot of hidden talent in my new acquaintances.

"Textiles," she replied. "I'm a weaver. My loom's down at the studio."

"Wow, I'd love to come and visit sometime."

"Well, we'll probably both be working there on Sunday, so why don't you pop in then? And how about tomorrow, are you going to join me?"

"Yes, why not?" I replied.

On Saturday morning I set out with Isla on the reverse of Monday's journey: by car, then a ferry to Oban. As we travelled, Isla intimated that she had several chores to carry out, and that Fraser had encouraged her to stay out in town for dinner as a treat and a break from cooking. I was invited to join her. So, once we had driven off the ramp from the ferry, she pulled over onto the side of the dock to let me off, and pointed out a sign farther down the pier.

"There's the fish restaurant I was telling you about. It opens at 5.30; that's plenty of time to get a bite to eat and be on time for the last ferry."

"OK, I'll see you then," I said, clambering out from her car.

After waving her off, I looked around. There was a brisk wind blowing in from across the bay. The water slapped against the pier wall beside me, and gulls coasted lazily in the air, following the currents with wings spread wide. I could see a round stone tower on the hill above me. Isla had explained that it was a ruin but worth the climb to enjoy the view. I began walking in that direction and was soon out of breath as I followed direction arrows up steep, winding streets. When I reached it, I found that McCaig's Folly was only a shell. Shaped like a mini Colosseum, it had a double layer of arches with amazing views over the town and the bay, out towards Mull. I wandered around the gardens, but despite the glow that I'd gained from my trek up the hill I quickly began to feel chilly and decided that a tour round the distillery might be a good way to warm up. I'd walked past it during my short exploration of the town on Monday, and began to retrace my route down the hillside into the town, looking out for the distinctive grey-and-black stonework and the red chimney to guide me.

I wasn't a whisky drinker; wine was my usual tipple. But the tour was interesting and I felt much warmer as I sipped my free 'dram' in the visitor centre. The fiery liquid burned as it travelled down my gullet and I had to make an effort not to cough, taking careful deep breaths. I didn't want to offend my tour guide or to be a source of amusement for my fellow tourists. Once I'd successfully drained my glass, I realised that it was almost time to meet Isla at the fish restaurant. I floated along the street towards the pier. The whisky had gone straight to my head.

The next morning, I set off walking from the guest house down the hill into the centre of Tobermory. Like Oban, the town was set in tiered streets, like an amphitheatre on the hillside curving around the bay, but on a much smaller scale. It was a bright, sunny day, and this helped to show off the vivid colours of the painted houses along the seafront. A church bell was ringing nearby, competing with mewling gulls and the clink of halyards against yacht masts in the harbour. I'd driven through the town a couple of times, but now I took my time, peering over walls into gardens where spring bulbs were in bloom, and examining window displays in the shops as I passed.

I found the McDonalds' studio at the side of the harbour. A large picture window revealed a display of small pieces of furniture. There was a sleek, long-backed rocking chair and two coffee tables; one still had bark-like material round the edges and the other was made from assorted woods of different colours and grains. Beyond this, in the interior of the space, I could see Isla sitting at her loom. A bell pinged as I opened the door, and she looked up.

"Hi, Claire, welcome to the studio."

"Hello. I don't want to disturb you now that I know how precious your working time is." Isla had told me about her weaving while we were eating dinner in Oban. It was mainly a winter occupation as the guest house kept her very busy from Easter until October, but she still had a few orders that she wanted to complete before the tourist season began. "What are you working on just now?" I came closer to see.

"This is a bespoke tartan for a small hotel on the island of Colonsay. They've chosen very muted colours to reflect the landscape. You can see the mossy green here and some lilac for heather, with some grey and very pale blue to represent the sea and the sky. They want to use it for upholstery, blankets and cushion covers. I've already sent them several bolts, but their tourist season is the same as ours, so they'd like the order completed as soon as possible."

"And is Fraser working too?"

"Aye, he's in the back. He has the doors shut to keep the sawdust out from this area. You can go through."

I pushed through a well-sealed double door. At once I smelled the fresh scent of cut wood. Fraser was using sandpaper to polish the top of a small chest of drawers. He stopped and pushed his goggles back when he noticed me.

"Hi, Fraser. I just love that rocking chair in the window. Do you make most pieces to order, or do you just get an idea and run with it?"

"A bit of both. If I've no paying work on the go I make what I like, but I do get commissioned work. In the summer people pass by the studio and wander in. I have a catalogue with examples of my work here in the studio and online, so folk will think about the idea and contact me later."

"So, will you ship pieces?"

"Aye, or sometimes people like the excuse of coming to collect their order to make another visit to the island. A lot of visitors return to Mull many times."

"So, in the summer you'll be around the studio most of the time and do the construction work in the winter?"

"Aye, Isla and I generally work here at opposite times of the year. But it means that we can usually man the shop by ourselves; saves on wages. And I think that buyers appreciate dealing with the craftworkers directly. I'm sure we make more sales that way."

"Well, I love your stuff. But I don't want to hold you up, so I'll head off now."

"Bye, then. Are you off up to the estate office?"

"Yeah, I'll probably spend most of the rest of the day there. See you later."

I waved as I retreated out of the workshop. Then I quickly said goodbye to Isla too, trying not to break her rhythm. The loom was clacking as I left the studio. I was hugely impressed by the quality of both of their work. It made me wish that I had a gift for something creative.

Chapter 6

Archie, who usually struck me as a talkative man, seemed quite reticent and shy when I asked him about his fiddling on the Monday morning.

"Aye, it's just a wee pastime."

I tried to draw him out, enquiring more about his performances over the past weekend.

"Friday, we were in one of the pubs in Oban. It was a work's do. Then a wedding dance on Saturday down by Inveraray."

"And will I get a chance to hear you play? Is there a local gig coming up soon?" I asked.

I was sure that there was a hint of redness building up on his cheeks and ears, the only parts of him that I could easily see, as we were both well wrapped up in hats and scarves against the wind.

"The weekend after Easter there's a ceilidh at Craignure. It's a charity dance for the lifeboats. I'm sure I could get you a ticket if you'd like?"

"Yes, I would, and maybe Fraser and Isla would come with me. I'll ask them and let you know."

He nodded.

The clocks had changed to British Summer Time at the weekend, so for my second week on the island it stayed light for longer in the evenings and it still wasn't dark when I arrived back at Taigh Dearg for dinner. I'd moved down to the second floor of the castle and was making progress with the bedrooms, aiming to catalogue the two rooms at the rear of the building this week, and move on to Murdo's room after that. In the second bedroom I found two carved wooden boxes tucked in right at the back of a high shelf in the wardrobe. The carvings were of wading birds in tall reeds; maybe herons, I thought. The boxes had no locks, and when I opened them each was filled to the brim with a jumble of jewellery. A quick rummage through gave me the impression that there were some valuable pieces mixed in with costume jewellery. It was going to take me some time to assess, and so I decided that the only way for me to keep up with my schedule was to bring the boxes back to the mainland with me on Friday and work on them over the weekend.

On Saturday I slept in later than I'd intended, but it still seemed to be very dark. When I opened the curtains I discovered why: the sky was grey and glowering, and rain fell in sheets. I could hear the wind howling round the eaves of the house, and I was very glad not to have to cross to the island today. It would be a good day to stay indoors and examine the jewellery more thoroughly. After showering, I went down to the kitchen. Rain lashed against the window and the room was empty. I found a note on the table; it was from Isla, asking me to help myself to whatever I'd like for breakfast and lunch. She and Fraser were at the studio. I peeled and segmented an orange, popping the juicy fruit into my mouth and licking my fingers. Then I made toast, spreading it with butter and honey, and drank a mug of tea.

When I returned upstairs, I prepared for work. I unfolded a black cloth that I kept for use as a photographic background and spread it over the end of my bed. Then I collected some polishing cloths and small brushes, and my magnifying lenses. Each piece of jewellery needed to be cleaned, numbered, examined, described and photographed. I worked for an hour and then went back downstairs to make coffee. Taking my mug through to the lounge, I found a copy of yesterday's newspaper, which I flicked through, browsing for articles that caught my interest.

My day passed peacefully; I continued my cataloguing, with additional breaks for lunch and a cup of tea in the afternoon. By the time Isla returned to make dinner I only had a few more pieces to assess.

"Do you not need a bit of air? You've been cooped up in here all day," she commented after I'd described my progress.

"Maybe it's the townie in me but I've been quite happy to avoid all that weather out there," I admitted. "And I've achieved a lot. If I go along to the office tomorrow I can send all of this down to London and I'll still be on schedule."

"But all work and no play... it isn't good for you, Claire."

I didn't like to say that there wasn't much else for me to do. "Maybe I'll go into town this evening for a drink. Is there a pub that's friendly?"

"Aye, there are a couple. Fraser and I will probably be going to the Mishnish ourselves. You're welcome to join us if you'd like. They often have some music on a Saturday."

"That would be nice, but I don't want to intrude on you and Fraser."

"Och, wheesht. We're an old married couple; we don't need to be huddled up together all the time. We like to be sociable."

So, after dinner we donned our waterproof jackets, pulled up our hoods and set out for the pub. It was cosy, with a welcoming peat fire, and I enjoyed listening to a guitarist playing some light classical music mixed in with folk tunes. I even surprised myself by ordering a whisky and enjoying it.

On Sunday I drove through the wandering sheep up towards the estate office. When I arrived at the gate there was a small, curly-haired girl climbing on it. Yesterday's bad weather seemed to have worn itself out and the day was bright and sunny, but there was still a bracing wind blowing. The girl was wearing a bright yellow anorak and a cream-coloured bobble hat, but wisps of her hair had escaped and were whipping around her head in the breeze. I didn't have much experience of children but I thought she looked about five years old. I stepped out of the car.

"Hello," I said.

"Hello. Are you here to see my daddy?"

"Is that Grant?" I guessed.

"Yes. My name is Laura Maclean and I'm six years old."

"Hi, Laura. I need to come through the gate. I'm going to work in the office."

She looked at me doubtfully.

"My name's Claire and your daddy said it was OK," I tried.

She slowly climbed down from her perch. "I'll get the gate for you," she offered.

By the time I got out of my car in the parking bay she'd caught up with me.

"Would you like to see my lamb?" she asked.

"Your lamb?"

"Yes, it's a wee baby one that lost its mummy and we've got to give it milk in a bottle. You can give it some if you want."

"Well…" I wasn't sure how to respond. I was wondering who was looking after the little girl – shouldn't she be under some sort of supervision?

"Come on, it's up in the barn. Catriona's there."

Maybe this was her sister, or someone who'd know where her mum and dad were.

"OK. I'll come with you." I decided to deliver Laura to this Catriona person.

We walked on together, up the track beyond the office, Laura skipping at my side. The rough road climbed a hill for a few hundred yards, then when it levelled out I could see a collection of buildings ahead: two large houses and a collection of outhouses that were probably stables or barns.

My companion chatted as she skipped. "My daddy's very busy with the lambing. I've hardly seen him since I got here," she said.

"Oh, do you not live here all the time?" I asked.

"Oh, no. I live in Edinburgh with my mummy. I just came here for my Easter holidays."

"Oh, that's nice."

"Well, it's not *very* nice, because Mairi went straight away to play with her friend Fiona and left me all on my own with no one to play with. And Daddy's busy."

"I see."

"And Catriona's here to look after me, but she isn't fun like my friends…"

Just then a teenaged girl appeared at the door of one of the barns. "Laura, there you are! Where did you get to? And who's this?"

"Hi, I'm Claire Ford." I introduced myself. "I guess that you're Catriona. I met Laura down by the gate. I'm here to do some work in the office."

"Oh, hello," Catriona greeted me, then turned to scold Laura. "Laura, you really shouldn't just wander off. But it's OK as long as she doesn't go out of the gate," she clarified to me.

"Claire wants to see the baby lamb," Laura announced, not at all put out by Catriona's rebuke.

"Well, I might as well now that I'm here," I added.

We all went into the barn and Laura led me to a hay-strewn pen with a heat lamp glowing red over it. The lamb was the size of a small dog; creamy white with a black face. It began to bleat excitedly as we approached. I put my hand down to stroke it;

it felt warm and very soft. It quickly turned its head and began to suck strongly on my fingers. I wasn't sure that I liked the sensation; its tongue was rough, and when I retrieved my hand, my fingers were covered in slobber. I tried to wipe them dry on a tissue I found in my pocket.

"See, it's hungry," Laura observed.

"It already associates people coming in with food," Catriona explained. "But it's not due its next bottle just yet. Anyway, we'll need to warm up the milk first."

"I think we should do that." Laura was hopping up and down.

"OK, let's go up to the house to get the milk and Claire can get on with her work," Catriona suggested.

"I'm going to call it Lulu," Laura announced as we left the barn.

"That's a good name," I said. "Is it a girl?"

"Yes, she is." Laura's reply faltered slightly; I guessed that she wasn't entirely sure.

Catriona shrugged.

"Well, Lulu it is," I said, waving goodbye as the girls headed for one of the houses and I retraced my steps back down the hill to the office. My first priority was to wash my hands to rid them of sheep slobber, then I'd get the coffee machine up and running.

Fuelled by coffee, I whizzed through my work and was almost finished when the office door opened and Grant appeared. He looked a bit rough around the edges; his curly hair more unruly than usual, dark stubble on his lower face, and his eyes rimmed with red. His clothes looked decidedly grubby, and I was sure I could see a dark smear on his lower left trouser leg. I didn't like to imagine its provenance. His arrival also brought a strong animal smell into the room; sheep, I presumed.

"Hi. I hear you're busy with lambing."

"Aye, you could say that. There's not too many left to drop now, though." He went through to the kitchen and reappeared with a mug of coffee. "You've got the hang of the coffee machine, I see."

"Oh yes, I need it to get me going in the morning."

"I gather you met my youngest. I hope she wasn't a nuisance."

"Oh no, she introduced me to Lulu the lamb."

"Is that what she's calling it? She's at a bit of a loose end, I'm afraid. Her sister still has friends on the island, but Laura was only two when she left and so she hadn't made any friends of her own here. I'll have more time to spend with her by the end of the week. Catriona's quite good with her really, and Mairi will be around some of the time."

"*Is* it a girl?"

"What?"

"The lamb."

"No, but don't worry, we won't tell Laura. She's not too impressed by boys at the age she is just now, and she doesn't need to know. By the time she's back in the summer it'll be just another sheep in the field."

"Well, I'm finished here for now, so I'll leave you to get on in peace." I'd been logging off and packing up as we chatted.

Grant was perched on the edge of his desk, cradling his coffee cup, with his long legs stretched out in front of him. "Aye. I was wondering. Next weekend's Easter. I wondered if you'd like to come on a trip with us?"

"A trip?"

"Aye, it's kind of a tradition; you could say a pilgrimage, not that we're over-religious. We've made it a habit to go across to Iona on Easter Sunday. The abbey's very famous and attracts a lot of visitors; I'm sure you'd find it interesting. The island itself is also worth seeing."

"That's a kind offer, but I don't want to intrude on a family day out."

"You wouldn't be; it's very relaxed, and Laura's already taken a shine to you."

I wasn't sure what to say. The idea of a day out and a visit to Iona was appealing, but I wasn't used to the company of children. I was an only child, none of my cousins had produced any children yet, and none of my friends had them either. If I was honest, I'd probably prefer to make the journey by myself, then I could take my time and follow my own agenda. But Grant seemed good company, and I could always revisit if there were things that I wanted to spend more time on. "Well then, thank you, I'll come," I decided.

"That's grand; we'll pick you up from Isla's about nine. Though maybe we'll bump into you again before then."

"OK, I'll see you then. Bye for now."

As I drove to Tobermory I decided to go exploring rather than back to the guest house. I was sure that I could buy a sandwich in the village where the ferry came in, and maybe I'd have a look at the castle there, a big cousin to my own castle. I enjoyed the leisurely drive down the coast; it had spectacular views out over the water to the mainland. By the time I arrived in the village I was hungry, stomach growling despite Isla's extra-large Sunday breakfast. I spotted the Craignure Inn, parked my car and settled in the bar with a glass of white wine while my sandwich was being prepared.

"Do you know if the castle's open today?" I asked the barman when he delivered my food.

"Not this early in the season, I dinna think – maybe after Easter," he replied. "But you can walk around the grounds; that's free of charge."

"Thank you, I'll do that." I found a *Sunday Times* in a rack on the wall and flipped through it while chewing on my smoked salmon sandwiches.

There was a long drive out to the point where Duart Castle stood. It had a commanding position looking out over the bay, and had obviously been built for defence. There were cropped lawns around it, and paths leading walkers down to the craggy rocks by the sea. To celebrate the millennium an enclosed area had been planted with native trees and plants. They were still small – saplings, really – but in years to come it would make a substantial wood. I explored, taking in the views out over the sea and back to the mainland. It was all very grand and impressive, but strangely I found the surroundings to be quite domestic compared to the stark, rocky outcrop that I'd grown accustomed to at Caisteal Glas.

Chapter 7

At five past nine on Sunday morning a dark red Range Rover drew up in front of the guest house. I'd been looking out for Grant and the girls from the lounge window, and was ready to leave. I called goodbye through to Isla in the kitchen and left by the front door, crunching across the gravel on the driveway to the passenger side of the vehicle.

"Hello. Happy Easter," I greeted them all as I hauled myself up into the seat.

"Hello, Claire. This is my big sister Mairi." Laura was leaning forward between the front seats so that her head was between me and her father. Her dark curls had been gathered into two high bunches which swung above her ears.

"Laura, sit back down and put your belt on. Let Claire get settled in." Grant tugged lightly on the bunch of hair nearest to him as he directed her to return to her car seat.

When I glanced back to smile at Laura and introduce myself to her sister I was struck by the resemblance between Laura and her dad. Mairi, on the other hand, had hair that was almost white-blonde and her skin looked very creamy and pink next to Laura's more olive complexion. She did have the same unruly curls as her dad and sister, though. She smiled in reply to my greeting. After some fumbling, Laura managed to buckle herself in safely. I fastened my seat belt and Grant swung the vehicle out onto the road.

"So, it'll take us about an hour and a half to drive to the Iona ferry," he began to tell me.

"But, Daddy, you've got to stop on the way. We always do," Laura interjected.

"Yes, Laura. I was just about to explain that to Claire." He smiled at me. "Another tradition. We have to stop off at a certain hill to roll their eggs."

"Eggs?"

"Hard-boiled eggs. They've painted them for Easter."

"Yes. Look, Claire. These are my eggs." A cardboard egg box was thrust between the seats. "Show her your eggs, Mairi," Laura instructed, and another box appeared.

When I opened the lid, Laura's eggs were vividly colourful against the grey carboard of the box. She'd chosen bright paints and her designs were bold, mainly zigzags and rather crude blobs. Mairi's eggs were much subtler; works of art in miniature. She'd given each one a springtime theme: a rabbit, a pale yellow chick, daffodils, bluebells, and, not surprisingly, a couple of lambs.

"We did six each and we're going to roll them down a big hill that Daddy stops at," Laura informed me.

"They're beautiful. It seems a pity to spoil them," I said. "I think the lamb on this egg here might be Lulu; it's got a black face."

"Is it, Mairi? Is it Lulu?" Laura shrieked.

"It could be." Mairi was much quieter than her sister. "But a lot of lambs have black faces, you know."

"Mairi." Grant's voice held a warning tone.

"Oh, I won't be offended. I admit that I know nothing about sheep," I said, laughing.

"In case you were worried, I have a big flask of coffee, so we can have our morning dose of caffeine while the girls are doing their eggy thing." Grant smiled at me again.

"Excellent," I said.

"Egg-sellent. Egg-sellent," Laura chanted from the back seat. "Ha ha. Egg-sellent – get it, Mairi?"

"She's a bit hyper today. The lambing is finished and she's luxuriating in having more of my attention now, trying to make sure that she gets all of it," Grant commented quietly under his daughter's noise from the back seat. "We'll have to give her plenty of chances to run around, then if she's tired out, she might tone down a bit."

The car bowled along the road and my higher vantage point and passenger status gave me a great chance to enjoy the scenery. There was a covering of hazy cloud which was thicker by the highest peaks, obscuring their tops. The sun was visible as a pale disc in the grey, so it looked as if the day might brighten. Once we'd passed Craignure and Duart Castle everything was new to me. The girls were now listening to music on headphones. I could hear sibilant suggestions of melody coming from the back seat.

"And how has your progress been this week?" Grant asked.

"Good, thanks. I've been working on the main bedroom and the dressing room, and so far there haven't been any great surprises. I've mainly found the clothes and accessories that I'd expect an elderly man to possess," I reported. "Although he had some Highland dress that's not so familiar to me. There are several kilts and different types of jacket to wear with them, and I came across five sporrans. Two are quite plain – just tooled leather pouches – but the other three are pretty ornate, with silverwork and spectacular long black-and-white hair."

"Aye, he'd have had plain sporrans for every day and dress ones for special occasions. Maybe some of the dress ones were passed down through the family if he had more than one."

"OK, and I was a bit surprised to find a small dagger in one of the sporrans. It's really sharp and has a silver hilt with a large amethyst on the top."

"That would be his *Sgian Dubh*. Traditionally blokes wore them tucked into their sock as part of the full Highland dress. Nowadays most people leave them at home; they don't want to be accused of carrying an offensive weapon."

"Yes, I can imagine. Then of course there are the bed hangings. They're really special, but so far I haven't come across any documentation that describes their origin, or a receipt for their purchase. I suppose I might learn more when I get down to the office."

"I'm not entirely sure, but I believe that they were a gift, made in Brittany especially for Murdo. The story is that the tapestries were presented to him in gratitude for the part he played there in the war."

"Wow, that's really interesting. I think Mr Stewart, the lawyer, mentioned something about Murdo's war service being hush-hush. Do you think he was involved with the French Resistance?"

"I think his role was mainly in transportation. He was a brilliant sailor, and used to the rocky coastline and strong currents around here. So, he was able to navigate around the coast of Brittany. He'd pick up people on the run – jettisoned airmen, escaping Jews, undercover agents – and bring them to Britain. And he'd deliver things – weapons, cash and agents – in the other direction. Sailing in a small boat, he was unobtrusive, able to dodge the enemy. Maybe you're right, and you'll discover some papers in his study to explain everything in more detail."

"That sounds like something from a spy novel."

"Aye, I believe it was called Special Operations."

"You have the same surname, were you related to Murdo?"

"No, not directly. You'll find that Mull is full of Macleans; Duart Castle is the clan seat. I suppose if you go back far enough, we would all have common ancestors. So, tell me. How did you get into the valuation business anyway?"

"Well, I suppose I got interested in art and antiques through my parents. They run an antiques business. Dad does the buying and some small repairs, and Mum helps out in the shop. I spent quite a lot of time in their shop as a kid, and on holidays and days out we visited a lot of galleries, museums and National Trust properties; that kind of thing."

"Aye, I can imagine that you'd either come to love it, or take a scunner to it."

"A scunner?" I guessed it was another of those tricky Scottish words.

"Mm… a dislike; could be after an overindulgence."

"OK." I was trying to remember the new words, mentally filing this one away.

"And is there a recognised career path, or a way of progressing in your line now?"

"Not really. I did a general degree in History of Art at Oxford. By the end of it, I'd decided on the direction I wanted to take, and then I did a postgrad degree in Art Market Appraisal at Kingston."

"Do you see yourself taking over from your parents in the long run? I guess I'm asking because that's effectively what I've done."

"You took over from your dad?"

"Aye. Way back, the estate was originally wholly owned by my family, but over time they needed to raise money. By the time my dad came along it was owned in partnership, and he was the manager as well as one of the partners."

"I see. I've never discussed it with them, but I suppose my parents might like it if I continue with the business. It's never been part of my plan. I've really enjoyed working in the auction and valuation business, and it was good that I could qualify as a registered valuer on the job."

"I guess I always wanted to come back to the island. I spent a good few years away, at uni and in New Zealand. But I always wanted to come home. Unlike my brother – he couldn't wait to get away, and he's hardly come back, even to visit, since he went off to uni."

"I don't have any siblings; I'm an only child."

"All the more precious, then," Grant said with a smile.

"You mean precious as in spoilt?" I asked, feigning indignation.

"I didn't say that, but if the cap fits…" Grant replied, grinning again.

A few minutes later he pulled the Range Rover off the road onto the verge just beyond a wooden gate. "Right, girls, this is where we get out. Jackets on, and don't forget the eggs."

We all pulled on our jackets and Grant collected a small backpack from the boot. Then we walked back to the gate and went through it into the field.

"We cut across this field to the stile up there," he said, pointing. "And then we can climb up the hill a bit for the rolling to begin."

The girls ran up the field ahead of us. "Watch out for cowpats, Claire," Mairi called back.

"I shouldn't worry. If there are any, they'll be old and dried up. I don't think Alasdair's had any beasts in this field for a while," Grant reassured me. Another sign that everyone here on the island seemed to know everyone else. However, I kept my eyes on the ground in front of me just in case.

We gained the stile and I managed to clamber over it without looking too ungainly. The sisters were already a good way up the hill in front of us and I noticed that Mairi occasionally stopped to wait for Laura, sometimes offering her a hand and pulling her up a particularly steep slope.

"Stop when you get to that big boulder. That should be high enough," Grant called. When we caught them up, he gave us a choice. "Snack first, or eggs first?"

I was beginning to crave my morning coffee and was out of breath after our climb, so I was pleased that the consensus was for snack first. The girls and I perched on the large, prominent boulder that jutted out from the hillside and Grant pulled out the contents of his rucksack. First, a carton of apple juice each for his daughters, followed by bags of mini cookies. The coffee from the thermos flask was divided between two melamine mugs and I cradled mine between my hands.

"Cookies?" he asked me.

"No, I'm fine," I replied, sipping my coffee.

I stayed on my perch and watched as Grant and the girls spread out just below the rock and began to release the eggs. Laura squatted down on her haunches and peered intently into her egg box. Eventually she selected a red-and-green egg and set it rolling. She jumped up and down as she watched its progress. It picked up speed on the steep slope, then veered to the side and smashed on a patch of scree.

"Yours is stuck, Mairi," she shouted, spotting that her sister's egg had become lodged underneath a gorse bush a short way down the slope to the right.

"Well, I'm not going in there to get it; I'd be prickled to death," Mairi declared, and set her second egg off on a different tangent.

As I watched the family and their interactions, I thought about their backstory that Isla had relayed to me when I'd told her about being invited on this trip. Apparently, Grant's wife hadn't liked island life.

"They met in Edinburgh when they were at university. Then they lived in New Zealand for three or four years after they were married, before Grant moved back here to run the estate. But Ruth never really settled into the island community; maybe she was just made for the city. I still find it hard to forgive her for breaking up her family, though, and we were good friends for a while. I tried to make her welcome, introduced her to people, and made suggestions for things she might do to fill her time."

"She must have been pretty unhappy here to break up her marriage," I'd suggested.

"Well, that wasn't the whole of it. You see, they bought a flat in Edinburgh so that she could easily spend some of her time there – for a break, you know? But while she was there, she started seeing a friend of Grant's. I'm sure it was probably just a friendly, sociable gesture of his to begin with; to keep her company when she was in town. But it grew into something more and she left Grant for Iain. They're married now."

I couldn't help but feel sorry for Grant. He'd been dealt a double blow, losing his wife and his friend. And it must be hard only seeing his daughters for holidays. As I watched him play with them, I could see how much he enjoyed their company. They were coming back up to the boulder now. All the eggs had been released, and several large hooded crows had already gathered on the slope below us and were pecking at the smashed hard-boiled eggs.

"Let's go, Daddy. I want to get the ferry now." Laura's attention had moved on to the next activity.

"Come on then, race you down the hill," Grant challenged her, and they all began to run down the grassy slope.

I slid down from the boulder and followed at a much more leisurely pace. I envied people who could throw caution to the wind and charge down hills. But I'd never been particularly sure-footed and I preferred to take my time, fearful of falling or going over on my ankle on the rough ground.

When I caught up with them back at the car the girls were sucking hard on the straws of their second cartons of juice. We set off again along the winding road towards Fionnphort and the Iona ferry.

"How often does the ferry sail?" I asked.

"It just crosses back and forwards all day with a short break at lunchtime, but we should be there well before then. It takes about ten minutes to cross and then around five to ten minutes at each side to load up. I suggest that we pop into the Argyll

Hotel when we arrive to book a table for lunch, and then we can go to see the abbey."

When Grant parked the car in the jetty car park, we could see the ferry on the other side of the channel, loading up at the Iona quay. "We leave the car here and just go over as foot passengers," he explained.

Laura began to fidget and squirm as soon as she jumped down from the car. "I need to do a pee, Daddy," she announced.

"You OK, Mairi?" Grant asked, and got a nod in reply, so Mairi and I waited by the waterside while Grant took Laura by the hand and led her to the public toilets.

"Dad says that you'll be going back to London once you've finished at the castle," Mairi said. I got the impression that she was just checking.

"Yes, that's where I live: in West Hampstead," I replied.

"I'll be going on a school trip to London next year, in P7. Everyone's really excited about it already."

"There's certainly lots to do there. I'm sure you'll have a great time. I've heard that Edinburgh's an interesting city too, but I've never been there."

"Yes, I like it. But I like to visit my dad here too."

"And I'm sure he loves having you. He must miss you when you go back."

"Well, he comes to see us for a weekend every month. We stay with him at his flat."

Grant and Laura returned, and soon the ferry docked and we were able to walk on board. As we crossed the water Grant sat on a bench and leaned against the boat's railing with Laura on his knee. Her body was relaxed back against his chest and their heads were close together, his face looking over her shoulder, his mouth next to her ear. I could just make out a tune and faint words above the thrumming of the ferry's engines and the screeching of the gulls. There seemed to be a refrain containing the word 'Iona'. He was singing her a song about the island.

Laura's eyes were closed and she was smiling. I moved farther away along the railing and feigned an interest in the spray thrown up by the ferry's wake to give them space. I didn't know much about complicated family dynamics, being an only child with parents who'd been married for nearly forty years now. But I could sense that Grant's girls needed time with their dad. One was overexcited, striving to grab his attention, and I'd sensed that the other had given me at least one put-down and a warning-off hint; and maybe there'd been others that I'd missed. I was beginning to wonder if I should have accepted Grant's invitation.

When we arrived on Iona, Grant suggested that I go ahead of them to the abbey. They'd catch up with me there after he'd booked a table for lunch and Mairi had paid a visit to the hotel toilets. As I walked away from the huddle of people disembarking from the ferry, I felt myself exhale deeply in a sigh and was conscious of loosening tension in my shoulders. I'd read the tourist blurb earlier in the week, with its description of the island as 'serene' and 'one of the most sacred places in all of Western Europe'. I couldn't explain the ambience exactly, but I definitely experienced a sense of tranquillity. Probably I was just feeling at ease in my own company again rather than submitting to the influence of a metaphysical phenomenon.

The abbey was busy. A service had recently finished and the congregation milled around, chatting. Spread out on the trail behind me, a snake of tourists was arriving from the ferry. In the main sanctuary I recognised pieces of the distinctive cream-and-green Iona marble, similar to the pillars in the castle, incorporated into the altar and the font. I wandered out into the cloister and lingered there, examining the carvings and the large central sculpture.

"I was just thinking that it would be nice to come back here when my parents come to visit," I told Grant when he and Laura caught up with me.

"Aye, I'm sure they'd like to see it. When are they coming?"

"They've arranged to take some time off in two weeks' time. They're planning to come up by train to Oban and then I can collect them from the ferry at Craignure. Isla has a room booked for them for five nights."

"Do they live in London too?"

"Tunbridge Wells. It's in Kent, a bit south of London. They've managed to arrange cover for the shop so that they can come. They would be really interested in the castle. Do you think it would be all right for me to take them there? Should I check with Mr Stewart?"

"Och, I wouldn't bother. Who's to know and what's the harm? I'm sure Murdo wouldn't have minded."

"Oh? That's not the impression I've got. I thought he was a bit of a recluse, very private."

"I wouldn't say so. He was a good friend of my father's, so he visited us often. I think he was contented with his own company but he also enjoyed meeting with like-minded people. He had a fair few visitors when he was still fit – a lot of scholars, bird enthusiasts and sailing people, mainly – and he travelled widely too. I think the 'recluse' label came from the remoteness of the castle, not the man himself."

"Yes, maybe you're right; interesting. By the way, where's Mairi?" I'd suddenly noticed that the older sister hadn't appeared.

"Oh, she met a friend and her family down in the village and they're playing together on the beach there until we get back."

"It's Emma and her brother. Can we go back now, Daddy? I'm hungry," Laura piped up.

"Yes. By the time we extract your sister I guess our table will be ready for lunch. Let's go. I don't feel too guilty about rushing you away when I know that you've got a plan to revisit with your folks, Claire." Grant gave me another of his smiles. I noticed how deep a blue his eyes were, and that the small lines at their outer corners were white against his tanned face when his smile relaxed.

Chapter 8

I watched Archie up on the stage, fascinated. His fingers were nimble and his bow flew across his violin; he was playing a fast and complicated tune. Without his waterproof jacket and woollen hat, which he was usually wearing when I encountered him, he looked even more like Elvis than usual; dressed in black shirt and trousers with his dark hair slicked back. The other members of the band were a middle-aged man playing a piano accordion and a teenaged boy on a drum kit. As I sat sipping from a glass of Coke, an intricate pattern was woven on the dance floor in front of me. I'd been pulled up onto the dance floor and initiated into the Gay Gordons by Fraser, and then he and Isla had made me their third in a Dashing White Sergeant. Consequently, I was hot and breathless and definitely in need of a rest and a cooling drink. Apparently, those first two were simple dances that even children would know. I could see that the reel taking place in front of me now was much more advanced. As I watched, I noticed a variety of different clothing. Some men wore kilts, the different tartans topped by a shirt or a T-shirt. Others, like Archie and Fraser, were in trousers. Most of the women wore skirts and blouses, or dresses; almost all had short sleeves. After only two dances I could understand why, and was glad that I'd listened to Isla's advice not to overdress. I hadn't packed a skirt for this trip, so I'd had to wear trousers. I'd matched them with a blouse, and after the first dance I'd rolled up my sleeves.

As I soaked up the atmosphere, I was conscious of my efforts not to look at the time, or towards the door for any sign of Grant arriving. I'd mentioned the ceilidh to him at the end of our outing last weekend, wondering if he would attend.

"I have a ticket and I might look in," he'd said. "But I'll be taking the girls back to their mother's next Saturday. We've arranged to meet at Tyndrum, which is about halfway between here and Edinburgh. The last ferry back from Oban is at eight o'clock, so I could come when I get off the boat. I'll see how I feel."

With each day that passed his attendance had seemed to become more and more important to me. I'd been up to the estate office on a couple of evenings after dinner, but I hadn't encountered him. Understandably, he might not be in a sociable mood tonight. He'd probably feel down, having had to say goodbye to his daughters. And the interaction with his ex could be stressful. I wanted to tell him that coming to the dance would be a distraction; take his mind off things. But what did I know about such feelings? And why was I so bothered anyway? Really, I was being ridiculous.

The dance ended and Isla flopped down into the seat beside me. Fraser had gone to the bar for more drinks. "Phew, I'll need to sit the next one out; get my breath back," she said. She blew upwards with her bottom lip pouting out, lifting her fringe off her forehead.

"Yes, I'm not surprised you need a rest. I've never experienced Scottish country dancing before. It's all very energetic."

"Aye, good in a cold climate. Thanks, Fraser." Half a pint of beer appeared in front of Isla on the table. She drank some, leaving a moustache of froth on her upper lip.

"We'll have to wait for the next simple one for you, Claire," Fraser said, sitting down next to his wife.

I really liked this couple; they were so friendly and inclusive, and such easy company. But I didn't want to be a constant gooseberry, so when I spotted Catriona, Laura's babysitter, standing on her own on the other side of the room, I excused myself to go and talk to her. "Hi – I met you when you were looking after Laura," I reminded her as I approached.

"Oh yes, Claire. My babysitting duties are over for a while now; Laura's away back to her mum's."

"Yes. But I'm sure you have a few other charges."

"I do, but after tonight it's down to studying for me. I've got my Higher exams coming up and I need to get good grades if I want to go to university."

"What would you like to study?"

"I'm hoping to get into Dentistry at Glasgow."

"Oh, you'll certainly need good marks for that. I hope it all goes well."

Catriona smiled. "Hey, come and do this with me." The next dance was being announced. "It's the Circassian Circle; an easy one, I promise."

I'd noticed earlier that there were several pairs of women and girls dancing together; not enough interested men to go around. So, I let Catriona lead me into the centre of the hall and I began to learn the steps of another dance.

When the time came for the band to take their break, platters of sandwiches and sausage rolls were set up on tables beside the bar. I was surprised by how hungry I felt as I began to load a paper plate with a selection of food.

"Aye, it's hungry work, the dancing." Archie appeared by my side.

"Archie, I'm amazed by the music, it's fantastic. You're so talented."

"Och, it's just a few tunes," he said dismissively. "I see you're beginning to get the hang of some of the steps."

"I feel like a terrible amateur and I'm sure I'll have some aching muscles tomorrow, but it's great fun."

"So, is your colleague finished with his work? Or will we have his company again on Monday?"

"No, he's gone back to Glasgow."

Last week I'd received an email from the office to let me know that a building surveyor would be arriving on the Thursday. I'd replied with instructions for him to meet me at half past nine at the jetty from where we'd set out for the castle. Archie and I had been waiting for twenty minutes when a red sports car came hurtling down the hill. A tall, thin man wearing a business suit, shirt and tie strode over to us with his hand extended.

"Miss Ford? Gavin Brown. I'm so sorry I'm late," he apologised as he shook my hand.

"Hi, I'm Claire," I replied. I reckoned that Gavin was a bit younger than me, probably in his late twenties. As I introduced him to Archie I couldn't help comparing his sartorial elegance with our sloppy jeans and sweaters.

Gavin explained his delay. I'd assumed that he'd stayed on the island overnight, probably in Tobermory. However, he'd been on the 8.15 Oban ferry and driven up from Craignure. "I came along the glen from Aros. What a fantastic road." He beamed.

"Aye, it would be a great trip in yon car," Archie agreed. I could see him sizing up the smart Porsche.

"I'm sorry. If I'd known you were coming on the ferry I'd have made our meeting time later," I said. I'd noticed that the islanders were all very good at gauging arrivals and departures according to the ferry timetable. "Anyway, now you're here, let's go over to the castle."

It was a dry day, but breezy. The wind made the crossing bumpy, but we could see where we were going and we didn't get wet. Just as well for Gavin's suit. He accepted a life jacket from Archie and during the crossing I noticed that he didn't look entirely comfortable. His knuckles were white, revealing the strength of his grip as he hung on to the side of the boat.

I was surprised by how difficult I found it to share my space with Gavin. He was a pleasant enough man and, although he wasn't dressed for the job, he seemed knowledgeable and got on with his work efficiently. But I'd grown used to having the castle and the island to myself. I liked to have my coffee on the roof terrace, watching the birds, and if it was a dry day I took my sandwiches down to the jetty to eat lunch in the company of the seals. On the Thursday, Gavin had no food with him. He pretended that it didn't matter but, when pressed, accepted a share of my packed lunch. The next day he arrived on time. He'd stayed overnight at the Western Isles Hotel in Tobermory and had arranged to be supplied with a packed lunch. He'd also dressed down a bit, in chinos and a sweatshirt.

"What do you think will happen to the castle?" I'd asked him as we drank tea from my thermos on the Friday afternoon. "I can't imagine that there will be a huge market for this kind of property."

"No," he'd replied. "It's pretty niche. It might make an upmarket hotel, but it's probably on the small side for that, and there's not much scope on this tiny island to extend. So maybe a holiday rental, or just a home for someone who wants a very quiet life."

"Now, Archie, you'll need to introduce us to the young lady." I was roused from my thoughts when the other band members approached.

Archie did the honours and I met Dougal, the accordion player, and Bruce, the drummer. They wanted to know about my job, and Bruce seemed very interested in my life in London.

So, we chatted together until they had to resume playing. As they climbed back onto the stage I made my way to the ladies' toilet. I was beginning to regret having offered to drive tonight. I'd enjoyed myself, but it was tiring making polite conversation and stumbling through the strange dance steps. I wasn't sure that I felt like staying for another couple of hours of the ceilidh. But I was committed to doing so until Fraser and Isla wanted to leave, and I could bet that they'd be here until the lights were turned out.

When I returned to the hall another fast dance was under way, with couples twirling and intertwining furiously. I saw Fraser 'setting' to a tall woman with a short blonde bob. Isla was still sitting at our table, and next to her I recognised Grant's dark, curly mop of hair. I took a deep breath to steady myself before joining them.

"Hi, Claire. Have you managed much of the dancing?" he greeted me.

"Oh yes. I've been pushed and pulled through some of the easier ones," I replied.

"Och, you're making it sound much worse than it was; you've been doing really well," Isla chipped in.

"Well, I'm at your disposal for the next one," Grant stated.

"The next *easy* one," I clarified.

That turned out to be a Strip the Willow, which was a fast dance involving a lot of turning, but it didn't have complicated steps. Grant and I stood at the bottom of the set as the fourth couple so that I could watch the others and try to learn the pattern. I had a great sense of achievement when the final chord sounded. I thought I'd managed pretty well. However, I was breathless again and could feel sweat running down my cleavage and under my armpits.

"I'm going to have to go outside for a moment to cool down," I panted.

"I'll come with you for a bit of air," Grant offered.

We went out through the door and into the car park. I could see a picnic table and a children's play park to our right, and I headed in that direction, relishing the cool evening air against my skin.

"Phew, that feels better." I sat on one of the swings and began to move it gently.

Grant perched on the end of the picnic bench, facing me. "Now, if you were Laura you'd be calling on me to push you, but Mairi can manage by herself."

"You must miss them when they go back to Edinburgh." I was cross with myself for stating the obvious. But what else could I say?

Grant didn't seem to mind. "Yes. The house will seem far too quiet for the next few days. Then I'll just get used to it again. I'll go down for a weekend soon, and I can use Skype to talk to them from the office. But it's not the same as being there. I feel that I miss a lot of the wee things that make up their lives. But you don't want to be bored with all of that."

"I don't mind. I don't really know any children but I liked your girls. Laura is very like you."

"Aye, everyone says that. I suppose Mairi is more like her mum, but no one in either family has the Scandi-blonde hair like hers."

I was beginning to swing in earnest now, reaching quite a height and enjoying the rush of the air through my hair as I whooshed up and down. "I haven't done this in years. I used to have my own swing in the garden and I'd spend hours on it."

Grant looked thoughtful. "You've just given me an idea. Maybe the girls would like a swing up by the house. I could get it all set up for the summer holidays as a surprise."

"Yes, I'm sure they'd love that, and you've got loads of space, so no problem."

I was taken aback as I experienced a sharp pang of disappointment. I wouldn't be there to see the girls' reaction to their new swing. I'd be long gone, back in London. I slowed the swing down and we went back into the dance hall together. Grant asked Isla up for the next dance.

"I'm being so illogical about this. I hardly know the man and there's a lot of baggage: a broken family and two little girls. You know I don't really do children, but suddenly I so wanted to be there to see their faces when they discovered the new swing. And I like his company. He's easy to be around; relaxing." I was on the phone to Jessica the day after the ceilidh.

"Well, Claire, you know that feelings aren't always logical. Despite his family situation and the fact that he lives in the back of beyond, it sounds as if you're quite attracted to this Grant. What about him? Are you getting any vibes that he likes you?"

"Well, he did ask me to Iona and he's always very friendly. But I think he's friendly to everyone. Maybe he's just being polite because I'm a visitor, but he's asked me round to his house for dinner next week."

"I think that's more than polite, don't you?"

"Hmm, possibly. I've been using his office because it's got the best internet connection, and his house is just next door. He's missing the girls and wants some company."

"But he wants *your* company, that's the important thing. I think you've made a conquest. You just need to think carefully about how to proceed."

"Oh, Jessica. I'm hopeless at this."

"No you're not, you're just out of practice. Anyway, isn't it next weekend that your parents are visiting? You should make sure that they meet this Grant and then you'll get your mum's impression. That should help."

"Why do you keep calling him 'this Grant'? His name is just Grant."

"Now you're leaping to his defence. Definitely smitten." Jessica gave her verdict.

Chapter 9

On Thursday evening I was back at Craignure, sitting in my car down by the ferry terminal. The sky was darkening as I watched the ferry approach from the bay, all lit up against the grey-black sea. Mum and Dad would be tired after their journey: three trains to get to Oban, and then the boat. Isla had prepared a selection of sandwiches, home-baked scones and shortbread for their arrival, and I was sure that they would be much appreciated. At the beginning of the week, I'd phoned the office in London to arrange to take Friday and Monday off from work so that I could spend time with my parents. I'd fully intended to use some of my annual leave, but Anthony had acknowledged all the extra hours I'd been working and given me the days as time off in lieu. I was pleased that he'd noticed the effort that I was putting into the project. I wasn't going to the castle to work tomorrow, but I'd asked Archie to take us over to Eilean Creagach for a short visit so that my parents could see the set-up there. I was excited about the prospect of showing them the castle. It occurred to me that I'd become strangely proprietary about the place. I remembered my initial resentment at having to share my days there with Gavin the surveyor. It would be a wrench to lock up and leave for the last time, although that day was still nowhere in sight. After five weeks, I still had to cover part of the great hall, the library, and all of the lower floor.

As the ferry drew nearer my thoughts went back to Tuesday night's dinner with Grant. I'd driven on, past the estate office, up the track to the yard by the houses and barns, feeling slightly nervous. I wasn't sure what to expect. Was my new friendship with Grant about to change its character? The old stone house was all in darkness, so I reckoned that Grant must live in the other building. It was a sprawling ranch-style bungalow, and some of the windows were lit up. When I got out of my car I saw Grant framed in the doorway; he must have seen my headlights approaching, and no doubt had heard the cacophony of dogs barking that was coming from one of the outbuildings.

"Come away in," he greeted me. "I thought we wouldn't stand on ceremony, so I've just set the table in the kitchen. It's cosier there when it's just the two of us."

I followed him into a modern kitchen with pale wooden units and a matching central wooden table. When I sat down, Grant poured me a glass of white wine and then returned to the stovetop to check on the cooking.

"It all smells delicious," I commented.

"Well, I hope it'll live up to expectations. I've had to learn how to fend for myself. This is my cooking bible," he said, holding up a copy of *Delia Smith's Complete Cookery Course*.

"Snap! I've got the same book," I exclaimed.

We had a simple but tasty meal of chicken casserole and potatoes followed by apple pie with cream. The evening was relaxed and Grant was friendly and chatty, but there had been nothing about the conversation or the atmosphere that I could interpret as being at all romantic. So I was left trying to push any silly ideas that I'd had about Grant to the very back of my mind.

Now I could see that the ferry had docked, vehicles were driving down the ramp and people were beginning to emerge from the walkway onto the quay. I left the car and went to look for my parents. I saw Dad first. He's tall with a full head of thick white hair, and that made him easy to spot under the docks' bright floodlighting. He was wearing a royal-blue rain jacket and carrying a small holdall. He had another bag on his back, and was scanning ahead to try and spot me. I began to wave. Just as he saw me and returned my wave, I caught sight of my mum behind him. Everyone has always said that I look like Mum. We're of a similar height and build, but she'd recently adopted a very short pixie-style haircut and coloured her hair a copper shade, so suddenly I didn't think we looked so much alike. She could see where Dad was heading, and began to wave too. Soon they were both wrapping me in strong hugs. Once I'd extracted myself, I began to lead them towards the car.

"So, how was the journey?" I asked.

"All very straightforward and easy," Mum replied. "We read our books and did the crossword, and your dad had a bit of a snooze. Luckily, the ferry crossing was calm; I'm not a very good sailor."

"We've got about half an hour's drive and then you'll be comfortably installed in the guest house. It's a pity it's dark now as the views on the road are great. But you'll see it all later."

We stowed their bags in the boot and they climbed into the car; Dad next to me and Mum in the back. I pulled out onto the road and joined a flow of vehicles heading towards Tobermory.

"It seems busy; I'm surprised at the volume of traffic," Dad commented.

"It's just the ferry offloading; that's the equivalent of rush hour on the island," I explained. "Generally, it's pretty quiet, although the locals complain that it gets congested during the summer tourist season."

The traffic began to thin out, speeding off and turning down side roads. I was still a cautious driver, especially in the dark, having been spooked by Fraser's stories of encounters with deer on the roads.

"Have you seen many deer?" Mum asked when I expressed my worries.

"Oh, yes. I often see three or four on the hillside up behind the guest house, and I regularly see them when I'm driving to and from the castle. Thankfully, none on the road yet, though."

"Well, just take your time. A few minutes longer will make no difference. What's happening now? Why are you pulling over?" Mum sounded worried.

We'd reached the single-track road and there were headlights approaching, so I'd turned into a passing place. I explained.

"Oh, goodness. What a lot to get used to!" Mum exclaimed.

I smiled to myself in the dark as the oncoming car passed and we continued on our way. I was pleased because, while not yet as carefree as a local, I had begun to adapt. My grip on the steering wheel wasn't quite as tight as it used to be.

Mum continued to be spooked by the island roads on our journey to the castle the next day. Every time we had to stop for an oncoming vehicle she gasped, and if someone stopped for us, she waved as we drove past them. The hairpin bends had her gripping the seat in front of her. By now I was accustomed to my commute, but Mum's reactions left me feeling frazzled by the time we arrived at the ferry car park. I was glad to hand over the responsibility for transport to Archie. I could see his familiar figure leaning against the bonnet of his van. He came forward at once to greet my parents, shaking hands and then helping them down the steep stone steps into the boat. He kitted them out with life jackets without asking their preference and cast off the ropes tethering us to the shore.

"It's a calm day for the crossing," he commented. "And clear – you can see the hills on Rùm." He pointed towards some distant mountains.

"I think there's some snow on that one. I wish I'd brought my binoculars." Dad was peering into the distance.

"There's a pair at the castle that you can borrow," I offered.

"Oh, and, Claire, I've a wee surprise for you on the island," Archie announced.

I wondered briefly what he could be referring to, but then I caught sight of the island. "There it is!" I called, drawing my parents' attention for their first glimpse of the castle.

"I can't believe that this is where you've been working every day!" my mum exclaimed.

"Yes, it's pretty special, isn't it?" I replied.

We were soon at the castle jetty, and Archie jumped out to fasten the boat and help us all onto the quay. "Just wait a wee minute here while I get the generator going," he instructed. "I've a special treat for Claire."

I was puzzled, but remained on the quayside with my parents while he strode round to the outbuilding to start up the electricity. As we waited, I pointed out a couple of my seal friends just offshore, heads bobbing out of the water, watching us.

"Now, come away with me," Archie commanded, striding ahead of us.

Instead of our usual route to the back door, he set off round the path leading to the front of the castle. We arrived at a stone staircase leading up to the impressive oak front door. Archie dug in his jacket pocket and produced the gigantic key which had been in the envelope from Mr Stewart. He held it out to me.

"I borrowed this a few days ago. You do the honours," he said. "I've been working away, freeing up the lock and hinges. It opens easily now."

"Wow, Archie, thank you," I said. As I ascended the steps and slotted the key into the keyhole, I explained to Mum and Dad that until now we'd always used the back door. "This one was all rusted up. It's going to be so impressive to come in through the grand hall."

The key turned easily in the lock and the door opened smoothly, without a single creak. There in front of us was the magnificent hallway, its walls hung with gleaming weaponry and stags' antlers, leading to the pale marble pillars.

"It's so much more impressive than coming in through the kitchen," I said.

I felt quite breathless, and realised that I was grinning. And I'd known exactly what to expect when the door opened. I could see that my parents were surprised by the scale of the hallway, and its grandeur. Archie was still hovering on the top step, and, before I'd thought about it, I ran back and gave him a hug. He looked pleased and began to blush.

"You dinna mind that I borrowed the key, then?" he asked. It wouldn't have been difficult, as I tended to leave the envelope of keys lying on the kitchen table. Then I knew where to find it if I needed to look for a key.

"Not at all. It was a brilliant surprise," I reassured him.

"Well, I thought we should show off the castle at its best. And I guess when it comes onto the market to be sold, they'll want to enter through this door. So, it was my wee project. Anyway, I'll away for now. When do you want me back?"

I asked him to return for us at 12.30. "That should give us enough time to look around, and then we can find some lunch."

My parents' visit gave me a relaxing break from work, and time to explore parts of the island that I hadn't seen. Over the long weekend we aimed to cover all of the main places of interest listed in our tourist guide. This included a return visit to Iona for me, with more time to spend in the abbey. We also went to one of Iona's beaches, where we walked along the tideline and searched for pebbles of Iona marble to take home as souvenirs.

On the Sunday evening Isla suggested an outing to the Mishnish Hotel for drinks after dinner. "I've heard that some of our local musicians will be playing tonight. I think Edward and Barbara would enjoy that."

So, we all walked down the hill to Main Street and joined the throng in the busy pub, managing to find seats at a table near the fire. When we arrived a woman with flowing red hair was singing a song in Gaelic and accompanying herself on a miniature harp. She was persuaded to give us another song, and then she was joined by a guitarist. I wondered if he might be her brother, as he also had red hair. They played together and sang in harmony, sounding well rehearsed. Next an elderly man with a drum-like instrument like a giant tambourine joined in, and the pace of the music picked up as he used a small stick to beat the rhythm.

"It's called a bodhrán," Fraser answered when I asked about the drum.

At around ten o'clock, just when you might have expected the players to be winding down, a fourth musician arrived. It was Archie with his fiddle. The mood of the music changed again, and I could see lots of people tapping their toes. If there had been more space, I'm sure that some of the audience would have been up dancing. When there was a break for refreshments we bought Archie a beer, and he joined us at our table. We were all very complimentary about the music.

"It's just a wee jam session. We try to get together here about once a month. People drop in as they're able, so it's a different line-up every time." Archie was his usual modest self. "Do none of you play an instrument?"

"Claire used to play the flute," my mum informed him. "She was really good; passed her Grade 8 exam."

"But I've not played for years now," I said.

"That's a pity; a flute would be a good addition to our gathering. We sometimes have Hamish on a penny whistle but he's away at the university just now. You should keep up with the music," Archie advised me.

I thought about it as they started playing again; a slow air this time. It had been easy to fit in with the orchestras at school and university, but once I'd moved to London and started working, I hadn't bothered to find another group to join. I made an effort to attend orchestral and chamber group performances several times a year, and had enjoyed hearing some very famous musicians who'd come to London on tour. But I'd definitely neglected my own playing.

Four weeks later I locked the door of Caisteal Glas for the last time. I stowed the key back in the brown envelope, ready to be returned to Mr Stewart the next day. I'd call in as I passed through Oban on my way back to Glasgow airport. The library had taken me longer to catalogue than I'd anticipated, and I'd arranged for a manuscript curator to follow up my work in order to produce accurate valuations. As I made my way down to the waterside, I wondered what Murdo's nephew would decide to do with his inheritance. Would he be curious enough to come and visit the castle? After all, a lot of second-generation emigrants were very interested in their roots, researching family trees and carrying on with old traditions.

There was no sign of Archie yet, so I wandered round to the front of the castle. Seabirds were wheeling around as usual, and I was now able to identify several species after studying one of Murdo's books. I could see common gulls, herring gulls, terns and guillemots. I heard the chugging of the boat's motor above the birds' cries, and arrived back at the jetty as Archie approached.

"I've turned off the generator," I called. Archie had me well trained after nine weeks on the island. I was now able to hop straight on board and we could set off without him having to leave the boat. "I can't believe that this is my last journey with you."

"Aye, well, you'll be glad to get back to the bright city lights," he commented.

"Yes and no," I said. "I've missed my flat and my friends, but I've enjoyed being here. Working at the castle has been amazing, and everyone has been so helpful and welcoming, especially Isla and Fraser. I feel that they'll be friends for life now."

"Aye, they're a couthie couple. They have a lot of return visitors at Taigh Dearg."

"Maybe I'll come back for a holiday sometime," I ventured.

"Well, if you do, I hope you'll maybe have learned to play a few tunes. Here, I got you this." Archie handed me a package.

I opened it to find a book of music; a collection of Scottish folk songs arranged for the flute. "Wow, thank you, Archie." I was touched by his generosity, and felt the prickle of tears beginning to form. "I'll need to dig out my flute now." I tried to think where it might be – probably gathering dust under my bed.

I said goodbye to Archie at the car park and drove slowly back to Tobermory, taking in all of the scenery for the last time. Before dinner I emptied the wardrobe and drawers in my room at Taigh Dearg, folding everything neatly to fit back into my suitcase. I was taken aback for a second time that evening when both Isla and Fraser presented me with gifts. Two packages were sitting by my place at the kitchen table.

"Oh, I feel so bad. I haven't got anything for you guys," I protested.

"Och, they're just wee things as a minding," Fraser reassured me.

"You just have to make us a promise to come back again," Isla said, giving me a hug.

When I opened the parcels, I knew that Fraser had lied. Each of them must have spent a lot of time making their gift. Isla had given me a woven throw in several shades of blue and grey, and Fraser had made me a marquetry wall hanging. It was a depiction of a castle on a rocky island, surrounded by the sea. "It could be Caisteal Glas!" I exclaimed.

"Aye – we don't want you to forget us when you go back to the big city," he said.

"Thank you both so much. There's no way that I'll forget you, or this whole experience," I promised.

Chapter 10

When I turned the key and opened the door to my flat, I was met by a waft of stale, musty air. I hauled my suitcase inside, then immediately went to open the windows. The lounge was west-facing and the early evening sun was shining into the room. I could tell that Mum had visited recently, as the surfaces were dust free and there was a vase of fresh freesias on top of my bookshelf. Knowing Mum, I guessed that she'd also have left me some essential groceries. I checked the fridge to find it stocked with milk, eggs, butter, cheese, tomatoes and orange juice. There was also a selection of fruit in the pottery bowl on the kitchen table, and a loaf of bread on the counter. I felt grateful that I wouldn't need to go out shopping tonight, and instead would be able to settle in after my journey. I took my jacket off and went back into the hall to hang it up on one of the pegs by the front door. There were a few envelopes and flyers lying behind the door. I picked them up and added them to the bigger pile of mail on the coffee table. I felt rather aimless, and decided to pour myself a glass of red wine and then phone

Mum to thank her for her housekeeping. The wine rack in my kitchen had a few bottles that I could choose from. I selected a Californian Zinfandel, unscrewed the top and poured a measure into a wine glass. Then I retrieved my handbag from the hall where I'd dropped it, fished out my mobile phone and rang Mum.

She answered almost immediately. "Claire, are you back safely?"

"Hi, Mum. Yes, I'm home. And thanks for the groceries and the flowers. I think you must have waved a duster around too."

Mum laughed. "Indeed, it's amazing how much dust can gather over nine weeks, even with the windows closed. What are your plans for the weekend? Do you want to come here for lunch on Sunday?"

I'd anticipated this, and had my reply prepared. "You know, I'm a bit whacked what with winding everything up, packing, and then all of the travelling. And tomorrow is threatening to be a pretty full-on day: I'm going shopping with Jessica for her wedding dress and maybe my bridesmaid's dress. So, I think I should keep Sunday free to get myself organised; get some shopping in, do the laundry. Things like that. I hope you don't mind. What I thought would be good would be to come down to you next weekend and maybe stay over, since it's the bank holiday. That is, if it suits you and Dad?"

"Of course. That would be lovely. When do you plan to come?"

"I guess late afternoon on Saturday and then come home on Monday afternoon. Will you be closing the shop?"

"No, I don't think so. Holiday weekends are often a good time for browsers, but we don't both need to be on duty full time. We'll work something out."

"Great – I'll look forward to seeing you both. I think I'll take advantage of your shopping and make myself an omelette now."

"Enjoy, and good luck with finding a dress. I'm not sure why you're complaining about it; you usually like shopping."

"I know, but Jess has been hassling me so much recently about not being available to go with her. She seems to be getting quite agitated about it all. I think she's done some scouting around over the past few weeks but she wants my opinion on her dress and to find one for me."

"When's the wedding again?"

"The end of September."

"Oh well, four months should be plenty of time to buy a dress and have any alterations done. How many bridesmaids is she having?"

"Just me and four flower girls: her two nieces and Chris's two nieces."

"Oh, so you'll have the job of keeping four little girls in check. How old are they?"

"I'm not sure. I guess I can find out from Jess tomorrow. Thankfully, they aren't included in the shopping trip."

"Mm, well, you can tell me all about it next weekend. Bye for now, love."

"Bye, Mum." I hung up, took a deep breath and a large gulp of my wine, and then scrolled up to Jessica's name on my contact list. I needed to find out where we were to meet tomorrow.

Jessica knew that I'd need a caffeine hit before any serious shopping could be done, so she'd arranged to meet me in a coffee shop on Pentonville Road, just around the corner from the Angel underground station. She'd told me on the phone the night before that there were at least seven bridal shops within a close radius of the station. She'd browsed around two weekends ago and had identified a few possible dresses. I was already sipping my Americano when she arrived in the café. I stood to give her a hug, then she went to the counter to order her own drink.

"Well, thank God you're back to help keep me sane," she announced as she sat across from me with her latte. "It's been no fun trying to arrange things, with my mum in the south of Spain and you away in the boonies."

Jessica's parents had divorced ten years ago and her mum had relocated to the Costa del Sol with her second husband. While this was handy for sunny holidays, it obviously wasn't so convenient for planning a wedding. I realised that my friend was genuinely upset, feeling that she'd been deserted when we should have been making her the centre of our attention. I hadn't been taking my role as bridesmaid seriously enough. I decided that I'd have to step up my involvement now that I was back in London, and give Jess more support.

"I'm all yours now," I reassured her. "Tell me about the shops and the dresses and we can plan our day."

She produced a list and a tattered *A-Z* from her handbag. We consulted the street map, which she had annotated by marking the bridal shops with a star, to make up an itinerary.

"So, number one on the agenda is to find you the perfect dress." I was totally in role now. "You're going to be the centre of attention and you have to choose something that looks amazing and feels comfortable. Then we can find something for me that will tone in, and it doesn't matter at all if we don't find it today."

"OK, but I want you to have a dress that you'll really like too, and could wear again to a function or a dance. Not a meringue creation."

"Well, that's a relief," I laughed. "I'm not really a sugary type of girl." Thankfully, we had similar taste in clothes. Jessica was about three inches taller than me, but we wore the same dress size and had dipped into each other's wardrobes during all the years that we'd shared a flat, swapping and borrowing outfits. So, I didn't think that our opinions would differ too much when it came to choosing dresses for Jessica's wedding.

All afternoon I followed Jessica in and out of the shops, helping with zips and buttons, asking assistants for shoes to borrow, and giving my opinion. She avoided the frothiest styles, but there were off-the-shoulder dresses, dresses with V-necked fronts or backs, and one dress with a high neckline and what seemed like a hundred tiny buttons up the back. The hemlines varied too: some had trains, some were straight and narrow, and there was one fishtail number. By three o'clock we had narrowed the choice down to two dresses. We decided to have a breather and something to eat before returning so that Jessica could try them on again.

We settled in a wine bar with stuffed paninis and glasses of Pinot Grigio. Jessica had messaged her mum, describing her two preferred dresses, and was waiting for a reply. I checked my phone too, and must have inadvertently made a comment.

"What?" Jess enquired.

"Oh, nothing really." I was loath to tell her that the text was from Grant. I'd hardly seen him in the last month of my stay on Mull, and was trying to keep thoughts of him out of my head. I didn't want to waste my time and hopes on something that wasn't to be. But I knew that if I mentioned him now, Jessica would want to examine all the details of our friendship and the implications of this message.

The text was to thank me for the bottle of whisky that I'd left on Grant's desk as a thank-you for the use of his office and broadband. Despite my best intentions, I'd succumbed and written my phone number on the accompanying card. Thankfully, Jess's mum had replied and she was distracted. I didn't need to share.

Many thanks for the whisky. Sorry I didn't get to say goodbye in person. It was a pleasure to be of assistance. Perhaps you'll visit us again. Slainte! Grant.

I decided that a response was unnecessary. And anyway, after the refreshments and her chat with her mum, Jessica was keen to get back to dress-hunting.

The next day, I had to tackle my domestic chores. I tipped out the contents of the suitcase that I'd ignored since returning home on Friday and sorted through the clothes, putting some into the washing machine and others into the laundry basket. There was also a small pile for dry-cleaning. Then I settled down to make a shopping list. I'd made a decision that from now on I'd try to eat more healthily. I'd so enjoyed Isla's home cooking, and knew that it was better for me than constantly relying on ready meals. I found my Delia Smith recipe book and sat at the kitchen table, flipping through, looking for ideas and adding the ingredients to my list. I'd also need to buy some plastic food containers, as my intention was to freeze some portions so that I'd have a stock to use on days when I was in a hurry.

There was another huge task on my mind. I had to act soon to make arrangements for Jessica's hen weekend. Back in January I'd contacted the guests she was inviting and asked them all to keep the August bank holiday weekend free. That was a month before the wedding and seemed an ideal time for us all to go away. But now it was only three months away, at a busy time of year, and I hadn't given any thought to our destination, never mind made a booking. As I walked to the supermarket, I began to turn over some ideas in my head. If we left on the Friday evening, we'd have three nights away. In my opinion it was therefore important not to spend too much of that time travelling, so it should be somewhere that was only a short flight away. Next, I considered the kinds of things that Jess liked to do. She liked culture: galleries, museums, the theatre. She also liked to have a bit of fun: cocktails, nice food, dancing. Pampering should be on the agenda; somewhere with a spa, and a pool or the sea for swimming. I was mulling over all of this while I pushed my trolley along the supermarket aisles, tossing in items from my list. I picked up a copy of the *Sunday Times* and put it into the trolley. I had a huge amount of stuff – no way could I carry everything home. I scrolled through my phone and found the number for a taxi.

At home, after I'd unpacked and stowed the shopping away, I made a small cafetière of coffee and sat down in the lounge with that and the newspaper. Was it serendipity? One of the first articles to catch my eye was about arts festivals. Maybe I was just hyperalert to all things Scottish, but I quickly noticed that the Edinburgh Festival takes place in August. Might that be a good focus for our hen weekend? Only an hour's flight away, with lots of culture and things to do. I went to fetch my laptop, excited and ready to carry out more research.

An hour later I was still enthusiastic, but also slightly discouraged. It was definitely a good idea, but accommodation prices in Edinburgh during the festival were sky-high, particularly for that weekend. We could stay in the suburbs for a more reasonable price, but the atmosphere wouldn't be the same. Then another thought came to me, but I tried to resist it. It would be too presumptuous. I knew that Grant had a flat in Edinburgh. He used it as a base when he went to visit the girls. I also knew, because Isla had mentioned it, that he'd let her and Fraser stay there for a holiday. But they were very good friends, and I was only a slight acquaintance. Plus, he'd already been kind to me. I couldn't ask him, could I?

I decided that I needed to put the subject out of my head, so I logged out from my computer and headed to the kitchen to begin cooking my first batch of home-made food. I collected my ingredients, opened my recipe book and began chopping and frying while singing along to Mariah Carey. I enjoyed cooking and eating the fajitas, but I couldn't let go of the idea of Grant's flat. Consequently, after dinner I gave in and phoned Isla.

"Hi, Isla, it's Claire."

"Hello, Claire. You got home safely, I hope?"

"Yes, I'm all settled in and ready to go back to work tomorrow. I've even done some real cooking, inspired by all of the lovely meals that you made for me."

"Well, that's all good."

"Listen, can I run an idea past you?" I then proceeded to tell her about the hen weekend, and my thoughts about Edinburgh and its downside of expensive accommodation. "Remember you said you'd stayed at Grant's flat? Do you think he'd let us stay there? We'd be willing to pay something."

"Oh, well, I couldn't say. I don't think he's in the habit of renting the flat out; it's kind of a home from home. And of course, he might want to be there himself for the festival. When we stayed, he just asked us to make a contribution towards the utility bills."

"Do you think he'd think it very cheeky of me to approach him about it?"

"No, I shouldn't think so. He's a pretty relaxed character."

"Where exactly is his flat?"

"It's in an area called Marchmont, just south of the city centre. There are lots of flats there, all built at the end of the nineteenth century. It's close to the university so a lot of students live around there."

"Would it be big enough for six of us to stay?"

"Aye, easily. The rooms are a generous size and it has three bedrooms as well as a lounge."

"Wherever we stay, it would mainly just be a place to dump our stuff, to shower and change, and to sleep. I'm sure we'll be out and about most of the time. That's part of the reason I don't want to spend a fortune on rooms."

"You can only ask."

I thanked Isla for her advice, but I still felt nervous about approaching Grant. I pottered around the flat, tidying, making a packed lunch for the next day, and looking through the neglected pile of mail that had accumulated in my absence. Eventually I went to bed, still undecided.

Chapter 11

The next day, I had to reaccustom myself to the London rush hour. I was swept along West End Lane, shoulder to shoulder in a mass of commuters as we all marched briskly to the tube station. The platform was crowded and I didn't get onto the first train. I squeezed into the next one, then had to stand, clinging to an overhead loop as the train hurtled along. I tightened my grip as we picked up speed, and then again as we decelerated coming into a station, and I readjusted my footing as we swung around bends. Strong scents mingled in the carriage: perfumes of toiletries from early morning ablutions mixed with the aroma of coffee from cardboard carry-out containers. A few girls were busy applying their make-up. I was always amazed that they didn't smudge it all, given the jerky movement of the train and possible jostling from other passengers. Our progress created a lot of noise: the carriages clanked and rattled; our motion through the tunnel made a constant whoosh which could change in pitch until, at its worst, it became an uncomfortable piercing scream. A woman's voice announced the stations as we approached, and repeatedly told us to mind the gap between the carriage and the platform. In contrast, the commuters were mostly quiet. A lot of people looked half asleep, but some were reading newspapers, books or e-readers. Many had earbuds inserted, locked into their own zone, listening to their chosen soundtrack.

At Baker Street station I had to change to the Bakerloo line. I was aware of the sound of my city shoes clicking along the corridors. They felt unfamiliar and decidedly uncomfortable, rubbing against my heels, after weeks of wearing trainers. After my second tube journey, I was relieved to emerge onto the street at Charing Cross into comparatively fresh air. I was in good time, and slowed my pace as I approached the office. I couldn't help comparing this journey with the meandering drive followed by a boat trip that had been my start to the morning up until three days ago. But this was my normal life and that was just an interlude, so I shook myself mentally and entered the office building via the revolving door.

During the course of the morning most of my colleagues found a reason to visit my desk for a chat and to hear about my extended absence. My descriptions of the castle and island life seemed to be met either with horror or disbelief. I deduced from Miles White's comments that, having returned to work in my absence, he judged that he'd been lucky to escape that particular assignment. But he was definitely playing to the small audience that had gathered around, as he asked for details about the location. I knew that he'd done research and set up the initial arrangements for travel and accommodation. I realised that he liked to be the storyteller, the centre of attention.

"You had to make a sea crossing every day?" He sounded incredulous, hamming it up.

"Well, just a short sail, about fifteen to twenty minutes."

"What if it was raining or rough?"

"The boat had a small covered area at the front and we were mainly in a sea loch and close to the shore, so it didn't get too bad."

"It seems quite a contrast to my last trip, to the palazzo in Tuscany."

"Yes, I suppose so," I agreed. "And will you be able to take on some travelling again? What about your father?"

"Oh, thank you for asking. I got him a place in a very pleasant care home. It's in a village close to our old family house. He's settled in there, so it's all taken care of and I'm a free agent again."

Didn't that sound a little callous, I wondered? "Well, that's good; I'm glad that you were able to sort everything out," I responded.

Speaking with Miles made me consider the likelihood of being assigned any more of the office's distant valuations now that I'd proven myself to Anthony. Or would Miles just take over completely again? I should definitely raise the subject at my next appraisal meeting; show that I was keen to continue in this line. In the meantime, I had some loose ends to tie up from Mull. Not all of the expert valuations had been received and collated. I also discovered a file containing details of a property in Hampstead. It must have been placed on my desk prior to my arrival that morning. Actually, that would suit me very nicely at the moment. I could walk there from home and avoid the horrors of the London public transport system while I reacclimatised to my old life.

By the end of the day I had a buzzing headache, probably, in part, from drinking too much coffee. My return journey home wasn't so busy; the end-of-day rush tended to be more spread out and less hectic. However, the aromas wafting through the tube carriages weren't so pleasant: stale cigarette smoke and sweat mingled with greasy food scents. I was glad to be able to kick off my pinching shoes when I stepped through my front door. I headed straight for the medicine cabinet above my washbasin and popped two paracetamol caplets out from their packet. I went to sit on my sofa with a glass of ice-cold water, closed my eyes and propped my feet up on the coffee table. Concentrating on deep breathing in an effort to relax, I inhaled the sweet perfume from Mum's freesias. After about twenty minutes I began to revive. As I unwound, I realised that at some point over the past twenty-four hours I'd come to a decision about contacting Grant. I hadn't been aware of actively thinking about it, but now my mind was made up. The only question was, should I phone him now or wait until after I'd eaten? No – I'd done enough procrastinating over the arrangements for Jess's weekend, so no time like the present. I went to fetch my phone from my bag, which I'd dumped by the front door. I brought up Grant's text message, then quickly tapped in his number before I could change my mind. It was ringing.

"Hello. Claire?" Grant's accent sounded much more Scottish than I'd remembered; the way he rolled the 'R' at the end of my name. It could be the effect of the mobile connection.

"Hi, Grant. I'm sorry I had to rush off without seeing you, but thanks for your message."

"And how're things back at home?"

"Honestly? It's lovely to be back in my flat, but I'm finding the pace of London hard to get used to again. I'm just in from my first day back at work and I'm shattered."

"No sheep jams today, then?"

"No, just a lot of people and a few pigeons to dodge. But I'm phoning with a request. While I was away, I ignored the fact that I'm supposed to be organising my friend's hen weekend, and now I'm in a bit of a jam."

"I'm not sure how I can help with that. It doesn't seem to be exactly my scene."

"Well, I've been thinking of going to Edinburgh for the August bank holiday weekend while the festival is on. Only, accommodation is scarce and very expensive and I wondered if we could stay in your flat." I gasped this last sentence out and then held my breath as I waited for his reply.

"OK… it would be a good time to visit with lots going on, but I don't really rent the flat out. It's my home. The house I live in here on the island belongs to the estate, so I needed to buy into the property market and to have a base in the city to see the girls."

"That's OK, I understand. It's just that Isla said that you sometimes let friends stay there. Anyway, it might not suit. You might want to spend some time there yourself during the festival."

"I will be down. I usually choose a week when the girls are still on holiday so that I can take them along to some of the shows. But I think your weekend would be after they go back to school."

"Grant, just tell me if I'm being cheeky. There will be six of us, and I promise we'd be very responsible if you should say yes."

"Can I think about it and check the dates? I don't want to promise you something I can't deliver."

"Of course."

"OK, I'll check with Ruth what the holiday dates are for the girls and get back to you."

"Thank you so much."

"I haven't said yes yet."

"I know, but you're considering it and you don't sound cross with me for asking."

"What are friends for? I'll be in touch. Bye for now."

"Bye, Grant."

I sighed after I hung up. I didn't feel comfortable. He'd used the word 'friend', but had he felt obliged, pressured? I wasn't sure if he'd thought me presumptuous and pushy. But he hadn't said no, so it might work – and I probably wasn't ever going to see him again anyway. I tried, not very successfully, to make myself feel better with that thought as I headed into the kitchen to consult Delia about that night's dinner.

The next day I set off for the Hampstead property in South Hill Park. It was quite a large house, but nothing close to the scale of a castle. Also, although furniture had been left in situ, there were no other contents to catalogue. All of the shelves, drawers and cupboards had already been emptied; it seemed soulless. However, I was quite relaxed as I set about my task. Comparing my stress levels today with Monday's, I was definitely beginning to feel more comfortable in my surroundings again. I'd enjoyed the morning walk through the leafy streets, and took my packed lunch to the Heath at lunchtime. I found a shaded bench overlooking one of the ponds, and was chewing on a bite from my cheese sandwich when my phone rang. I rootled around in my bag to find it. Maybe it was Grant. My heartbeat gradually returned to normal after I read the name on the screen.

"Hi, Jess."

"Claire, I need your advice about the wedding invitations."

"Uh-huh?"

"I've got them back from the printers and they look gorgeous. I want to send them out straight away, but Mum says it should only be six or eight weeks before."

"You've already done a save-the-date, haven't you?"

"Yes, to some people, but not the whole list. I don't see the point in holding off."

"What does Chris say?"

"Oh, he doesn't care; he says to do what I want."

"Well, why don't you do what you want? I don't think anyone really bothers too much with all the old protocols so much now."

"You really think that'll be OK?"

"Yes, I'm sure it will." I tried to use my most soothing voice. Her anxiety about what I reckoned to be such a small detail seemed out of character for Jess. "Is everything else OK?"

"Yes, yes, I'm fine." But she sighed.

"Do you want me to come and help you with the invitations? I could write the addresses."

"Oh, would you? That would be brill."

"I could come to you tomorrow after work?"

"Cool, you're such a star, Claire, thanks."

"Fine. I'll call in at Marks on my way past and get us something to heat up. Keep our strength up."

"I'll have a bottle of white in the fridge."

"See you tomorrow, then. Bye."

I was pleased that my friend sounded happier when I rang off. I finished up my sandwich, ready to set off back to work. I'd saved a few pieces of crust for the pair of green parakeets that had been squawking from the tree across the path, and scattered them in front of the bench as I left. When I glanced back from the pathway, they'd already swooped down to retrieve the food.

That evening I had another date with Delia. I'd bought the ingredients for beef stroganoff and was pleased with the result. I treated myself to a glass of red wine as an accompaniment. Determined not to obsess all evening about a possible phone call from Grant, I needed a distraction. I remembered the music book that Archie had given to me and, after my meal, I decided to look out my flute. It was under my bed, along with abandoned tennis and skiing gear, a Mexican sombrero, and an unopened three-thousand-piece jigsaw puzzle of New York. I took the flute case through to the kitchen and wiped away the dust with a damp sponge. Once it was assembled, I raised the flute and blew a few notes. They were quivery and breathy; I was badly out of practice. My joints felt stiff and awkward as I worked through some fingering. I had to begin somewhere, so I flipped through the book of songs, hoping to find one without multiple semiquavers that would require maximum dexterity. But on the other hand, a slow tune with long, sustained notes would need steady breathing. I settled on a tune called 'The Birks of

Aberfeldy'. It had two sharps in the key but apart from that it looked quite simple.

After three or four runs through I felt I was getting the hang of it, and began to search for another piece to play. If I practised, I should be able to tackle all of these. It was something to aspire to. I could even try some of my previous repertoire; look out my old collection of music. Where would it all be? Probably in the attic at my parents' house. It was so long since I'd played. Well, I was going to Tunbridge Wells at the weekend. I could hunt for it then.

Chapter 12

The train journey from Charing Cross to Tunbridge Wells takes just under an hour. I stowed my holdall on the overhead shelf and settled into a window seat. As the train pulled out from the station, I sent Mum a text to let her know that I was on my way. She replied to suggest that I call in at the shop as she and Dad were both there that afternoon. When I glanced out of the window, I could see that we were level with Canary Wharf. It wasn't an area of the city that I'd visited much, but I knew that Jessica's Chris worked for an accountant's firm based there. I returned my gaze to my phone and looked for the umpteenth time at the text that I'd received from Grant on Wednesday.

Hi, Claire. The dates are OK for you to use the flat. I'll get in touch nearer the time to make arrangements, but letting you know that you'll need to bring bed linen and towels, and probably a sleeping bag for the 6th person. There are 2 double beds and a single; the 6th will have to be on the sofa. Hope that's fine. Grant.

It was a businesslike message. Practical, but not unfriendly. I didn't think I could read any more into it than that, no matter how many times I read through it. I'd fired off an immediate reply full of thanks. It was a huge relief to have the question of accommodation settled. It meant that I could get down to more detailed planning for the weekend. I'd already looked at the Festival Fringe programme online and been overwhelmed by the choice of entertainment that would be on offer. I'd also researched some spa deals. From information on the Edinburgh tourist guide site, it seemed that we could easily spend a whole day on the Royal Mile, visiting the castle at one end and Holyrood Palace at the other, with lots of shops, pubs and restaurants in-between.

I was gazing out of the window at the passing countryside as I mulled through these nascent plans. Suddenly I focused on two rounded turret roofs with stubby white chimneys emerging from their tops. My first oast house sighting of this journey. These traditional buildings were dotted all around the Kent countryside, and my first glimpse of their familiar structure was always a symbol of coming home.

When I arrived at Tunbridge Wells railway station, I made my way to the exit, then turned right onto the High Street, heading for The Pantiles where the family business was situated. This historic street was for pedestrians only. Today it was busy with stalls selling crafts, fudge and home-made sweets, toys and bric-a-brac. They were set up along the upper walkway; a common occurrence for a Saturday. I weaved my way through families and browsing tourists and stopped outside Ford's Antiques. The shop bell pinged as I opened the door. Immediately I was enveloped in the scent that I associated with my parents' business: dusty mustiness, lavender, and a hint of spice. My mum harvested the lavender flowers from our garden every year and put them into small home-made drawstring cloth bags which she then distributed around the shop. She'd started doing this years ago to mask any stale odours from the second-hand merchandise. Gradually the number of scented bags had increased with time, and they'd become a signature feature of the shop.

The bell having alerted her to a possible customer, my mum appeared with a swish of the beaded curtain that shielded off the back of the shop. "Claire, how are you, love?" She wrapped me up in a warm hug.

"I'm fine, Mum – been busy today?" I asked.

"Well, a steady flow of browsers, but not so many sales," she replied. "I'll call your dad up; he's down in the storeroom." She stuck her head back through the beads and called, "Edward, it's Claire. She's arrived." Before he appeared, the shop bell pinged again and Mum turned her attention to the new arrival. "Can I help you?"

As I stood by the till, my attention was caught by some of the objects around me. The elephant's foot umbrella stand was still a feature; it seemed to have always been there, never having been sold. The walking canes and shooting sticks it contained did turn over, but the stand now seemed to be a permanent fixture. Another piece that had stuck was the stuffed barn owl in its domed glass display case. It was a beautiful specimen, but perhaps, like the elephant's foot, not something that most people felt comfortable to have in their home. To one side of the shop, I could see a new array of luxurious, vividly coloured Persian rugs. I made my way towards them and stroked the soft, velvety pile of the closest carpet. From my new vantage point, I could see a display table with a glass cover which had appeared since my last visit. Moving closer to examine the contents, I found that it contained perhaps two dozen Japanese netsuke. I particularly liked a little mouse – it was a pale, creamy colour; I guessed that it must be carved from ivory.

"Ideally I'd like that to be an open display so that people could pick them up and handle them. But I was afraid that they might be pocketed, hence the locked case." My dad had appeared at my shoulder.

"Hi, Dad." I turned around to give him a hug, and noticed that Mum was now showing the elderly woman who'd come into the shop a selection of cameo brooches.

"Come on through to the back." Dad led the way. "When your mum's finished serving that customer, you and she can go home. I'll be fine on my own for the last half hour."

"Good idea – we can get a meal on the go."

"That would be very welcome. So, how has it been settling back into the routine?"

"Actually, much stranger than I'd thought," I admitted. "I've felt a bit overwhelmed by the noise and the busyness, and I seem to crave open spaces. Luckily, I was working near Hampstead Heath this week, so I've been able to chill out there at lunchtimes."

"Oh well, you can always go for a walk on the common tomorrow."

I found it hard to explain. What was this urge that I had to see the sky? Also, while the greenery and openness were welcome, somehow the manicured space of a town park didn't seem wild enough anymore. The job close to the Heath had been a godsend this past week; the time spent in the open air a tonic, I was in no doubt.

Dad sat down at the table, returning to the task he'd interrupted to greet me. He was polishing up a set of tiny silver coffee spoons. Their handles were intricate and he was using a baby's toothbrush to reach into all of the interstices. The table also held other pieces which required cleaning or mending: a broken picture frame, a hand mirror with a space where a jewel was missing, a wooden elephant with only one tusk, and a murky brass plant pot.

Mum joined us, pleased that she had made a sale. "What an interesting lady." She proceeded to tell us all about her American customer, who was a huge fan of the Regency period and of Jane Austen in particular.

Dad and I exchanged grins. We were always amazed by the amount of information that Mum could extract from people. We joked that her talent was wasted as a shopkeeper. She should work for the secret service or as an undercover police officer, as people seemed to just naturally confide in her without any obvious effort or questioning on Mum's part. She gathered her jacket and handbag, searching around for her glasses as she chatted. She eventually located them on top of the filing cabinet, and then she and I were ready to set off for the house.

"Bye, Edward, don't stay any later than five." Mum gave Dad a peck on the cheek.

"Bye, Dad, see you soon."

When we left the shop some of the stallholders on the street outside were beginning to pack up. A few of them greeted Mum as we passed by. Our route home took us along Mount Sion and Claremont Road. We chatted as we meandered along the leafy streets, taking our time and looking into gardens, catching up on our news.

My weekend stay was very relaxing. I'm not sure if it was the familiar surroundings or Mum's cosseting, but I could feel myself gradually letting go of the tension that had built up over the past week. I enjoyed hearing about the house sales that Dad had attended, and he was inquisitive about the future for my castle and its contents. Mum and I spent a lot of time together in the kitchen, chopping and stirring as we prepared meals. I also assisted her in the garden, following her instructions closely as I had no knowledge of plants and was likely to pull up a prized specimen mistaking it for a weed if left to my own devices. On the Sunday morning we all went for a walk on the common, and later that day I pulled down the attic ladder and rummaged around among the dusty boxes until I found a leather briefcase which contained some of my old flute music scores.

Somehow, the visit to my parents grounded me and helped me to begin the process of settling back into my old life, picking up the reins and taking charge of my leisure time. Over the next week I began to contact friends and fill up my diary with drinks evenings, dinners, concerts and cinema outings. I researched amateur orchestras online and made a plan to apply for a place in the autumn. Meanwhile, I practised my flute two or three times a week. The dexterity of my fingering, and my breathing pattern both improved as I revisited some of my old repertoire and learned more of Archie's tunes. A lot of my free time was spent with Jessica; the arrangements for the hen weekend and the wedding seemed to be never-ending. Then both of those events came around, were enjoyed tremendously and, suddenly, were in the past.

At the beginning of October, after the bustle and excitement had died down, I experienced a strong sense of anticlimax. Restlessness seemed to creep up on me during the week after the wedding. Jessica was away on her honeymoon in Mauritius. Maybe I needed a holiday too. Apart from the weekends in Mull, Tunbridge Wells and Edinburgh I hadn't had a break all year. I searched for inspiration. I wasn't sure about the prospect of holidaying alone, and I couldn't think which of my friends might be free to accompany me on a trip, especially at short notice. I'd have almost a full holiday allowance to use up before the end of the year. Perhaps I should visit my cousin Louise in South Africa. She lived in Cape Town, and had extended several invitations. I could spend some time with her and arrange a safari tour. That might work. Then I wondered if I knew anyone who might be up for a group skiing trip between Christmas and New Year. That could be fun. The snow might not be reliable, though. I decided to research both trips on the internet. After brewing up some coffee I spent a happy Saturday morning looking at travel sites on my laptop. I decided that both of my ideas were good, but I'd need to gauge the amount of interest there was for skiing. I'd left my phone charging in the kitchen and went to collect it, meaning to fire off some messages. But when I reached the kitchen, I realised that I was starving. No wonder – it was nearly two o'clock. Making and eating a sandwich suddenly took priority over holiday plans. I sat down in the lounge to eat and flicked through the list of shows that I'd recorded onto my set-top box from the TV. I picked *The Graham Norton Show* to accompany my lunch. So, it was an hour later when I eventually retrieved my phone in order to contact my friends. That was when I discovered a text message from Grant.

I'm going to be in London this week and wondered if you might be free to meet for a drink or dinner? Grant.

Chapter 13

'd arranged to meet Grant on the steps of the National Gallery and was in position there just before 6.30 on Tuesday evening, scanning the crowd. From my vantage point I spotted a tall figure with an unruly mop of dark, curly hair approaching from the direction of the Strand. I thought that was probably him, but I'd never seen Grant dressed in smart city clothes before. As the man approached, I took in his appearance. He was wearing a charcoal-coloured suit with an open-collared blue shirt and shiny black brogues. It was definitely him. He waved a greeting as he caught sight of me, and when he smiled his eyes crinkled up at the corners in a familiar way. Unsure, I stuck out my hand to be shaken. He obliged, grasping my hand and leaning in to kiss my cheek. At close proximity I caught scents of sandalwood and peppermint. As he stood on the step below me, his eyes were level with mine. They looked intensely blue, shining out from the deep tan of his face.

"Hello. I wondered if I would recognise you in office apparel. You look extremely elegant," he said.

I'd come straight from work and was wearing a navy shift dress under a cream-and-navy jacket, and court shoes with heels. My hair was neatly drawn back in a French plait, restructured in the office toilets before I'd left. I'd also refreshed my make-up. It was certainly a different look from my wild, wind-tossed and mist-frizzed hair, and clear, make-up-free skin on Mull.

"Funny, I was just thinking the same thing. I've never seen you looking so smart."

"No straw or sheep shit on my trousers today, then?" He laughed. Obviously no offence had been taken. "So, where are you thinking of eating? I'm starving."

"Well, as long as you like Chinese, I thought we'd visit Chinatown. It's not far from here."

"Great idea." He fell into step beside me as I began walking, heading towards Wardour Street and Shaftesbury Avenue.

"What brings you to London?" I asked.

"Oh, some very boring and complicated legal stuff. It's come up because my parents have decided that they want to buy a house in France. To do that, Dad has to take some of his assets from the estate in a lump sum."

"He's retired now, right?"

"Aye. He used to do my job and the estate pays him a pension, but it's not quite as simple as a regular job with an old-age pension. He has other rights and assets tied up in the business which are part of his family inheritance. The lawyers have to work it all out. Obviously, we'd prefer not to sell off any of the land if we don't have to, and the family aren't the only stakeholders anymore."

It did sound convoluted.

"Where in France do they want to buy?"

"They've been renting a property in the Charente area for the past six months. That's in the west, north of Bordeaux. Anyway, it seems that the current owners would like to sell up and Mum and Dad are keen to buy."

"Have you been there?"

"No, but it sounds idyllic. You can bet that I'll be visiting for my holidays if the deal goes through."

"Speaking of holidays, I have to thank you so much for letting us use your flat."

"Oh, I think you already did that several times. It's fine, Claire. I'm glad that the weekend was a success. And how about the wedding? I guess that's all happened now."

"Yes, it was ten days ago. Thankfully, everything went really well."

As we walked on, colourful Chinese signs and decorations began to appear to either side of us, adorning the buildings and street lamps. Lanterns were strung across the street, swaying in the breeze. Gold-and-red dragons, banners with Chinese script, and pagoda-style awnings all vied for our attention.

"We'd better start looking at menus to decide on a place to eat," I said.

We wandered up and down, perusing the shopfronts and the menus on display.

"I only had a small sandwich for lunch. It all looks great to me." Grant didn't seem to want to look much farther.

"OK, let's go for this one." I made up my mind and we entered underneath a crimson arched tunnel.

The decor inside the restaurant mainly followed a theme of bamboo and giant pandas, but there were also wall panels with a lotus flower design, and a huge tank of tropical fish took up most of one wall. We studied the large selection of food on offer and decided to order a banquet for two with dim sum. I asked for a glass of white wine and Grant chose Snow beer; very popular in China, according to our waiter.

"So, how are the girls?" I asked once we'd given our order. "Did you get that swing for Laura?"

"Aye, I did, and it was a huge success. I had Laura to stay for a month over the summer, but Mairi only came for part of that time. She was off at a pony-riding camp. She's suddenly mad about horses."

"Maybe you'll have to buy a pony if you want her to visit more."

"Aye, you could be right, that's not a bad idea."

"Actually, I was joking," I said. "But I suppose you've got plenty of space for the odd pony."

"What's more, I could beat her mother on that. She's not going to be keeping a pony in Trinity. That is kind of a joke, but not completely," he clarified. "I try hard in front of the girls not to show that there's acrimony between us. But, if I'm honest, I don't mind scoring some extra points on the popularity scale. I expect Isla filled you in on our backstory."

"Mm, a bit," I replied. I felt my face begin to flush, embarrassed to confess that we'd been discussing him. I didn't like him to think that I was a gossip. I was glad that my wine arrived just then, and I thanked the waiter and took a sip, trying to compose myself.

"Ach, don't worry," Grant said. "I know that on a small island like Mull, in that kind of close community, everyone's business is in the public domain. It's not a place where you can easily keep a secret."

"How is Isla?" I asked, trying to change the subject. "I know that she's expecting."

"Definitely blooming. You know that she always looks great, statuesque. With her height she carries the pregnancy so well. And she's absolutely delighted. She and Fraser were trying for a while before this happened. So, all in all, she just seems to glow."

"Well, that's great." Bowls of food began to appear on our table. Our waiter described the contents of each.

"How are you with chopsticks?" Grant asked.

"Not great, but I won't starve," I replied. "Are you going to have a go?"

"Sure."

As we tucked into the food, our comments were mainly about the different flavours and textures of the various dishes, and we giggled over our ineptitude with the chopsticks. The meal was delicious, and by now I was feeling much more relaxed in Grant's company. I realised that I'd been really nervous about meeting him again.

"Has your work sent you on any more adventures since Mull?" Grant asked. Our initial hunger was sated and we were picking much more daintily at the remaining food.

"Nothing out of London. I did raise it at my appraisal last month. Said I'd enjoyed the challenge and was up for another similar project. I got good feedback too."

"Maybe there just hasn't been anything."

"Well, most of our work is in the south-east. But I know that there have been a few jobs farther afield. I suppose that my boss, Anthony, has had the people to cover them. I was just a substitute for Miles on the Mull valuation. There's always a pecking order in a firm like ours."

"You like your job, though?"

"Yes, I do. But I have to admit that I found it hard to settle down to the same old routine when I got home from Mull. I suppose I enjoyed the autonomy I had there, working at my own pace. I was busy but I felt more relaxed. I'm not so restless now, but maybe I should be looking for a change."

"How long have you been with this firm?"

"Just over ten years now. But I'm still one of the juniors."

"Well, there's no harm in keeping an eye out for any new opportunities that come up," Grant suggested.

"Yeah, I guess." I wasn't sure that I was sufficiently motivated to make a career move right now. To steer our conversation in a different direction, I told Grant about my holiday plans. He'd visited South Africa in the past and was able to give me some tips about places to visit.

"And you know that you're welcome to come back to Mull for a holiday any time," he told me.

"Isla keeps asking me," I said. "I'll definitely come sometime next year once the baby has arrived."

"Claire, I want to apologise for blowing hot and cold with you earlier in the year."

"Oh, I—"

"Let me explain," he interrupted. "I want you to know that I was, and am, attracted to you and I enjoy your company. I think I let that show early in your visit. Then I sort of panicked. It was hard for me to really envisage a new relationship, and my priority has always been to do nothing that might upset or confuse the girls. So those ideas started to get in the way of how I felt about you, and I began to freeze you out. I know that you must have wondered at the change in me. Anyway, I've really missed you since you left; my office just doesn't feel the same. I realise that I've probably ruined my chances and put you off forever. Isla gave me a terrible row too. She can read me so well; she knew I liked you but had pushed you away. I suppose what I'm trying to say or ask in all of this is whether there's any hope for me. Is there a chance that we could start over again?"

I was taken aback by Grant's declaration, but also extremely pleased. His right arm was stretched out on the tabletop, his hand close to his empty beer glass. I reached out and took his hand. "Thank you for being so honest. I can understand that you feel cautious about relationships, and why."

He bowed his head a little and smiled ruefully.

"I think if we're going forward, we should both be open and truthful," I continued. "I admit that I was confused and disappointed by what seemed to be a big change in the way that you reacted to me. Then I thought maybe I'd read too much into your earlier friendliness and I was embarrassed. But overall, I was just sad that things had changed."

"So, you're saying that we can start over again?"

"Yes, I'd like that," I said, and squeezed his hand. He squeezed back, then lifted my hand to his lips and kissed it.

"Thank you, Claire. I'm so pleased."

After these speeches, we both seemed momentarily awkward and tongue-tied. Grant suggested that we order coffee, and I decided to pay a visit to the ladies'. Whilst washing my hands I looked up and caught sight of my face in the mirror. My grin would have outdone the Cheshire cat's.

We managed to regain our equilibrium over coffee. Grant described a few projects that he was planning on the estate over the coming year, and I filled him in on my flute practice and told him about the orchestra that I'd joined. "It's all thanks to Archie and that book of music he gave me," I explained.

Grant hadn't known about the gift, but he promised to tell Archie about the revival of music in my life. "He'll expect you to take a turn at the next ceilidh you attend," he warned.

"I think I could manage that. It would be fun."

After coffee we collected our coats and made our way back out onto the street.

"Where's your hotel?" I asked.

"Russell Square."

"OK, why don't we make for Piccadilly Circus underground? Then you can catch the Piccadilly line to Russell Square and I can go in the other direction to Green Park and change to the Jubilee line there."

"Sounds like you have the underground map etched onto your brain."

"Not really, but I go to Russell Square sometimes for the British Museum."

We set off for the tube station and, as we walked along side by side, Grant took my hand in his. "Would it be very forward to ask you if you're free to meet me again tomorrow night?" he asked.

"Not at all, and yes, I'm free," I replied, immediately deciding to give orchestra rehearsals a miss this week.

We met every night that week. On Wednesday we ate at a tapas bar on the South Bank. I managed to get tickets for *The Phantom of the Opera* on Thursday, then we went for a drink after the show. Grant was catching the sleeper to Edinburgh on Friday night so that he could spend most of the weekend with Mairi and Laura, and then he would travel on to Mull on Sunday afternoon. So we met at Albertini's, a family-run Italian restaurant five minutes' walk from Euston station, for dinner.

The kiss that we shared before he left for the train station was intense. I didn't want him to go; we were just getting to know each other and I'd enjoyed his company so much. However, we'd agreed that I would go to Edinburgh in two weeks' time and we'd meet up there for a long weekend. My current wealth of holidays might come in handy. And of course, we could phone and text each other every day until then.

Chapter 14

Grant's first text message arrived the next morning.

Missing you already. At a hockey match supporting M. G x

I replied:

Hope she wins! C x

Jessica and Chris were due back from their honeymoon later that day. I planned to visit their flat to check that the heating was on and deliver some groceries. I also had a lot of my own chores to catch up with this weekend; I'd hardly set foot in my flat since Tuesday, just coming in to sleep and then rushing out to work in the mornings before meeting Grant every evening. I put a load of washing into my machine before setting out for Jess's flat. Her nearest tube station was Clapham Common, so I needed to change to the Northern line at Waterloo. It would be easiest to shop at that end; maybe I'd have some lunch in Clapham.

When I arrived, the flat looked as if a bomb had hit it. I didn't know how much tidying up I should attempt – after all, it wasn't my mess. Clothes were strewn around the bedroom; I guessed that they were the rejects from the holiday packing. In the lounge there were piles of presents on almost every surface. Some were still fully wrapped, others had been put into boxes, and more were just lying loose. Wads of discarded wrapping paper had mainly missed the wastepaper bin, but were scattered around in that vicinity. The kitchen was definitely the worst room, containing dishes with dried-on food, coffee mugs and glasses with dregs of drink remaining, and a very smelly bin. I looked in the fridge and found mouldy cheese and wilted salad vegetables. I decided to tackle this room, as it would be the most unpleasant to face on coming home from an idyllic holiday. I opened the kitchen window and tore off a large refuse sack from the roll that I found in the cupboard under the sink. I emptied the offending rubbish and food into it, tied it off and carried the bag outside to the communal bins. Then I rinsed all of the cups and mugs, ran a sinkful of hot, soapy water and put the dishes in to soak. They could stay there while I did some shopping.

I picked up the essentials at a Sainsbury's Local, along with a newspaper for myself. I came across a patisserie with a very tempting display of cakes. I almost walked past on my way to the common, but the cakes called to me, making me stop. I chose a wedge of fruit tart, ordered a coffee, and settled down to read my newspaper. I was looking at the film reviews when my phone buzzed with an incoming text.

We won 3:1. Talk tonight? G x

Drinks do at 6, home by 10. C x

I attached a smiley to my response, and realised that it matched the smile on my own face. I felt so excited and happy, but there was still a niggle of doubt. I didn't quite trust this sudden romance. I hadn't mentioned it to anyone yet – would a sounding board help? If I told my mum, or Jessica once she was home, would it jinx everything? And if I did tell them, they were bound to mention Grant's children and ask how I felt about them, and I hadn't worked that out for myself yet. I'd have to say something before my Edinburgh trip, but that was two weeks away. I knew that Mum was hoping I'd meet someone and settle down soon. She was always tactful and didn't ask direct questions, but the odd comment or searching look gave her away.

I hadn't had a serious boyfriend since Johnathan. We'd met not long after I came to London to do my MA at Kingston. He was a software engineer and worked for a firm running projects for financial institutions. We'd both seemed to enjoy city life, but after four years together, he'd suddenly decided that he wanted to get away from the stress of big business. This also seemed to involve moving to Australia. At the time, I was just six months into my new job with Braithwaite, Crosshall & Greene, and really excited to be there. So, I didn't want to go to Australia. I'd often wondered since then: what if Johnathan had suggested the move six months earlier while I was still at Rosebery's? Would I have gone? Would we still be together? As far as I was aware, he was still living in Australia in the Melbourne area. Since Johnathan I'd dated sporadically, but I'd never found anyone who could make me smile just thinking about them, or cause the fizzy excitement that I was currently experiencing. I folded up my newspaper and settled my bill.

Back at Jess's flat, I restocked the fridge. Then I brushed off the dishes vigorously, stacked them in the dishwasher and turned it on. I wiped down the surfaces and swept the floor. Last, I closed the window and put the flowers I'd bought into a vase which I left on the kitchen table. That would have to do.

As I retraced my journey home, I wondered what I should wear tonight. One of my colleagues, India, had bought a flat and tonight she was hosting a house-warming drinks gathering. We'd clubbed together towards a gift voucher from the whole office, so I didn't need to buy a present to take along. I'd know a lot of the people there, and normally it would be something that I'd look forward to. But now I wished that Grant could come with me, because I knew that his presence would make it much more fun. How was I going to cope with this relationship when we lived five hundred miles apart? I hadn't considered that when I was holding Grant's hand and agreeing that we should make a go of things. But then, of course, it hadn't been a problem when I was with him.

That was almost the first thing that Jess asked me when we spoke the next day. She rang to thank me for tidying her kitchen and to enthuse about her holiday in Mauritius. She was my best friend; I had to tell her about Grant.

"Wow, he showed up in London? And you're going to keep seeing him? How's that going to work exactly?" Jess wasn't well known for tact.

"Well, we'll just have to see. To begin with, I'm going to Edinburgh for the weekend in two weeks' time."

"Of course, he's got the flat there. That makes it a bit easier." She sounded doubtful.

"Jess, can you not be happy for me? I like him."

"Sure, yes. Yes, I am happy for you. But he's got kids, hasn't he?"

"Yes, but they mainly live with their mum."

"Where's that?"

"Edinburgh," I muttered.

"So, will you see them on the weekend?"

"I don't know. I might. I've met them before; I like them."

"OK, listen, Claire. I just don't think you should rush into this. I don't want you to get hurt."

"It's fine, Jess."

"Hey, will we meet for drinks on Friday at the wine bar? Then I can talk some sense into you."

"Yeah, I'd like to meet up."

"OK, see you on Friday at six."

"It's a date. See you then." I knew that Jess was pointing out the difficulties in my blossoming relationship, because she was protective. But she hadn't met Grant, and I hoped that she'd approve of him when she did. It was good that she wanted to maintain our old routine. I hadn't been sure if her marriage would change things. Although, thinking about it, why should there be a difference? She and Chris had lived together for nearly three years already, so really her circumstances were much the same as before.

In the end, when I told Mum that I was going to Edinburgh for a weekend break I didn't mention a boyfriend. I kept the details vague, saying that I was meeting up with someone I'd made friends with while I was working on Mull. It wasn't that I planned to keep the whole thing a secret, but I decided that I could wait to tell her properly once there was more to say.

I arranged to take a half-day of holiday so that I could travel up to Edinburgh on the Friday afternoon, leaving the evening free to spend with Grant. This time I travelled by train. As I sped northwards, I imagined the distance between Grant's car and my train gradually diminishing as our routes converged on the city. I knew that he was driving to Edinburgh from Mull that day, planning to arrive ahead of me so that he would be there at the flat to let me in.

I took a taxi from the station. Grant answered almost immediately when I pressed the entryphone buzzer at the building's entrance. The door clicked open and I paced myself climbing up the three flights of stairs. I didn't want to arrive sweaty, flushed and out of breath. As it was, I did feel breathless when I caught sight of Grant standing in the doorway of his flat.

He was barefoot, wearing jeans and a pale blue sweatshirt, and he was smiling at me in his crinkly-eyed fashion. Since this visit had first been suggested, I'd speculated over the likelihood that it would result in our relationship moving on to the next stage. I'd wondered if the move to having sex might be awkward. I had to admit now that just the sight of this man was making me feel weak at the knees, and I didn't think that it was from climbing the stairs.

"Hello, you're here," he greeted me.

He caught me by my hand and pulled me towards him into the hallway of the flat, my little suitcase clattering behind me. The door closed, I dropped the suitcase and was immediately enveloped in Grant's arms, inhaling his soft sandalwood scent and feeling his lips on mine. I didn't have to wait long for my question to be answered; we progressed from the hallway to the bedroom, shedding layers of clothing as we went.

Grant had booked a table for dinner at a nearby Italian restaurant in Bruntsfield. We held hands as we walked there through damp residential streets. We sipped glasses of Prosecco as we studied our menus.

After we'd ordered I tried to describe my mixed feelings over the past two weeks. "I want to be totally honest with you. I think that the time spent apart is going to be difficult."

"Aye, but we can make sure that our time together makes up for it. I'd rather be with you for some of the time than not at all. That's what I discovered after you left the island."

"Will it not be hard for you to arrange to see me? You already have to travel every month to see the girls."

"It will be tough at busy times of the year; you might have to come to see me then. But I have a lot of scope to organise my own workload. I think that we can make it work."

"OK, but you have to promise that you'll be straight with me, and tell me if there's a problem."

"I promise," he said, picking up my hand and kissing the palm. "Now let's tuck in and enjoy our meal." Two steaming bowls of pasta had just been served.

Our weekend together was quite different from my previous visit to Edinburgh with Jess and the group for the hen weekend. The city was much quieter outside of festival time, although there were still plenty of visitors. Grant took me to places that were less well known, steering clear of the main tourist attractions. We were lucky to hit a dry spell of weather, so could mainly be outdoors. On Saturday we climbed Arthur's Seat so that I could get a bird's-eye view of the city. We stopped for lunch at a delicatessen on our way back to the flat, then bought ingredients to cook our evening meal. After a romantic interlude in the flat followed by cooking and eating, we headed out to a small cinema to watch *Atonement*, based on the novel by Ian McEwan. We both enjoyed the film, and Grant explained that it was a particular treat for him to go to the cinema to see an adult show. Usually he was taking the girls to see the latest Disney or Harry Potter release. On Sunday we drove east out from the city to an amazing beach at Gullane and walked for miles. That made us hungry again, and we found a pub with good food on our route back into town.

"So, we have to arrange our next few meetings," Grant announced when we arrived back at the flat. "Have you firmed up on your South African holiday yet?"

"Not fully, but I was thinking of taking two weeks off, probably the second half of November."

"Well, why don't I come and join you for a week?"

"Would you?"

"Like a shot. We could take a safari trip together, and then you can enjoy time with your cousin for your other week."

Grant fired up his laptop and we spent the evening looking at travel sites, working out dates and making plans. We agreed that I would make the bookings next week.

"And I'll schedule two or three days in London with you before then," Grant promised. "I've got to wait for some confirmations from shooting parties to come through before I can give you exact dates. But it will happen."

On our walk that afternoon Grant had described how he was working to increase and diversify productivity on the estate. In addition to sheep farming there had always been some deer hunting, but only ever carried out by locals in a small way. Grant was actively marketing the estate as a location for shooting deer, and in addition he was introducing game birds to widen the market. He hoped that he'd soon be able to employ a full-time gamekeeper to help with this venture, but at the moment it was mainly down to him, with some part-time help on actual shooting days. This was his main work over the autumn, and his growing success might now make it difficult to take time off. However, I was learning that Grant was an optimist, and he kept reassuring me that, between us, we could find time to spend together; that we could make things work if we were both committed to doing so. His certainty was beginning to rub off on me, and when I left Edinburgh at the end of the weekend, I felt a lot more confident that our relationship was grounded and solid.

Chapter 15

That first Edinburgh weekend marked the beginning of our roving relationship. Grant and I met for holidays and weekends. We enjoyed city breaks in Paris, Amsterdam, Milan, Nice and Barcelona; not to mention London, Edinburgh and Glasgow.

Our safari week at Kruger National Park was amazing. Grant had visited before, so he knew what to expect, but I'd never been up close to any of the African wild animals. I soon became engrossed in keeping a written record of our sightings, and I tried to obtain supporting photographic evidence for each one. My favourite encounter was with a family of female elephants with a young calf among them. The baby was obviously inquisitive, and came ambling up very close to our vehicle. It raised its trunk towards us, as if it was sniffing, and we could almost have reached out to touch it. Meanwhile, it was completely ignoring the deep warning rumbles coming from its mother. On our last day in the park, I was disappointed because we still hadn't seen a leopard to complete my tally of the 'Big Five' animals. When he heard this, Matome, one of the reserve guides, offered to take us out for a final evening drive. He told us that he knew where a leopard had been sighted the previous night, and that there was a good chance that it would still be in the same area. He explained that leopards are solitary animals, extremely elusive and most active at night, and so often tricky to spot. But he had a hunch that this animal had stored the remains of a kill in the area, so he was willing to take us there. At dusk we were bumping along a sandy track towards a large tree where Matome thought the leopard's kill might be stashed, when he suddenly stopped the vehicle and pointed. There, crossing the road in front of us, was the leopard. Even in the fading light I could see its beautiful markings. The animal was sleek and muscular, packed with power. It seemed to ignore our truck completely, despite being momentarily caught in the headlights, and it padded slowly and steadily towards the tree, then leapt up and stretched out along a large branch. I grappled for my binoculars; once I'd focused, I could see that the creature appeared to be looking at us, locking gazes with me. We stayed there quietly for about thirty minutes, with neither side moving, apart from Grant and me passing the binoculars between us. Then the leopard suddenly moved to climb higher in the tree, to a branch around the other side, presumably to eat its dinner in peace, having ascertained that we weren't a threat. I was delighted to have seen the leopard, and to have completed my 'Big Five' sightings. But the combination of its distance from us and the poor light meant that the photographs I'd shot just looked like shadows and blobs; so I have no record of it.

At Easter I made a return visit to Mull. It was a busy time for Grant, with the lambing, but I wanted to visit Isla to meet her baby son, who had been born in January. I followed the same route that I'd travelled just over a year ago. As I drove away from Glasgow airport, I was conscious that although the scenery looked the same, so many other things had changed. Last year I had been nervous, but excited to be travelling into the unknown. This year I was still excited, but for such different reasons: I was going to visit the man I loved, and to see good friends that I was keen to catch up with.

I found Isla in her studio, working the loom. Her baby, Calum, looked sturdy and had a mop of ginger hair which stuck up comically in multiple directions at once. Motherhood didn't seem to upset Isla; she carried Calum around in a baby sling and continued with her weaving.

"You look amazing, Isla," I commented after our initial greetings. "I can't believe that you're back in shape so quickly."

"It's nothing special that I'm doing; just feeding this hungry wee man." She kissed the top of Calum's head where it peeped out from the papoose.

"And he's sleeping well?"

"Aye, only one overnight feed now. He's very contented."

"It's the effect of all the whisky that she's drinking coming through in her milk," Fraser joked. He'd just come through from the back shop.

"He's joking. You know I don't even like the stuff," Isla objected.

Fraser and I embraced. "So, you and Grant…" he said, grinning and giving me a playful punch on my shoulder as he released me.

"Yes." I was grinning too.

"I thought it was never going to happen when he didn't make a move while you were still here with us."

"Aye, we were both urging him on," Isla confirmed.

"Well, better late than never," I quipped, blushing.

"Aye, he's a deep one," Fraser commented. "Not a bad thing, though; now you know that you've got a keeper."

"Do you want to come round for something to eat tonight? Then we can all catch up properly," I said.

"Are the lambs all in now?" Isla asked.

"I'm not sure," I admitted. "But Grant suggested that I ask you, so he must think he'll be around."

We agreed on a time and I set off to see Archie next. We'd arranged to meet at the Mishnish for a drink and a light lunch. I wanted to tell him all about my progress after starting to play flute again. "I even persuaded Grant to come to one of my orchestra's concerts a few weeks ago," I added.

"Well done, but he's obviously smitten. What kind of programme was it?"

"It was very accessible, mainly popular classics and film scores. I think he even enjoyed it."

We both laughed. Grant was famous for only liking country and western music and some Scottish folk songs.

I'd been pleased that he'd agreed to come down to London for the concert. It also meant that he could meet Jessica and Chris for the first time, as they would be there too. I was definitely on edge that weekend. I wasn't nervous about the performance as, being part of such a large group, I was well supported. But I so wanted my best friend and Grant to like each other. We met up in a pub near the concert hall and I could tell that Jess was quickly won over by Grant's good looks and charm. He ordered a malt whisky, and Jess began to tell him about the advertising campaign she'd worked on for one of the other malts.

He pretended to be horrified that she hadn't ever sampled the drink, or compared it with any other whiskies. "We'll need to get you up to Scotland for a whisky-tasting tour."

"I've been round the distillery at Oban," I boasted.

"But not the Tobermory one?" Grant asked.

Then I had to admit that, although I'd sampled one or two other whiskies since then, I still had to steel myself when drinking it, not completely enjoying the taste. And I was convinced that I would be totally unable to tell any difference between one type and another.

"Aye, it's probably an acquired taste," Grant admitted. "What about you, Chris?"

Chris admitted to liking Irish whiskey and bourbon.

"That crowns it. Claire, you'll need to organise an educational tour."

The banter continued, and I was happy that everyone seemed to get on well together.

On another of Grant's visits to London I arranged for us to go to Tunbridge Wells to visit my parents. Mum had volunteered to cook lunch. By this time, Grant and I had been a couple for more than six months. My parents had heard lots of references to him and I'd told them some of his history, so they were aware that he was divorced with two daughters. I knew that Mum was dying to meet the man in my life. Dad was subtler in his approach, but I was sure that he would also be eager to meet Grant.

We caught the train to Tunbridge Wells, and from the station I took us on a detour to The Pantiles to show Grant where the shop was. It wasn't open on a Sunday morning, so I couldn't take him inside. "They'll have one of their helpers covering this afternoon so that they can both be at home to meet you," I explained.

"I'm honoured, and also a wee bit nervous," Grant admitted.

We held hands as we walked through the town, and I pointed out some local landmarks from my youth. "That's where I used to play tennis, and my Guides troop used to meet in that church hall over there."

"It's a pretty town," Grant said. "I'm sure it was a good place to grow up."

"Yes," I agreed. "Small enough that my parents would let me be quite independent, but big enough to have activities and friends around."

"Do any of your friends still live here?"

"No. I think we all went away to uni, and so far no one has drifted back."

"Aye, I'm one of the few out of my group of friends to have come back to Mull."

The lunch was a success, although I hadn't really been worried. I'd known that my parents would make an effort to be welcoming and warm to any friend I brought to meet them. But, beyond that, I felt that they both genuinely liked Grant and didn't have to work hard at accepting him. It helped that Mum and Dad had visited Mull and even Eilean Creagach. They'd also met Archie and stayed with Isla and Fraser, and all of this gave the four of us some common ground for chat.

My first meeting with Grant's parents required a much longer trip. They now lived permanently in the west of France. So, Grant suggested that we have a holiday in the region, and stay with them for a night or two. We flew separately to La Rochelle, and met up there in a hotel overlooking the iconic harbour. It was September, but the weather was still warm, allowing us to eat lunch outdoors at a port-side restaurant. Having eaten my breakfast in London, it felt very luxurious to drink a local wine and soak up the French seaside atmosphere just a few hours later. After two nights in La Rochelle, we collected our hire car and drove inland to Saint-Jean-d'Angély. We passed through very green countryside and row upon row of grapevines. At this time of the year clusters of ripe grapes were almost ready to be harvested. Grant's parents lived in a converted barn and steading a little way out of Saint-Jean. Their approach road was a pothole-strewn track with tufts of grass growing in the middle. Grant's dad had obviously been keeping a lookout for us; we spotted him sitting on a bench at the entrance to a cobbled courtyard. He sprang to his feet, waving, as we approached slowly along the rough track. He directed Grant to park just around the corner and we got out of the car to greet him. I could see immediately that Grant took after his father. Colin's hair was grey now, but it was still thick and curly like Grant's, and his build was very similar. He was wearing shorts and a casual short-sleeved shirt, showing his arms and legs, which were very tanned. He wrapped Grant in a bear hug, clapping him on the back.

"You made it here at last, son. I hope our directions were easy to follow?"

Grant was able to reassure him that we'd found the place easily.

Then Colin came to shake hands with me and kissed me three times on alternate cheeks, in the French style. "So glad to meet you, Claire. Sheelagh is inside, but I know that she's looking forward to your visit too." He led us through the archway into a sunny courtyard and suggested that we sit at a wooden table which was shaded by a striped parasol. "Now, what can I get you? Coffee? Tea? A cold drink? Something stronger?"

We both opted for coffee and Colin disappeared through a doorway to make it. A few seconds later Grant's mum appeared from the same door. She was wearing a summer dress and strappy sandals. She looked very elegant; her silver hair neatly arranged in a low chignon. I stood up to greet her and, with our eyes level, noticed that hers were the same navy-blue hue as Grant's. We did the three-kisses routine, then she moved over to embrace her son.

"I can't believe that it's taken you so long to come to see us," she chided Grant. "But now that you've done it once, you'll have discovered that it's not so hard. There are flights to La Rochelle or Bordeaux and then it's not that long a drive. Have you visited this area before, Claire?"

I told her that I'd only been to Paris and a few ski resorts, but that I'd loved La Rochelle and the drive that morning. "Did you move into this already converted, or have you done much to it?" I asked, gesturing at the building.

This was an inspired question, as Grant's mum, and his dad when he reappeared, proceeded to tell us all about their property-hunting experiences, and how in love they were with their eventual choice.

"You did well," Grant confirmed later. "French property is their number-one topic of conversation."

"It seemed to break the ice, anyway," I said.

I felt comfortable with Grant's parents, and we enjoyed our stay. It was fun to move on and explore other parts of the Poitou-Charentes area for the remainder of our week, but I knew that I'd always be welcome at Saint-Jean, and that I'd look forward to revisiting.

Meeting up for holidays was pleasant, but after almost three years Grant and I agreed that we needed to live closer to each other. Of course, he couldn't relocate as his job was tied to the estate. I suppose I'd always known that if we were going to stay together, I would have to move to Scotland. Although Grant made it plain that I was welcome to move in with him, I wasn't quite ready for that step. It therefore seemed fortuitous that, one afternoon on a visit to Oban, I bumped into Mr Stewart the lawyer walking along George Street. He recognised me from our association over Murdo's estate, but was surprised to see me back in town.

"We could use someone with your expertise in the town right now," he declared. He went on to explain that the firm who normally carried out local valuations had one member of staff on maternity leave, and another who had just been diagnosed with cancer and would be absent for the foreseeable future.

This seemed to be just the opening I needed. Within a week I'd applied and been accepted as a locum in the local company. And I'd found a cottage to rent in Oban. My contract obliged me to work out a month's notice at my job in London, and that gave me time to register my flat with an estate agent who would arrange and oversee tenants for me. Then I was living and working in Oban, only a ferry sailing and a drive away from Grant. Some people might think that would still be quite a hassle, but for us it was amazing to be able to meet for an evening and have dinner, or to spend a weekend together without one or both of us having to get on a plane.

The only significant family member left for me to meet was Grant's brother, Malcolm. I'd gathered, from comments dropped by Grant, that the brothers weren't close. But when we eventually met, I realised that Grant seemed to actively dislike his younger brother.

"My brother will be in town tomorrow," he informed me during a telephone call. "Wants to meet up with me, he says. He's staying at the Best Western, so I'll just book us a table there for dinner – say, around seven?"

"OK," I replied, at a bit of a loss in the face of Grant's cool attitude. "Will he not be staying with you, then?"

"Oh no, he doesn't want to waste time crossing over to the island. He's only in the country for a few days, apparently; been at a reunion in Glasgow. So, we're honoured that he's even making it up to Oban."

"Are you sure that you want me to join you?" I asked.

"Aye, it will be a lifesaver – if you don't mind."

I couldn't help but be intrigued. What could be so awful about the man to deserve Grant's animosity? I knew that Malcolm was a dentist and that he'd worked abroad for many years; that was about all. I decided to ask Isla, as it sounded as if it would be prudent to be better informed.

"Och, it's nothing really," she replied. "It's just family stuff. The boys were aye different characters. Grant liked the land and the estate; Malcolm couldn't wait to shake the dust from his heels. He's never really been back since he went to Glasgow to uni. Once he qualified, he seemed to move quickly into private practice and cosmetic procedures; first in Glasgow, then London. Later he was in Hong Kong for a while, until it was handed back to the Chinese. I believe he's settled in Dubai now."

"So, he's not some kind of monster?"

"Naw, far from it. A very smooth operator."

Isla was spot on, I thought as I shook hands with Malcolm the next evening. He was slightly built and immaculately dressed in a beautifully tailored navy suit with an open-collared light blue shirt. His hair was blond, straight, silky and well behaved, reminding me of Sheelagh's. Quite unlike Grant's chaotic curly mop. The only obvious physical similarity between the brothers was their intense blue eyes. When he spoke, Malcolm's Scottish accent was very faint.

"So lovely to meet you, Claire. I believe that Grant has lured you up here from London. How on earth has he managed to do that?" he asked with a smile.

"Oh, just his general charm. Plus, I was ready for a change of pace," I replied.

He shuddered theatrically. "I've only been back in the country for three days and it's already been raining for two of them."

"Well, hopefully you don't dissolve in water like the Wicked Witch of the West," Grant commented acerbically.

"How was the reunion?" I asked.

That gave Malcolm plenty of scope to describe the varying careers of the dentists he'd studied with. He was scathing about some of their practices, seeming to equate success only with a high income. It became apparent that he didn't rate research, charity work or ordinary dentistry. Grant and I didn't know any of the people he mentioned, but that didn't seem to worry Malcolm, who managed to maintain his monologue for the time it took to give our orders and eat our starters.

"The estate's doing well," Grant eventually managed to interject as our plates were switched to deliver our main courses.

"Oh, that's good. You'll be pleased, then," Malcolm replied.

"And the girls are fine," Grant informed him.

"Oh, yes. How old are they now?"

Grant filled Malcolm in on his daughters' latest achievements.

"Do you have a family?" I asked.

"Good God, no. No wife, no dependants, footloose and fancy-free," Malcolm declared.

"Right. Your parents seem to enjoy life in France." I tried a new subject.

"Yes, lovely weather, but a bit too rural for me. I had to escape down to the casino at Royan after twenty-four hours in the sticks with them."

By the end of the evening we knew all about the nightlife in Dubai, and how it compared to Hong Kong as it used to be. We'd also covered sailing and tennis quite thoroughly. I had to wonder, though: why had Malcolm taken the time to make a two-hundred-mile round trip to see us? Apart from his opening sally, he hadn't asked me for one other detail about myself. And if Grant hadn't taken the initiative to inform him, he would have learned nothing new about the estate or his nieces. I didn't think I'd ever met anyone quite so self-absorbed. Now I could understand Grant's antipathy, and guessed that we wouldn't be seeing much of Malcolm in the future.

Part Two

2017

Chapter 16

I was peeling onions for French onion soup when the phone began to ring. I wiped my hands on my apron and went to answer.

"Hello."

"I need to speak to Grant, urgently." It was a woman on the other end, and I was fairly certain that it was Ruth, Grant's ex-wife.

"He's not here right now. Can I take a message?" I asked, trying to exude cool efficiency.

"You need to get in touch with him. It's Laura." I heard a sob. "She's seriously ill, in intensive care."

I shivered, experiencing a sudden chill, and immediately became more sympathetic and cooperative. Checking the clock on the kitchen wall, I replied, "Ruth, Grant's up on the hill right now and he doesn't have his mobile." I could see it lying on the worktop by the back door. Grant hated to take it with him when he was working on the estate. "But I'm expecting him back by 12.30. We can be on the 2.15 ferry."

"OK, tell him to phone me. She's in the Western General."

"I will. I hope she'll be OK."

Ruth had already rung off. I felt agitated. What to do? Well, we'd need to go to Edinburgh. So, while I was waiting for Grant, I should pack a couple of bags and make sandwiches for the journey. Should I see if I could book the ferry to be on the safe side? It would be terrible if we couldn't get on, though midweek in January it probably wouldn't be full. Nevertheless, better to be safe. I fired up my laptop and logged on to the Caledonian MacBrayne website. A few minutes later, booking made, I went through to our bedroom to pack.

Laura's health had been a matter of concern for the past six months. I hadn't seen her myself in that time, but Grant had been travelling to Edinburgh every two or three weeks. I knew that she had anorexia and that she'd been seeing a psychiatrist, but I didn't really know what the present crisis was. What was I going to tell Grant? I should have asked Ruth for more details, but the sudden call and Ruth's obvious panic and distress had flustered me. I hoped that Laura hadn't done something drastic; taken an overdose or harmed herself.

I gathered a change of clothes and pyjamas for each of us and piled them on our bed. Then I went to the cupboard in the hall to look for our overnight bags. We still had the flat in Marchmont, and kept toiletries and a few clothes there. When had Grant last been down? I thought back. It was only five days ago, and he'd seemed calm enough on his return. Although Laura was ill, it hadn't seemed to be deadly serious. Back in the kitchen, I scraped my semi-prepared onions into the compost bin and began to make some sandwiches. Grant would probably be here in another twenty minutes or so. I'd get him to phone Ruth immediately for more information. I would drive; Grant was bound to be upset, so more likely to be distracted. We didn't want to have an accident to add to our problems. Of course, I'd need to cancel my own arrangements for the next few days, but

I could do that from the ferry. I'd better pack my laptop, and remember to take its charger, and the ones for the phones.

The sound of the Range Rover's tyres spitting up gravel in the courtyard alerted me to Grant's return. I hurried to the door to meet him. I suppose that was unusual, and probably my face and body language raised his alarm.

"What's wrong?" he asked immediately as he approached the house.

I explained about the phone call and my preparations, and held out his mobile.

"OK, I'll need to go to the loo first," he said, grabbing the phone on his way past.

I guessed that he wanted to make the call in private, and started to load our bags and picnic into the back of the car. I threw in jackets, gloves, hats and scarves too. Then I climbed in and adjusted the driver's seat and mirrors, ready to set off. I knew that we'd be early for the ferry, but I didn't imagine that Grant would want to hang around. We could eat our sandwiches down by the terminal.

His face looked strained and grey when he emerged from the house. "Do you have the house keys?" he checked.

"Yeah, in my bag," I replied. I watched him unlatch the snib, pull the door shut and cross to the passenger seat.

He settled in, but didn't fasten his seat belt; he'd have to get out again at the sheep gate a few hundred yards down the drive. He was silent.

I waited until we'd reached the tarmac road before I questioned him. "What did she say?"

He looked stricken. "Apparently Laura collapsed after getting out of the shower this morning. Ruth called an ambulance. There's something wrong with her heart and she's in the coronary care unit."

"Her *heart*?"

"Aye, Ruth said it can happen with severe anorexia."

"But she's OK just now?"

"They're monitoring her and doing the best they can, but it's serious, Claire."

"Yes, I can understand that." But really, I couldn't understand how Grant's bubbly, chatty daughter had come to starve herself until she was lying at death's door. It made no sense to me at all.

Our journey south was tense, and we couldn't find much to say to each other: a few comments about the scenery and the traffic. A few 'what if' scenarios petered out before long. It was too cold to sit out on the ferry's deck, so we found places in the lounge and tried to read the books and magazines that I'd packed. I sent off a salvo of texts, cancelling some appointments and asking Jamie, our ghillie, to look after the dogs. Luckily there was no snow or bad weather, so we made good time once we reached the mainland. The darkness closed in by four o'clock, sealing us into our small space. I turned the radio on to keep us company.

We eventually arrived at the Western General at 6.30. Grant had phoned a couple of times during the journey, but there was no new information. I'd already decided that I'd drop Grant off at the hospital and go directly to the flat. I knew that there were likely to be visiting restrictions for intensive care. Also, I'd never met Ruth before, and I didn't think that this would be the best time and place to do that. I stopped at the main hospital entrance and got out of the car with Grant.

"Do you have your wallet and your phone?" I checked, handing him a thick jacket from the back of the vehicle. "Call me soon to let me know what's happening. I can come and get you later if you want."

"It's all right, don't wait up. I can get a taxi." Grant gave my hand a squeeze and pulled me into a hug.

"I hope she's OK."

"Aye, I'll let you know what's happening. Thanks for driving," he breathed. Then he approached the automatic glass doors, which swallowed him with a double swoosh.

It took me another fifteen minutes to drive across the city to Marchmont. Then I had to search for a place to park. The flat was cold and my first actions were to start up the central heating boiler and water heater, then I filled the kettle to make a hot drink. I was exhausted after the long drive and the worry. I made a cup of tea and settled down in the lounge, pulling up an armchair in front of the electric fire, which was already lifting the worst of the chill from the room.

My mobile rang and I grabbed it, thinking it would be Grant. But it was Isla. She was one of the people that I'd messaged earlier.

"Claire, is everything all right?" she asked.

"Well, we got here safely and I've dropped Grant at the hospital, but I haven't heard from him yet. So, I don't have any more information."

"They usually say that no news is good news, so hopefully that means she's stable."

"Yes. I hope so."

"I won't keep you, Claire, I just wanted to touch base with you and let you know that Fraser and I are here for you. Let me know if there's anything I can do."

"Thanks, Isla, I will. And I'll keep you informed."

"You do that. Bye, now."

I swithered about phoning my parents, but then decided against it. I'd wait until there was more information. And anyway, I should keep the line clear in case Grant needed to speak to me.

I must have dozed off in the chair. Next thing I knew, I was coming round, feeling groggy, and with a crick in my neck. I checked the time; it was ten past ten. No messages or missed calls on my phone. I didn't think that I should call Grant. Wasn't there some rule about not having mobile phones switched on around hospital equipment? I decided to send him a text and then go to bed. The central heating had done its job and the rooms were all cosy now. I made up the bed with clean sheets, then changed into pyjamas and brushed my teeth. There was still no message on my phone, so I attached it to the charger and set it on the bedside table in case I was needed in the night.

Over the next few days, I felt that I was in limbo. Grant appeared sporadically and crashed out, exhausted. Then he'd shower and head off to the hospital again. I tried to make sure that he had something nourishing to eat, and of course I wanted to be on hand to give him my support. Laura was, thankfully, out of immediate danger. The medical team had been able to normalise her hydration and salt levels by attaching her to an IV line, and this had a stabilising effect on the rhythm of her heart. They would monitor her in the cardiology department for a few more days, and then she would be transferred to a specialist psychiatric unit dealing with eating disorders.

Once Grant told me that she'd been moved out of the intensive care unit, I asked if I could go with him to see Laura. I'd known her for ten years: first as a visitor, then as her dad's partner and wife. She came to stay with us for a few weeks during school holidays; initially with Mairi, but more recently by herself. Grant always tried to rearrange his workload to make himself available so that they could spend as much time together as possible during her visits. Now, I tried to define my relationship with her; how it really worked in practice. I didn't spend much one-to-one time with her; maybe I was a bit like an aunt. Or, since we weren't genetically related, perhaps I was more like a godmother; a responsible adult who took an interest in her.

"Yes, of course, I'm sorry. I didn't think about it. It'll be good for her to see another face," Grant responded.

So, later that day I followed Grant through a maze of hospital corridors towards the cardiology wards. He explained that Laura was now on the general cardiology ward, as she didn't require one-to-one supervision anymore, but that she was still hooked up to a monitor and a drip. I hadn't much experience of hospital visiting, so I was grateful to be forewarned about what to expect. Also, I suspected that Ruth would be there, so I tried to prepare myself to meet her.

We swung open the double doors to the ward and used the squirty hand sanitiser on the wall.

"She's in the middle bed on the left," Grant directed me, striding into the six-bedded ward.

But I froze. The woman who rose from the bedside chair to greet us could have been my double. Well, maybe she wasn't an exact clone, but she looked uncannily like me; enough to stop me in my tracks. No one had ever mentioned this resemblance to me. I don't suppose it was the kind of thing that my in-laws were likely to bring up, but Isla, or Fraser, or Archie – wouldn't they have told me? And what must Ruth be thinking – that I was some kind of a statue? Had she noticed the likeness too? I forced myself to move forward and shake her hand, and then tried to focus on Laura.

That wasn't much easier. She seemed to be dozing, and I got the impression that her eyes were darting backwards and forwards under her partially closed lids. It was warm on the ward – Grant and I were already carrying our jackets – but Laura was wearing several layers of clothing. I could see pyjamas, a sweater and a dressing gown. She was also lying under a thick duvet. Her arms were on top of the covers and one hand was swathed in bandages where a drip was attached. Her wrists, where they emerged from the layers of clothes, looked literally like skin and bones, with no padding under the skin. Her face was pale, her skin and lips dry and flaky, and her cheekbones were like cliffs above sunken dips where her cheeks should be.

"She drank some of the build-up drink tonight," Ruth reported.

"That's good," Grant replied. "Not chasing you away, but do you want a break while we're here?"

"Yeah, OK."

She stood up, and now I could see that her build and figure were also very like mine. Her hair was definitely a lighter shade of blonde, and curlier, but it was a similar length. Her skin was probably paler; maybe reflecting city rather than island living. Her eyes were paler, more grey than blue. I tried not to keep staring at her. Of course, I'd heard of men having a 'type'. Rod Stewart was an example. All of his wives and girlfriends were leggy with long blonde hair. But I'd never considered that I might be such a direct replacement for Grant's first wife. Did it even matter? I wasn't sure; I'd need to think about it.

Ruth unhooked her handbag from the back of her chair. "I'll go out for some air. Back soon."

Meanwhile, Laura was stirring. "Hi, Dad. Hello, Claire." Well, thankfully she could tell the difference between me and her mother. And her voice sounded normal. Somehow, I'd expected it to be changed; maybe hoarser, or higher in pitch.

"Hi, Laura. I hope you're feeling better. Everyone's been so worried about you, and hoping that you'll be well soon."

"That's nice. I'd like to get out of here, that's for sure."

"Well, have some more of your energy drink; that'll help to speed you on your way," Grant suggested.

Laura screwed her face up, but consented to be helped into a sitting position, with pillows providing padding behind her back. She took a sip of the milky pink liquid through a straw. "It's pretty foul," she complained. "Strawberry flavoured, and warm. You know I don't like warm milk."

Now that she was sitting up, I could see how prominent her neck muscles were with no flesh to hide them. And her ears protruded through her wispy hair.

"It's because you've taken so long to drink it. I'm sure it was cold to begin with," Grant suggested.

Tears gathered and pooled in Laura's eyes but didn't spill over her lids. "It's just really yucky. You wouldn't like it either." She sounded genuinely hurt.

"OK, we'll speak to the dieticians tomorrow to see if they have something that you'll find more palatable," Grant promised, squeezing her unbound hand and kissing the top of her head. I had the impression that she was going to be hard to please on that score.

To change the subject, I began to tell them about the plot of a film that I'd seen at the cinema the day before; a kind of Agatha Christie 'whodunnit' spoof.

Then Laura told us about a documentary that she'd been watching on television. It was about vets, and she said that it had made her think about Mairi and wonder if she would be doing the kind of surgery featured in the series. "I mean, I like animals, but I wouldn't have the stomach for that," she declared.

"Mairi was always interested in any animal, no matter what it looked like: snakes, frogs, crabs, slugs. She was into all of them. Whereas you were more conventionally girly, I'd say. You liked the wee fluffy animals, like puppies, kittens and lambs." Grant gave his opinion.

"But remember, Mairi came a cropper because of a slug," Laura commented.

Then we began to laugh, recalling the time when Mairi had chased Laura down the farm track waggling an enormous orange slug on a gardening trowel in front of her. Laura had been much smaller, so her big sister was catching her up when she leapt to one side over the ditch, trying to escape. Mairi followed, but misjudged; she'd tripped and fallen into the ditch, soaking her foot and pitching herself face first into a heap of sheep dung.

Ruth reappeared while we were giggling and reminiscing. "Ah, the joys of farm life," she commented wryly.

I took her return as my signal to leave, so made my farewells to Laura and nodded to Ruth. As I navigated back to the car park, I checked my watch. I'd only been there for forty minutes, but I felt totally drained. I supposed that meeting my predecessor and discovering that she was my mirror image, then coping with the terrible change in Laura, had both been major events. But I felt pleased that I'd left on a positive note; we seemed to have managed to cheer Laura up.

Chapter 17

Unfortunately, Laura's recovery didn't go as smoothly as we'd hoped. It seemed that even a small amount of physical activity caused her heartbeat to become irregular again. This gave her pains in her chest and made her feel faint and breathless. So, she had to stay for longer than expected on the cardiology ward and couldn't even walk to the toilet or the shower, but had to be pushed in a wheelchair. Also, although she was confined to bed and her calorie intake was carefully monitored, her weight didn't seem to be increasing much. Consequently, by the beginning of February, Grant and I were still living in the Edinburgh flat.

Luckily for us, January and February were the quietest months on the estate. The main shooting season was over and the lambing hadn't begun. There were still a few parties booked in for pheasant shoots but Jamie, the ghillie, was easily able to cope with them. Also, my business was quiet. I'd only planned to open the shop on Saturday afternoons for the first three months of the year. Those were the weeks when Grant and I would normally work through a lot of our administrative tasks. It was also the time of year when we usually arranged to go on holiday. Work was quiet, and we could escape some of the Scottish winter weather. This year we had booked a trip to Mexico; I'd been looking forward to exploring the Mayan ruins and snorkelling on the coral reef. But we were going to have to cancel.

I was working on the computer when Grant eventually appeared for breakfast. These days he always seemed to be exhausted, with the result that he slept in late most mornings. After he'd settled himself at the table with toast and a pot of tea, I approached with my paperwork.

"Grant, I've contacted the travel insurance company and we need to get one of Laura's doctors to complete this medical form. I've done the first part. Could you ask them about it?"

"Aye, just put it beside my jacket, then I can't forget it."

"Is there any word about her being transferred to the eating disorder unit yet?" I sat down beside him and poured myself some tea from the pot.

"Maybe next week. The psychiatrist was in to see her again yesterday and he spoke to her cardiologist too. They're not keen to move her until her heart's stable. Apparently, they don't have much medical backup on their unit, and no doctor on site overnight."

"I suppose I'm wondering when we might go back home."

"I don't know." He sighed. "I guess I could take a trip up for a few days before she's transferred, since everything seems more stable. I could do with organising some things around the estate. Jamie's been great at filling in, but I'd like to see things for myself."

"Well, maybe we could go on Thursday or Friday. They're not likely to move her at the weekend, are they?"

"No, I wouldn't think so. I'll speak to the consultant today and see if that would be OK. You know, you could stay up there if you want. It's been great having your company, but I think Laura's out of danger now and I know you've a lot to prepare for the start of the season."

"Yeah, it might be good to stay on Mull, if you don't need me here."

Grant nudged his chair closer to mine and put his arm around me, hugging me close. "I've really appreciated you being here looking after me, but I think I'll be spending more time travelling back and forward from now on. And I'm sorry that we've got to miss our holiday." He kissed me.

"We'll go another year," I said when he eventually released me.

I was pleased to be back on Mull. Normally I enjoyed our trips to Edinburgh and what I called 'civilisation'. I always made the most of the culture on offer: booking theatre tickets, going to the cinema, attending art exhibitions and, of course, sampling the variety of food on offer from the many restaurants. But on this trip, Grant had obviously spent a lot of time at the hospital. When he wasn't there, he was understandably preoccupied and I didn't like to suggest an activity that he might consider to be frivolous. We'd also stayed for much longer than our usual visits, and I'd come to realise that I didn't really have any friends of my own in the city. I knew people through Grant, mainly couples that we'd socialise with together, but there wasn't anyone that I felt I could call on to accompany me on an outing, so I either had to go on my own, or not at all. On Mull I had my own friends: Isla, my musical buddies, and others that I'd come to know through my business and the estate work. I definitely felt much more grounded on the island; less of a visitor. As if I belonged.

Over the weekend Grant and I attended to a lot of chores around the house and the estate, and then he set off back to Edinburgh on Monday morning, leaving me behind. I'd arranged to go to Isla's for coffee, so at 10.30 I parked my car in my old spot outside Taigh Dhearg. The car park was empty, but it was unlikely that Isla would have any visitors at this time of the year. I tried the front door, which was unlocked, so I stepped into the hall, calling, "Hello, it's me."

Isla appeared from the kitchen, drying her hands on a towel. She swooped me up in a tight hug. "How are you, lass? It seems so long since I last set eyes on you. Come away through to the kitchen and I'll put the kettle on."

I followed her into the cosy kitchen.

"Have a seat," she instructed. "Has Grant gone back already, then?"

"Yes. He's hoping that it'll only be for a few days. We're expecting Laura to be transferred to the psychiatric hospital this week."

"So, that's a good thing, eh?"

"Yeah, she's a bit better physically. Her heart seems stronger and she's gained a few pounds."

"And have you any idea yet what on earth set all of this off?" Isla placed a cafetière onto the mat in the centre of the kitchen table and then produced a plate of buttered scones.

I thought back. It was about eighteen months ago that Grant and I had first begun to notice changes in Laura, but it had been easy to put them down to normal teenage angst. When she'd come to stay over the Easter holidays last year, she was very quiet, much less bubbly than usual. She wasn't interested in the lambing, though in previous years she'd have been out in all weathers helping Grant, and have spent hours bottle-feeding any abandoned lambs. We weren't too surprised that, at the age of fifteen, she'd outgrown the habits of painting and rolling hard-boiled eggs and hunting for chocolate eggs. But most teenagers still seemed to enjoy eating an Easter chocolate hoard. I found all of Laura's in her sock drawer, uneaten, when I was putting away clean laundry after she went back to Edinburgh. We'd both noticed that her shape had changed, and thought she'd lost some weight, but we put that down to her age and the shedding of 'puppy fat'. It wasn't unreasonable to think that her newly developed moodiness was part of being a teenager too. It's simple to say with hindsight but, when everything was added together, it should have made us more uneasy.

"Well, beyond the divorce I don't know of anything upsetting in her life," I answered eventually. "But I'm not involved in her family therapy sessions. I have to rely on what Grant tells me."

"I did wonder if, subconsciously, she was trying to bring her parents back together again," Isla mused. "They'll have been spending a lot more time together through all of this."

"Speaking of which, I got quite a shock when I met Ruth," I said as I accepted a mug of steaming black coffee.

"In what way?" Isla sounded puzzled.

"Well, she looks just like me – hadn't you noticed? It's freaked me out a bit."

"Oh, you're maybe a wee bit similar. But I wouldn't say it was that obvious."

"It seemed like more than a wee bit to me."

"Well, I haven't seen her for a few years now and she might have changed. But her hair was a lot lighter than yours; although not so white-blonde as Mairi's. And it was a lot longer than yours, and more frizzy than curly. I'd have said that she was a bit heftier than you, too."

"Well, she's obviously had her hair done differently and maybe lost weight. I was probably being daft, but it got to me. I've never doubted how Grant felt about me before. He's always seemed so genuine and open. But after I met Ruth, I wondered if I just fitted into some sort of stereotype."

"Have you asked him about it?" Isla sounded concerned.

"No. I thought he had enough to cope with, without me being needy."

"There's no way that I believe Grant has used you to fill empty shoes. He's mad about you. You have to trust in that."

"I want to…"

"Here, have a scone." Isla pushed the plate towards me and I accepted one. It was buttery, crumbly and delicious.

"Claire, I think you're overreacting. You've been under a lot of stress. Meeting Ruth would have been tough for you whenever it happened, but these circumstances have maybe made it all too vivid and difficult."

"Mm, maybe," I conceded while munching more of my scone.

"Then there's what I said about Grant spending a lot of time in Ruth's company – that could have made you feel more insecure."

"Well, he's never said much about her; he certainly hasn't criticised her."

"Did you come across Iain at all?"

"No, and Grant didn't mention him either, but you'd think that he'd have been visiting too. I only went in about once a week, but Laura lives full time with Iain; you'd expect him to turn up."

"Could be that he avoided times when he knew Grant was there. Ruth probably let him know when the coast was clear."

"Yes, it wouldn't have been good for Laura to have a lot of tension around."

"Have another scone," Isla coaxed.

"I really shouldn't, but they're just too tempting." I helped myself. "Tell me what you've been up to," I encouraged her, wanting to change the subject. But I felt more cheerful and confident after our chat. Maybe I'd got the idea about Ruth's and my likeness out of proportion.

Grant called that evening.

"Hi, how're things?" I asked.

"Not too bad. Laura's been moved. I'm just back from there."

"What's it like?"

"I'd say that it's an institutional attempt at homely. You know? It has soft furnishings and smaller rooms, but it's still lino on the floor and magnolia walls. It reminds me a bit of the first student flat I stayed in."

"Yeah, I know what you mean. How did Laura seem?"

"It's a bit hard to tell. She didn't say much. Obviously, the other patients are around her age, whereas she was quite the baby in the cardiology ward."

"I suppose that can be awkward for a teenager; trying to fit in with a new crowd."

"Well, before I'd have said that would be no problem for Laura. I always thought of her as outgoing and confident. But she doesn't seem that way now. And, Claire, I'm not sure how to express this, but all those wee, thin, stick-like lassies... it depressed me. It doesn't seem at all a healthy or wholesome environment for Laura."

"All the more reason to work hard with her to get her out as soon as possible."

"Aye. There was one lass who only looked about ten or eleven years old. It's a terrible affliction."

"Have you eaten yet yourself?" I asked.

"I put a fish pie from Marks & Spencer in the oven when I got back, so it'll be ready in about ten minutes. I've got some frozen peas to have with it."

"Well done. I pigged out on scones at Isla's this morning, so I just had an omelette and salad for dinner."

"Sounds healthy. How's Isla?"

"She's fine, and busy with lots of weaving orders. Fraser's working on a cottage renovation down at Aros."

"Maybe you could set up a date with them for the weekend. I'd like to catch up."

"You're definitely coming back, then?"

"Aye – I asked about the unit schedule, and they don't have family sessions at the weekends. Later on, once she's a bit better, she might get to go home for weekends. A sort of trial for discharge."

"That makes sense. OK, I'll check with Isla for Saturday night."

"Great, I'll phone again tomorrow. Love you."

"You too. Enjoy the fish pie. Bye."

Chapter 18

looked at the kitchen clock again to find that it was only a minute since I'd last checked it. I sighed; clock-watching was pointless anyway. Grant had phoned as the ferry left Oban to let me know that he'd caught the four o'clock sailing. I knew that the crossing and the subsequent drive took at least an hour and a half, so there was no chance of them arriving before 5.30. I pulled another shirt from the ironing pile and smoothed it out over the board. Ironing was a task that I thoroughly disliked, but it was mindless and would fill up some time.

I was anxious about how we were going to cope with Laura. We'd agreed that we should try to act as normally as possible; just be relaxed. But things weren't normal. The girl had almost died. That was three months ago and I knew that she was a lot better now; they wouldn't let her out of hospital otherwise. But since the beginning of the year I'd been reading a lot about anorexia. It seemed that it could last for years and often recurred. I worried that we'd need to be on the lookout for any kind of relapse. We weren't to make a big deal about eating, while at the same time making sure that Laura was eating according to her contract. Grant had explained all of this to me, but those two instructions seemed to contradict each other.

My phone rang, breaking into the whirl of my apprehensive rumination. It was Mum.

"Hi, Mum."

"Hello, Claire. I was just wondering if Laura's with you yet."

"Not yet; I'm expecting them around 5.30."

"I hope that this relocation will work out."

"Yes, me too. But remember, it was Laura who said that she wanted to live with her dad. The idea came from her, not from us."

"And you said that Grant was quite firm with her and wouldn't say yes until she'd reached a target weight."

"Yeah, it was tough for him to hold out and make himself be so strict. But the consultant was very supportive."

"It's hard to think of Laura having these problems; she always seemed to be such a sunny child."

"She was always very much a daddy's girl too. Maybe living away from Grant was hard for her. I don't know."

"Well, let's hope that she's motivated to get better now."

"Yes."

"Give me a call tomorrow; let me know how things are going."

"I will; thanks for phoning. Love you, Mum."

I gazed out of the window to the hillside, still clutching my phone. What I hadn't said to Mum, or to anyone, was that I'd never been consulted about Laura coming to live with us. I understood it. Faced with his seriously ill child, Grant had agreed to her request out of desperation and love for her. He hadn't intended to disrespect or hurt me. I don't even think that it crossed his mind that I might object. To be honest, I'm sure that I would have agreed; only, I wasn't given a choice. I was trying to let it go, but it niggled.

I decided to go and check that Laura's room was warm enough before returning to the ironing. Because she still had so little body fat, she would be very susceptible to the cold. I'd turned up the thermostat on the radiator that morning and made up her bed with a high-tog duvet and an extra blanket, just in case. I opened the door and met a wall of hot air. It felt stifling to me; I'd have to hope it would be OK for Laura. Everything looked neat and tidy, which was very unlike the Laura of old. In the past, her room had hosted a riot of colours and objects reflecting her enthusiasms. The walls had been hung with posters, mainly depicting cuddly baby animals, that vied with pieces of her own artwork. Half-finished creations, coloured pens and crayons had littered the floor. Her dream at that time had been to draw and paint wildlife, perhaps to illustrate books. One wall of her room had been covered in shelves full of books, stacked higgledy-piggledy. As a girl she'd had a huge collection of soft toys spread over every available surface including her bed.

Then, the year that she'd reached fourteen, she'd asked if she could redecorate her room, declaring that it was babyish. We'd agreed to her request and helped her to choose colours for the walls, curtains and bedding. It all became very subdued: silvery-grey walls, and pale blue materials for the soft furnishings. Her toys and books were relegated to the attic. She hung two prints on one wall. One showed colourful hot-air balloons against a clear blue sky; the other was a misty sea scene with a lighthouse semi-engulfed by spumes of sea spray. These were both her own work. Her new passion was for photography; now she wanted to be a famous wildlife photographer. The balloon shot had been taken at a weekend balloon festival held at Strathaven in the south-west of Scotland. The seascape was only a few miles along the road from our home, at Rubha nan Gall lighthouse, just north of Tobermory. I was no expert, but I thought that she had a good eye – some of her shots were seriously impressive. But how much had she changed since her illness? Was she still keen on photography? Would I have to get to know her all over again?

I closed the bedroom door and headed for the kitchen. Time to get a meal on the go. I'd studied Laura's eating contract, emailed to me by her consultant. It came with lots of information and tips. She had to eat three proper meals and three snacks every day, and drink two energy drinks. She needed more calories than usual, and was likely to do so for many months after regaining a normal weight. A prescription had been sent to our local pharmacy and a huge box of energy drinks had been delivered yesterday. I'd put a selection of flavours into the fridge, remembering that Laura had made a fuss when her drink wasn't chilled. That morning I'd made a salmon and spinach oven bake with sliced potatoes on the top. Now I turned the oven on, put the dish inside and began to prepare some vegetables. Luckily ice cream counted as an adequate dessert for Laura, as Grant and I usually only ate one course. I hadn't known which flavour to choose, so had bought vanilla to start with. I'd have to ask Laura what she'd like, although there would be nothing very exotic available until my next trip to Oban.

I'd just scraped the vegetable peelings into my compost bin when the dogs began to bark in their kennel across the yard. They must have heard the car. I dried my hands and headed for the outside door, waiting on the step. Grant's black Range Rover pulled up, passenger side nearest to the house. He jumped out and waved to me, then came around to open the passenger door. He helped Laura down from the high seat. She looked tiny, enveloped by a black, puffy down coat. The hood was up and it was hard to see her face beyond its shadow and frame of furry trim. I stepped into the yard and approached, instinctively opening my arms to give Laura a welcoming hug. She didn't respond; passive, but not pulling away. She felt very insubstantial in my arms. I didn't attempt to kiss her.

"Hi, Laura, it's good to see you. Come on in, your dad will bring your things."

As I took her arm and led her towards the door, I felt her leaning on me slightly for support.

"Hi, Claire," she replied. "I'm a bit stiff after sitting for so long, and I definitely didn't have my sea legs on for the ferry crossing."

"Oh, was it rough?" I asked. I didn't remember Laura suffering from motion sickness before.

"No, not really, but I felt quite shaky."

Grant appeared, laden with bags, and kissed my cheek in passing. "I'll put these in your room, Laura."

"Thanks, Dad."

We made our way into the lounge and Laura plonked herself down on a settee.

"Don't you want to take your coat off? Make yourself at home?" I asked.

Laura shook her head, but did concede in pushing her hood down. I tried not to stare at her but, despite preparing myself, I was shocked that her face was still just a tiny, thin triangle. Her lips were pale and her eyes looked absolutely huge. She'd always had a mane of luxuriant brunette ringlets. Now her hair looked thin, dull and straggly. "I'll wait till I warm up a bit," she said.

"I can light the fire," I offered.

"That would be nice. It's been a while since I smelled peat."

As I was busying myself laying the open fire, Grant reappeared. "That's a good idea, Claire. It'll be fine and cosy. I think I'll have a dram before we eat. Can I get you girls something?"

I asked for a gin and tonic and Laura for a glass of water. Grant and I exchanged glances over her choice before he went off to fetch the drinks. But we kept quiet.

"Could you turn on the heat under the veg?" I called after him.

"Sure."

"Oh, Claire, I had something to eat on the ferry. Didn't you know? I won't need anything else," Laura announced. It was starting already.

"I think that would be your afternoon snack," I replied, trying to keep my expression as neutral as possible. "So, evening meal and supper-time snack are still to go."

Laura darted me an appraising look. Then she nodded once. Had I passed the test?

Grant arrived carrying a tray with our drinks and a small bowl of peanuts. "Welcome home, Laura." He raised his whisky and we all clinked glasses, joining in with his toast.

I took a long first swallow. "How was the drive?" I asked, and tried to relax as he described small changes on the familiar roads.

The room was heating up and Laura was sitting closest to the fire. After about ten minutes she shrugged off her coat. She was wearing a baggy jumper which hid her torso, but I could see her wrists and hands now, still skeletal. I tried not to make a comparison to photographs I'd seen of concentration camp victims during the Holocaust.

That first meal together was to set the pattern of how we ate for the next few months. At the time it seemed interminable. Laura spent ages cutting up all of her food into very small pieces. Then she chewed each tiny forkful for what seemed to be a hundred times. I'd given her a paper napkin, and she dabbed her mouth with it after each mouthful and then carefully rearranged it on her lap, smoothing it out thoroughly. At one point one of her legs started to shake, her knee bouncing up and down ferociously. Grant said her name and leaned over, placing his hand firmly flat on her knee, and the movement stopped. Grant and I had finished our meal and two cups of coffee each by the time Laura's main-course plate was empty, and we were trying to make light conversation throughout. I got up to fetch ice cream, two scoops, then made my apologies and headed to the lounge to read a book, leaving Grant to keep Laura company. He picked up a newspaper and read it at the table while the ice cream was slowly eaten, a teaspoonful at a time. After our meal Laura pleaded tiredness and disappeared into her room.

"I can see that we're going to spend a lot of time on eating," I commented to Grant, who'd joined me in the lounge. "I'm not sure how we're going to fit the snacks in when mealtimes take so long."

"Aye, it's painfully slow, isn't it? But actually, that's better than she was a few weeks ago."

We agreed that only one of us would need to continue the full vigil for each meal, and that it would be a good idea for that person to arrive armed with some kind of reading material.

"Maybe background music could help," I suggested. "Be a bit of a distraction. Not that I know what kind of music Laura's into these days. But I can ask her." It felt sad that I needed to have topics of conversation in mind. Laura used to be so chatty that it could be hard to fit in a word of my own when she was in full flow.

We settled down to watch a documentary about the impact of aerial photography on Scottish archaeological findings. The programme finished at nine o'clock.

"Should Laura have her snack now?" I asked. We hadn't seen her since finishing our evening meal. "I'll look in on her."

I tapped lightly on her bedroom door. There was no reply, so I eased the door open and called her name. The room was in darkness and there was still no reply, so I tiptoed in. Laura was in bed, asleep. I checked her breathing; it seemed regular.

"She's fast asleep," I reported back to Grant, who was now loading the dishwasher. "What are we supposed to do? It doesn't seem right to wake her."

"No, let's cut her some slack today. It's been a long, tiring journey for her; she was probably genuinely exhausted. Remember, she has very little energy and next to no reserves."

"OK, but we'd better make a clear rule going forward that she has to have the snack before bedtime, otherwise she'll think she can skip it. It's quite a few more calories, you know."

161

"Thanks, Claire. I appreciate how seriously you're taking her contract. I think you're right; we have to stay firm to make it work. The consultant hinted at this; he said that if we make very firm rules and give her no choice about eating, then it takes away some of Laura's guilt about it and actually makes it easier for her."

That night in bed, Grant seemed wakeful, despite the long drive from Edinburgh.

"You OK?" I asked, touching his shoulder.

"It's hard to explain," he said. "I don't think I've felt so overwhelmed by responsibility since the day we brought Mairi home from hospital as a new-born. The fact that a person depends on you totally for care, but that you really don't know what you're doing; if you're competent…"

"But Laura can look after herself to a degree; certainly more than a new-born baby can."

"Aye, she should be able to. But it didn't work out, did it? She nearly died."

Then I had to take my husband in my arms as I felt him begin to sob. His tears wet my neck.

"We'll be all right," I crooned. "We're together, and we've got friends to help, and the doctors and hospital for backup. She wants to get better now," I added hopefully.

Chapter 19

The bell on the shop's front door jangled, alerting me to a possible customer. I minimised the screen showing the stock ledger that I'd been working on, and made my way through to the front of the building.

"Hello, Claire, I thought I'd call in to see how things are going." It was Isla. My antique shop was located by the harbour, next to Isla and Grant's workshop.

"We've been OK, thanks." I sighed. "It's mainly been tedious spending so much time watching Laura eat very, very slowly. There haven't been any major problems, but she still tries to skip snacks and energy drinks; keeps us on our toes."

"Do you have to watch over her all the time?"

"One of us is always in the house with her, but not necessarily in the same room. I don't know how long it will be before we can ease back a bit."

"I suppose you just need to take it a day at a time."

"Yeah, tomorrow we've got the first appointment with the practice nurse for her weekly weigh-in. Before she left hospital, she worked with Grant and her consultant to come up with a series of privileges that link to target weights."

"So, as she puts on weight, she gains more autonomy?"

"Exactly, that's the plan. And her progress gets reviewed every month."

"Is she going back to Edinburgh every month?"

"No, they'll do it by phone. Maybe see her after a few months, depending on how it's going. Do you have time for a coffee?"

"Sure, Fraser's in the shop and he knows where I am."

I went back into the office to turn on the kettle. "How's Calum? Is it next week that school breaks up for Easter?" I called.

"Aye. Thankfully there's a football club running for the second week; that'll help to keep him busy."

"Yeah, he's always on the go," I agreed. I brought through two mugs of steaming coffee and gave one to Isla. She was perched on my stool behind the counter, so I dragged over a chintz-covered nursing chair and relaxed into it. "Do you have many bookings for the holidays?"

"Aye, we're pretty full. And a scattering booked for May and June already."

"That's good. Mum and Dad are driving a van up next week for a stock exchange. I'm looking forward to seeing them. And maybe their presence will lighten the atmosphere in the house a bit."

"Is it that grim?"

"Oh, not really, just a bit intense. I think we all need to lighten up."

"How about Mairi? Is she not going to visit soon?"

"Mm, I think she'll spend part of her Easter break with us, but she's got an assignment due for her degree and some horse show that she's competing in soon. So, I expect it'll be a flying visit." I paused. "Isla, do you think that you could persuade Laura to get her hair cut?"

"Me?" My friend looked surprised.

"Well, you always look so stylish and I think it might come across better from you. I feel like I'm always nagging her about eating, and if I mention this, she might take it the wrong way. But her hair is so thin and straggly, it makes me feel depressed. If she got it cut it would look better, and I'm sure that would make her feel more confident again. Hopefully it'll start to grow in and thicken up now that she's eating."

"OK, I'll give it a try. But it's not going to be the first thing I say to her; I haven't even seen her yet."

"Well, why don't you and Calum come up to the farm sometime at the weekend? We've got a couple of lambs in the barn that Calum might like to see. Or is that too babyish for him now?"

"He might like to think so, but I'm sure that he'd still enjoy feeding them."

"It would be good for Laura to have some visitors. At the moment she isn't allowed to exercise or to walk anywhere, so apart from going in the car she's stuck in the house."

"Is she getting bored, do you think?"

"I don't know, maybe. She sleeps a lot, which is probably good for her recovery, and she's been watching a lot of TV."

"I wonder what we could suggest to help keep her occupied."

"Once she puts on a bit more weight, I'm hoping that she can come down here and help me in the shop. Or maybe she could man your workshop if you're busy at the guest house. It wouldn't be strenuous, just sitting by the till, but it would get her out. And I wondered if we could encourage her interest in photography again. I could offer to display some of her photos for sale if she prints them up."

"That's a good idea; I'm sure Fraser would frame them for her. But remember, she has to do things by herself for herself; make her own decisions. We shouldn't try to organise her too much, Claire. It might actually annoy her."

"I know, but if we can make her feel that she belongs and has something useful to contribute I'm sure that'll help. After all, she hasn't actually lived on the island since Ruth left. There's a difference between staying here permanently and visiting for two or three weeks during the holidays."

"Aye, I suppose you'd know about that from your own experience. How about friends her own age? I take it that she won't be fit to go to school yet."

"No. For this term they're going to send some work for her to do at home, and a teacher will visit once a week to bring back marked work and discuss her progress. Hopefully that will help her to catch up and she can join Year Four after the summer holidays."

"Well, I hope it all works out." Isla drained the last of her coffee. "I'd better get back to my weaving; this order is due by next week. I'll give you a ring and arrange to come up to visit at the weekend. Probably Saturday, but I'll need to check with Calum and Fraser."

I heaved myself up with difficulty from my low chair and accompanied Isla to the door. She hugged me and I watched her make her way along the cobbled walkway to her workshop. I paused to look at the day. The sun was shining but an icy north-easterly wind blew white clouds across the sky and chopped up the water in the harbour. The wavelets sparkled in the bright spring light and boats bobbed up and down. A crowd of noisy seagulls squabbled around a rubbish bin beside the harbour wall, pulling out paper and spreading the litter in the hope of finding some food. Looking across to the main street, I saw that one of the houses had a scaffolding stack erected. The blue walls were emerging brighter, refreshed for spring.

I rubbed my arms, aware of goosebumps forming, and turned back into the shop. It was an airy, square, modern space, quite unlike my parents' shop in Tunbridge Wells. But the contents were very similar. When I'd first relocated to Mull I'd continued with carrying out valuations, including as a freelancer once my locum job was finished. Through this I came to realise that there was a huge source of antiques stock coming up for sale locally in Argyll and in the wider Highlands. When my parents visited, Dad and I were chatting, and it was his idea to expand the business and open a branch of Ford's Antiques in Tobermory. I kept a lookout for a suitable venue and this space came up for rental about five years ago. The following months were exciting. I had a wonderful time attending auctions and sales, building up my stock. Then Dad and I had begun our system of swapping over some items between the shops two or three times a year. That was why Mum and Dad were due to visit next week. It would be lovely to see them, and I always enjoyed unloading the van and examining the treasures that they brought with them. Now I needed to get back to my stocktaking so that I could pick out items for the journey south, although my parents would have their say too. After browsing around, they'd form their own opinions on objects for transport.

When Helen arrived to take over from me, I was amazed that the remainder of the morning seemed to have suddenly disappeared. Helen was my main assistant in the shop, and I was so glad to have her. She'd lived on the mainland and worked in a jeweller's shop in Oban until she was sixty. Then she'd decided to retire to Mull, where she'd grown up. Luckily for me, after making the move and settling into her renovated cottage, she'd grown bored and looked for a part-time job. I have to admit that on our first meeting I was rather doubtful that she would fit in. She arrived wearing a kilted tartan skirt, a white blouse and a black waistcoat. Her grey hair was neatly tied back and fastened with a matching tartan bow. Even to an incomer like me, this outfit seemed naff. It reminded me of a trip I'd once made to Austria, where the workers in the tourist areas were all clad in lederhosen and dirndls. However, she'd grinned at me knowingly and said, "The visitors will love it." Since then, she had proven her worth many times over. Her experience in retail was invaluable and she was so good with customers, seeming to intuit exactly what they wanted.

"A good morning?" she asked me now, as she shrugged off her coat to reveal her habitual 'Highland' dress.

"Yes. I finished the stocktake and I've got a good idea of what to transfer south. And I sold that Rennie Macintosh-style quaich."

"To tourists?" she guessed.

"Canadian," I confirmed.

"Good. Well, off you go for your lunch. Grant will be busy with the lambing these days."

"Yes, it's almost done now."

"Well, that's a lot to be thankful for," she commented as she began a tour of the shelves and displays, armed with a feather duster.

I waved as I passed the front window to collect my car. Helen was attending to a collection of Dresden figurines, examining each one carefully, dusting it, and replacing it to make a different tableau. I was happy to leave things in her safekeeping.

When I arrived back at Fearann Soirbheachail, Grant and Laura were installed at the kitchen table. Grant was reading a newspaper and Laura was stirring a half-finished bowl of soup and taking minute bites from a sandwich. The radio was playing softly in the background, tuned into Radio Clyde.

"Hi. Busy morning?" Grant asked as he folded up the newspaper.

I rubbed his shoulder as I passed behind his chair. "Yes, it was good. Would you like that soup to be heated up, Laura? I'm making some for myself."

"No, it's OK," she sighed, supping a third of a spoonful.

"I'll go, and let you sit here, Claire." Grant stood up and cleared away his dirty dishes. "I want to check on those last ewes. It shouldn't be much longer until they produce. What are you up to this afternoon?"

"I need to look at the new music that Archie dropped off. We're playing at the Mishnish on Saturday night and I haven't been practising enough."

"Well, you'd better get to it, then. You have to keep up to Archie's standards."

"Do you play with his band a lot now?" Laura asked.

"Yeah, quite a bit. Last summer we had live music slots about twice a week, and there are ceilidhs and weddings throughout the year."

"You and I could go along to listen, Laura," Grant suggested.

"Yeah, OK." The response sounded lacklustre, but coming from Laura it could be interpreted as verging on enthusiastic. Nothing had seemed to excite her much since she'd returned.

I sat down with my soup and sandwich and Grant kissed the top of my head as he made for the door.

"See you girls later."

Chapter 20

I t was refreshing to see a smile on Laura's face as she listened to Calum's chatter. He was trying to explain to her how he'd perfected the butterfly stroke and, not content with waving his arms around, he lay down prone on the floor and proceeded to give a wriggling demonstration across the carpet.

Laura laughed. "I think you'd drown," she judged.

"Naw, I'm getting the hang of it. Amn't I, Mum?"

"Aye, he's braw at the swimming. Coming on quite the thing," Isla confirmed.

"You'll all need to come and see me at the gala," Calum announced.

"When's that, then?" Laura asked.

"Next term, I think."

"OK, then. I'll come."

Calum looked delighted. He was obviously smitten, and in awe of the older girl, keen to keep hold of her attention.

"Finish off your lemonade and shortbread and then maybe Laura will take you over to see the lambs," I suggested. "Would you mind?" I checked with her.

"No, that's OK. I'll get my coat and a couple of bottles of milk. Would you like to feed a lamb, Calum?"

"Cool." Now Calum was jumping up and down, a bundle of energy. He sprayed crumbs around as he crammed the last piece of shortbread into his mouth. The nine-year-old boy had a tousle of red hair and a crop of freckles across his cheeks. He gulped down the last of his drink and set off after Laura. He looked so sturdy next to her waiflike figure, but really he was just a well-proportioned little boy, warmly dressed in jeans, trainers and a Fair Isle sweater. "Do we need to warm the milk?" I heard him asking as he followed her into the kitchen. I noticed that Laura's shortbread was still sitting on her plate, hardly touched, but I refrained from calling her back.

"Wow, I always forget how lively Calum is."

"Aye, he's even restless in his sleep; tosses the bedcovers off onto the floor. Probably playing football in his dreams," Isla commented indulgently. "So, how did the weigh-in go yesterday?"

"It was fine. She's gained two pounds. That maybe doesn't seem much, with all of the effort we're putting in, but it's an increase. That's what counts."

"And she was OK with it?"

"Yeah, she seemed to be. Nothing much gets a reaction from her. She's the liveliest I've seen her just now, with you two here."

"Maybe goes to show that she needs more company, more visitors."

"Yes, I'm sure that would help. Grant is bringing her down to the gig tonight."

"Oh, that's good. There might be some other young folk around too."

"Will you and Fraser make it?"

"One of us will come, or maybe we'll swap over so that we can both be out for a wee while."

"Don't you have a babysitter for Calum?"

"The trouble is that he runs rings around them. They're all nice girls but they can't get him to settle down to sleep. We come home to find him swinging from the lampshades."

"Not literally, I hope."

"Naw, but totally wound up. So, it's not really worth it. Did you hear that there's to be another diving expedition in the bay?"

"No. For the Spanish galleon? I thought they'd found everything that was worth salvaging."

"Apparently this team are from Spain, so it could be that they have more background information."

"Maybe." I was doubtful.

"They've taken a long lease on a house at Salen, right through until the summer. Rhona at the tourist information told me."

"Could be interesting."

Just then Grant strode into the room with a face like thunder, letting the door slam behind him.

"What's wrong?" I asked him.

"Something's been among the lambs." He flung himself down into a chair and raked his hands through his hair. Recently I'd noticed a sprinkling of grey appearing amongst his curls. "Sorry, Isla. I didn't know you were here. Hello."

"That's OK. Are they missing? Or injured?" she asked.

"I thought they were still close by, just next to the barn?" I said.

"Aye, they are. There's one dead, ripped up, and I think another missing."

"An eagle, do you think?" I asked.

"I'm not sure. An eagle would usually carry a whole animal away. The butchered one looks more like a dog's gone for it. They're often not hungry enough to eat the carcass; they've got the instinct to kill and then they just mess it up."

"It might be worth phoning round some of the other farms, see if they've had any trouble," Isla suggested.

"Aye. We always expect to lose a few, but it's frustrating when we've only just got them all safely delivered."

"Want a cup of tea?" I offered.

"Naw, I'll go down to the office and phone around. See if there's any word of something similar. Where's Laura?"

"She took Calum out to the shed to feed the lambs there," I reported. "She was on good form."

"Well, that's encouraging at least. Maybe see you tonight, Isla?"

"Aye, I'll try to make it along."

"It should be a good night. Did Claire tell you she's been working on some new tunes?" With that, he saluted in our general direction and hurried out of the room.

I lingered over the last poignant notes of 'Dark Lochnagar'; the flute was left to carry the tune alone. Then I lowered my instrument and there was a slight pause before the bar patrons gave their applause. It was the end of our set, and Archie announced that we would take a short break for refreshments. I joined Grant, Laura and Isla at their table.

"Was it OK?" I asked.

"Aye, really good, well done." Grant leaned over to kiss my cheek.

"I liked the last one," Isla added. "Didn't The Corries used to sing that?"

"Don't ask me, I'm not an expert on Scottish music. Archie could tell you." I craned round to see Archie standing at the bar. "He's supposed to be bringing me a drink." But he seemed to be deep in conversation with a young man who was sitting on one of the tall bar stools.

"I'll go and get you one," Grant offered. "What do you want? White wine? Anyone else need a top-up?" He took our orders and joined Archie at the counter.

"I didn't realise that you were so good at playing the flute, Claire," Laura said. "Don't suppose I've heard you before." She had wedged herself into the corner where two bench seats met, and seemed to be making herself look even smaller than she was by sliding down low on the bench and hunching forward. Was she trying to escape any recognition or attention?

"Thanks." I grinned at her. "It's all down to Archie that I started playing again. I'd let it peter out, but he gave me some music as a farewell gift that first time I came up here to evaluate Caisteal Glas. Back in London, I got into it again; even joined an orchestra for a couple of years."

"I wish I could play something. I've got a guitar, but I'm useless at it."

"Maybe you could get some lessons," Isla suggested.

"Is there anyone on the island who teaches it?"

"There's bound to be," I said. "There might be a music teacher at the school. We can ask about it once term begins."

"Here we go." Grant returned with our drinks and some packets of crisps which he deposited on the table. "That lad Archie's talking to is one of the Spanish diving team you were telling Claire about earlier, Isla."

"I thought he was a visitor; not from around here," she said.

"He looks quite tanned; a good clue that he's not spent the winter on Mull," I added.

"Apparently he's a flamenco guitar player as well as a diver," Grant informed us as he squeezed in to sit beside Laura. "Archie is trying to persuade him to play something."

"Oh, that would be cool." Laura sat up straighter. "We were just talking about guitar."

"Well, Graeme has volunteered to go and fetch a guitar; he only lives along the road. So, you might be in luck, Laura." Grant smiled at his daughter and, draping his arm around her shoulder, gave her a hug.

I took a sip of my wine and tore open one of the bags of crisps, leaving it on the table for sharing. It was good to see Grant relaxing. He'd been in touch with a few of the neighbouring landowners that afternoon and it seemed that we weren't the only ones to have lost lambs to some kind of predator. They had contacted the police and were all going to be on the lookout for a stray dog.

"I hope Graeme'll come back soon," Isla said, looking at her watch. "I'd like to hear the lad play, but I should be getting along the road to let Fraser come down."

"Well, look. Archie's rearranging the seats." I drew Isla's attention to the front, where Archie was now setting up a microphone. Then Graeme appeared and handed a guitar case to the Spaniard.

"It'll need tuning. It's not been played since Lewis went off to university," I heard him explain.

Then Archie made an announcement. "Ladies and gentlemen, we're privileged tonight to have a visitor all the way from Spain. This is Alejandro and he's going to play some traditional Spanish music for us on the guitar. Give him a warm welcome."

The bar patrons clapped and cheered. Alejandro sat on the chair that Archie had provided and worked on tuning the instrument. "I thank you," he said. "I hope that I will not disappoint you with my playing, especially with an instrument that is not my own. But I will try to play a piece in the flamenco style. It is called 'Entre dos Aguas'."

He then proceeded to amaze us; his playing was assured. The notes streamed from under his fingers – lively, intricate and rhythmic – and he tapped his feet and thumped on the body of the guitar to add to the sound. When he finished there was clapping, cheering, stamping and whistling from the audience.

"Well, I'll be scared to go back up now," I said. "I don't think we can compete with that."

"You can," Isla reassured me. "It's just different; not what we're used to. But you guys are good at what you do."

"Thanks." I still had my doubts.

"Anyway, I'll need to be away. I'll send Fraser down to hear your second set."

"Bye, Isla," we chorused as she rose and put on her jacket. As she was leaving, Archie approached our table with Alejandro in tow. Isla shook hands with Alejandro and gave Archie a kiss on her way past.

"Everyone, meet Alejandro." And Archie introduced us.

"Take a seat, man." Grant invited him to join us.

"That was some virtuoso playing," I said.

"Thank you, you are kind. My teacher would not say it was so good. But I am happy that people enjoyed."

"Have you been playing guitar for a long time?" Laura enquired.

"Since five years old."

"And you speak English so well." Laura again. She really seemed to be coming out of her shell today. "My mum's a Spanish teacher and I'm starting to learn at school."

"Ah, *eres profesora*," he said, looking at me and smiling.

"Oh, I'm not her mum," I replied. I was flustered, but didn't know why. Anyway, I decided not to try and explain our relationship.

"*Lo siento*, I am mistake. I hope anyway that my English will be getting better now that I am here for many months."

"I'm sure it will. And I can assure you that you're at least a hundred times better at English than anyone here is at Spanish. Drink up; it's on the house." Grant handed him a pint of beer that had been provided from the bar.

"Where do you live in Spain?" I asked.

"In Malaga, in the south," he replied.

"Oh, I've been there. Or at least to the airport; we actually stayed in Marbella."

"Is a good place for holidays," he said, grinning. His teeth looked incredibly white in contrast with his dark, tanned face and black hair. I'd noticed that he had a habit of tossing his head to flick his hair out of his eyes. It was short around his ears and at the back, but longer on top and floppy at the front. The gesture reminded me of a spirited horse tossing its mane. I could see that Laura was watching him very closely.

By the time I'd finished my drink and had to leave the table to play our second set, we'd ascertained that Alejandro was studying archaeology at university in Barcelona, and that the diving expedition was going to count as a research project for his course. Also, Laura had dropped into the conversation the fact that she was looking for a guitar teacher, as if it had been on her mind for any longer than the past half-hour. And it seemed that Alejandro had agreed to teach her some basic fingering, but in a few weeks' time once his research was more established.

Chapter 21

We paused on the headland by the rope sculpture of a woman. It had been drizzly and dull for the past three days. Although the rain had stopped now, the sky was still heavy and there was little definition between the clouds and the sea. The turquoise figure stood out boldly against the grey background.

Mum walked around the figure. Wearing wellington boots and a heavy rain jacket, she looked short and dumpy beside the slim but curvaceous statue. "She has a definite air of poise about her," she declared eventually.

"Yeah, and sometimes she has a great view; on a clear day without all this cloud and smir," I replied.

"Well, I'm glad to get out in the fresh air even if it is a bit damp. Can we walk down to that beach there?" She pointed down to Calgary Bay.

"Why not? You're right; it's good to be out of the house."

We began to make our way down from the headland towards the road that would take us along the coast to the beach.

"The atmosphere's a bit tense, isn't it?" Mum remarked.

"You're right. And this is actually better than it was. I'd say that things have been a little easier since the weekend, and having you and Dad around has helped too."

"Oh, well, that's good."

"I think that Grant and I find it hard to relax with this whole contract thing, and Laura is probably getting bored of our company."

"Can't she start to get out more?"

"If her weight is up again tomorrow it could be on the cards. We go down to the right here."

I directed Mum to a narrow path which led to a stile over the fence. I held her hand as she negotiated the steep step at the top, then clambered over behind her. We continued on a grassy track towards the sand. A few sheep were grazing, and scattered at our approach. They must have reminded Mum of our conversation over lunch.

"What exactly was Grant saying about a predator among the sheep?"

"Well, something has been taking lambs. It could be an eagle, or more likely a dog. But apparently old Alasdair Colquhoun was telling a tale in the pub last night about having seen a gigantic cat. So now the story's going around."

"What kind of cat?"

"I don't know, and I'm not sure that Alasdair can be relied on. He's an old shepherd with a liking for drink. Too much alcohol and living on his own might make his imagination run riot. He likes to have an audience when he comes into town, so he probably spun out a good yarn."

"I've heard things before about wild cats. Wasn't there a puma caught one time?"

"I don't remember hearing about that. Oh, look." I picked up a piece of royal-blue sea glass which had caught my eye. I rubbed it clean with my fingertips. It was smooth to touch, like a pebble. "This is an unusual colour. There might be more; often you find sea glass in clusters. Keep an eye out; Laura likes to collect it." Then I caught myself. "Or she used to. Maybe she'd still like it."

We continued to walk, heads down now, scanning the white sand for glimpses of colour. I picked up a few more pieces. "It reminds me of the colour of a Milk of Magnesia bottle. You used to give me that when I was little if I had a stomach ache."

"Yes, so I did. I want to ask you, Claire, while I'm here with you. This has all been so stressful with Laura, but are you all right, you and Grant?"

"Yes, Mum, we're fine."

"Really fine? Have you stopped trying for a baby?"

I sighed. When Grant and I first got together I'd been desperate to have a baby with him. Because he already had the girls he wasn't so bothered, but he could see my point of view and agreed that we should try. "After the fifth miscarriage I put it all behind me. I just couldn't go through it again. And there's my age."

"But maybe if you saw a specialist?"

"We did have a consultation and some tests, but the results weren't conclusive and I didn't want to go on to the next stage. I didn't like the idea of a whole lot of medical intrusion, and we'd have to keep travelling to Glasgow. It didn't seem fair to spend so much time and effort on something that might not work and that Grant wasn't wholehearted about anyway."

"You mean he didn't want another child?"

"Well, if it had happened naturally, I think he'd have been fine about it. But he wasn't so invested in the concept. Also, he hated how it affected me. I got so anxious, and then I was devastated and low each time when things went wrong. We both thought that we should stop trying."

"And it hasn't changed things between you?"

"I suppose it has in a way, but every relationship should move and change if it's going to survive. What we went through and the decisions we made have probably made us a stronger couple. And now we've got Laura to cope with, maybe it's just as well that there isn't a little half-sibling around to complicate life even more." I looked Mum in the eye. "I really am all right with it now, Mum. I'm quite content with Grant, the business, my music and a share of his girls."

We continued to wander slowly across the beach, drifting apart slightly, each on the lookout for blue glass. What I'd said about being over the whole baby thing was partially true. Mainly I was OK because I didn't allow myself to think about it. But now that Mum had dredged the subject up, I could feel my emotions bubbling up towards the surface.

I hadn't had any trouble falling pregnant, and when my first pregnancy was confirmed I was overjoyed. I'd suspected it even before I missed my period, as my breasts had begun to tingle and my nipples were incredibly sensitive. Grant and I agreed not to tell anyone until after my first antenatal appointment, as everyone knows that the first three months are risky. I tried not to get too excited, but of course I'd worked out when the baby would be due, and I'd started to look at a pregnancy website that showed the embryo's development, and imagine what was happening in my womb. When I began to bleed at eleven weeks, just two days before my appointment, my hopes plummeted. I suppose that the physical process wasn't much worse than a heavy period. I swallowed ibuprofen, which helped me to cope with the cramping as I passed tissue and clots. But I was a weeping, teary mess for days on end, and I hated everyone who told me that early miscarriages were common and assured me that my next pregnancy would be fine. This was my baby, not just some anonymous pregnancy.

It took me six months to be able to consider trying again. This time I made even more of an effort not to plan ahead, not to get my hopes up. I was edgy, and forever rushing to the toilet to check my underwear. This happened several times every day. I'd imagine that I felt wetness, or experience a tummy twinge; then I couldn't relax until I'd been to look for any bleeding. When it did start, at just over ten weeks, I was devastated. Our GP sent off a series of blood tests from both of us and swabs from me to test for infection. Then she arranged for us to see a specialist in Glasgow. I had a pelvic ultrasound scan there, and all of our other results were available, but there didn't seem to be any obvious answer or cause. As I'd said to Mum, I wasn't keen on further tests. And we were told that there was still a good chance that another pregnancy would be successful.

It took a lot of courage to try for the third time, and the fourth. The fifth was a mistake. It never got any easier; my five failed babies. I still wanted to cry if I thought about them, so I distracted myself, keeping busy. Usually it worked and I was genuinely happy with my life.

I reached the end of the bay and saw Mum approaching me holding out her hand, palm up, to show me her findings. She had some green and clear glass in addition to the blue. "It's amazing how you get your eye in once you start to look for it," she said, tipping the pieces into my hand. Then she noticed my wet eyes, and drew me into a hug. "I'm sorry, Claire. I didn't mean to upset you, bringing it all back."

"It's OK. I just don't think about it much anymore. But when I do, it still hurts."

Eventually Mum let me go and rubbed the back of her neck, turning her head from side to side. "Ooh, my neck's sore from looking down at the beach all that time."

"Let's head back to the car. I think the rain's due to blow back in soon."

We set off, returning along the curved bay, this time at a good pace and with our heads up, taking in the view. A crowd of black-and-white oystercatchers waded along at the tideline, looking for food. Intermittently they took to the air and we could hear their distinctive 'wheeep-wheeep' call. I could see a curtain of rain out at sea which would soon be coming our way. Hopefully we would outpace it.

When we returned to the estate, I found Grant in the office. He was on the phone.

"Thanks, Sandy. I'll make a note of that. I'm compiling a record." He listened. "Aye, it is a job for the police, but there's no harm in giving them a wee bit of backup, is there?" He laughed at the reply. "Right, I'll keep you informed of any news. Bye, then."

He put the receiver down and rummaged in the top drawer of his desk, extracted a drawing pin and crossed over to the map of north Mull hanging on the wall. He stuck the pin into the map at Ballimeanoch, then stood back, contemplating the map, which now had eight pins stuck in it.

"Another lamb?" I asked.

"Aye." He sighed.

Just then there was a tap at the window and my dad waved to us from outside. Grant went to meet him at the door.

"You heading out for a stroll?" Grant asked.

"Yes, I thought I'd wander a bit farther up the hill track. I've been stuck in front of a computer screen for long enough, and I reckon the rain will hold off for a little longer. Barbara is up at the house with Laura. She said you'd had a good walk, Claire."

"Yes, it was good to blow away the cobwebs. I'll join Mum in a few minutes; get our meal on the go. Grant's just heard from a neighbour about another lamb being attacked."

"Oh dear. That's not good, but I suppose you expect to lose a few."

"Aye, but not so many in just a few days, and over quite a scattered area. There's no doubt that something is after them. Can you keep an eye out while you're walking? It was farther up the road that the latest one was found," Grant explained.

"OK, I will do. See you later." Dad strode off towards the gate and the estate road, while I headed for the house, leaving Grant to finish up his admin tasks in peace.

When Dad returned, Mum and I were busy in the kitchen. Mum was peeling and chopping vegetables and I was whisking up egg whites in a bowl.

"Did you have a good walk, Dad?"

"Yes, it was refreshing; good to be out and about," he replied.

"Hang your jacket up to dry, Edward, and get out of those wet boots," Mum instructed as she leaned her head back to receive Dad's kiss.

"Half an hour till we eat, Dad. Can you see if Grant is around to get us a drink? I think he came in from the office a while ago."

Dad saluted us and made a hasty retreat. A few minutes later Grant appeared to take our orders for aperitifs. As he gathered glasses, bottles and ice cubes together he enquired, "Claire, would you be able to take Laura down to the nurse tomorrow? The time clashes with the public meeting about the wind farm proposal and I feel I should go along to that."

"Yeah, it's OK with me. I have to be in the shop tomorrow morning, so she can come with me and go to the health centre from there."

"I didn't know there was going to be a wind farm," Mum commented.

"Well, it's just a proposal; it may never happen. Thank you." I smiled at Grant, accepting a glass of white wine.

"And it's the usual tension between development and jobs, versus scenery and the environment," Grant explained.

"Although this time you could argue that it's a positive for the environment as it's renewable energy," I added.

"What do you think?" Mum asked Grant.

"Well, I probably lean on the side of development and jobs. It often seems to be the incomers to the island who get most het up about the scenery. I know that tourism's a big part of the island's economy, but the use of the land has changed a lot over the ages, and people need to make a living. Anyway, I'll find out more details at the meeting."

Dad joined us and accepted a gin and tonic. He swirled the mixture around, making the ice clink against the glass. "I was impressed when I visited the shop this morning, Claire. You and Helen seem to be a good team. I thought that everything was really well set out. You have some beautiful pieces and they're arranged to catch the eye."

"Thanks, Dad." His approval meant a lot to me.

"And I went through the accounts this afternoon; it all looks very satisfactory. You're making a good profit. So, I think you're well set up for a successful summer season."

"I hope so. Let's drink to that," I suggested.

We all clinked glasses and took a sip.

"Come on, we don't all need to stand around the kitchen. Let's move through to the lounge while the veg is cooking," I suggested.

In the lounge we found Laura reading a magazine, and settled into comfortable seats around her.

"Where did you get to on your walk, Edward?" Grant asked Dad.

"I went up the hill as far as the cattle grid. After that the ground looked very wet so I didn't venture much farther; didn't fancy getting stuck in a bog. But for a moment I thought that I might be the one to discover the sheep predator."

We all looked at him, and, knowing that he'd caught our attention, he continued with his story. My dad loved to tell a tale, and was working to draw in his audience.

"Well, just as I was about to turn back, I glimpsed something moving up on the hill, and felt that something was watching me. And there it was, a magnificent beast; a stag standing halfway up the hillside. I have to say that the sight of it was less dramatic than it might have been because it only had one antler. I was close enough to count the points on the one it did have, though: twelve."

"A royal stag," Laura confirmed.

"After a few seconds it ran off up the hill."

"Someone would value those antlers," Grant commented. "It might be worth taking a look up there in a day or so to see if we can find them."

"Doesn't Angus down at Salen use them for craftwork?" Laura asked.

"Aye, there are a few craftworkers on the island that use horn. Claire, is that the oven timer ringing?"

"Yes, so it is. Dinner will be served," I announced as I returned to the kitchen.

After our meal I was folding laundry in the utility room while my parents, at their insistence, dealt with the dirty dishes in the kitchen. I couldn't help overhearing their conversation over the clinking of dishes and cutlery, and the swishing of water in the sink.

"Did you speak to Claire about the business while you were out?" Dad asked.

"No, it didn't really come up," Mum replied.

"Well, I think we need to talk to her soon, mention our plans."

"It's good that her shop is doing so well."

"Yes, knowing that she's in a healthy position makes it much easier for us to retire. But she'll need to be part of the decision about what we do with the Tunbridge Wells end."

"Well, it seems to me that there are three options: we could sell up, we could take on a manager, or Claire might prefer to find another business partner."

"I don't mind what happens, so long as we get enough capital for us to live off comfortably."

I heard a clunk as the dishwasher door was closed, and then the machine began to hum and draw in water.

"So, when are we going to ask her?" Mum put the question.

"I don't know. She's got a lot going on right now with Laura. Maybe we should leave it until after the summer." Dad's voice faded as they left the room.

I was surprised that my parents were considering retiring, but after all they were well into their sixties, so why not? They'd worked hard on their business, and should stop and enjoy some leisure time before they got worn down or ill. Somehow, though, I didn't think of them as being at that stage. Luckily, they'd both had good health. I realised that having parents of retirement age made me feel older; positively middle-aged. I wasn't so keen on that thought.

Chapter 22

"Laura, I need you to speed up. I have to leave in five minutes." I was frustrated by the length of time that Laura was taking to eat her breakfast. I had an appointment at the shop at half past nine which I hoped could lead to some good business. The designer responsible for interior decoration at the new boutique hotel under development at Connel, was coming to look for objects that might feature in the hotel's decor. And I imagined that, once I'd met with him and knew the kind of things to look out for, I would also be able to source other pieces, either from Tunbridge Wells or at future house sales.

"That's OK, I can come now." Laura wiped her mouth with her napkin and made to stand up.

"Oh, no. You haven't had your toast yet. Look, I'll see if my dad might run you down. Your appointment isn't until eleven, so there's no need for you to rush." I didn't want to be responsible for any skipped calories.

"Where was Dad off to, anyway? I thought he was taking me."

"He's gone to the meeting about the wind farm down at Fionnphort. You eat your toast; I'll check with Dad."

I found my dad in the lounge, reading the newspaper. He readily agreed to take over supervising Laura's breakfast, and to act as chauffeur. "Well now, what do you think about this article about wild swimming? Apparently, it's becoming all the rage in Scotland, even in winter." I could hear him trying to engage her in some chat as I grabbed my handbag and jacket and rushed out of the door.

Just over an hour later, the pair appeared in the shop. I immediately wondered what magic spell Dad had cast, as Laura looked so completely different from the moody girl at the breakfast table. She'd made some effort with her appearance, wearing jeans and a pale pink, fluffy jacket. Her legs still looked much too thin, accentuated by the skinny jeans, but she'd tied her hair back in a ponytail so it didn't look as sparse, and had applied some mascara, eyeliner and lipstick. But most surprising were the shining eyes, wide smile, and slight blush of colour on her cheeks.

"Hi, you two."

"Hello, dear, how did the meeting go?"

"It was good. The chap, Gregory, bought five items from me and is interested in several from the Tunbridge Wells catalogue. I said that you could send them up for him to look at."

"That sounds encouraging."

Meanwhile I could see that Laura was engrossed, looking out of the window. She seemed to be watching something outside.

"Is something happening out there?" I asked.

"Oh, we met a young Spanish man just as we were coming into the shop. He has something to do with a diving expedition," Dad explained.

"That would be Alejandro. Are they diving today, Laura?" I asked, joining her by the window.

"No. He said that they're doing a sonar sweep today to locate the best places to concentrate their resources." We could see an orange inflatable dinghy containing several figures out on the bay. "He said that he'd try to look in at the shop later if he's finished before we close."

I took note of the 'we' when referring to the shop and, putting that together with Laura's sudden animation, decided that it was Alejandro who was the magician and not Dad. "Well, you're welcome to help me out here sometimes if you want to."

"It might be good for a change sometimes. I'm getting a bit bored at the house, and it'll be worse once Edward and Barbara go home."

"Remember Mairi's coming at the end of next week. That'll be good; to catch up with her."

"Mm."

"What's the diving all about?" Dad asked.

"It's the Spanish galleon that sank in the bay," I replied.

"I don't think I've heard about that, despite all of our visits here." Dad sounded surprised.

"Well, I don't know much about it, but I think it sank sometime after the battle with the Spanish Armada."

"Gosh, I must look that up on the internet; it sounds very exciting."

"Alejandro's an archaeology student, so he must know lots of details," Laura chipped in.

"And maybe I'll get a chance to speak to him about it later," Dad commented.

"Meanwhile, we'd better get along to the nurse. Can you mind the shop for half an hour, please, Dad?" I asked.

"I'm sure I could go on my own," Laura complained.

"Maybe next week, but today your dad asked me to go with you, so that's what's going to happen. Let's go."

Dinner that night was the last with my parents, who were setting off for home in the morning. Isla had helpfully sent along a pre-cooked moussaka which only needed to be heated up. I'd prepared a Greek salad and cut up crusty bread as accompaniments. Dessert would be baklava, bought from the Island Bakery and served with crème fraiche. I decided to set the table in the dining room rather than the kitchen to make the occasion a bit more special.

"First of all, a toast to Laura, who's gained another two pounds this week."

I cringed as my dad made this announcement. According to the rules we'd been given, we weren't supposed to make a big thing about any weight gain. However, I smiled and raised my glass with everyone else, and Laura actually looked quite pleased. Grant raised his eyebrows, then winked at me, easing my tension about Dad's faux pas.

"Also, congratulations to Claire for making a good business deal today. I think it could be lucrative."

We raised our glasses again. Then Mum cut in. "OK, let's serve up this lovely food before it gets cold. You know what Edward can be like once he gets going. We'll be raising toasts until midnight."

I laughed and began to dish up the moussaka. "Help yourselves to salad and bread," I encouraged everyone.

"I've found out a lot about that Spanish ship this afternoon. Grant, you probably know all of this, being a local, but the rest of us seemed to be in the dark." Dad consulted some written notes. "It was called the *San Juan de Sicilia*, and it exploded here in the bay on the 5th of November 1588."

"Hey, that's Guy Fawkes Night; a bit of a coincidence to have another explosive event on the same night." Laura sounded excited. "I must tell Alejandro."

"It predated Guy Fawkes by a good few years," Grant commented.

"Anyway, the ship was damaged and needed repairs, so they were laid up in the bay and the captain did some kind of a deal with the local laird," Dad continued.

"Aye, and then there was a falling-out and someone blew it up," Grant added.

"I'm surprised that there's enough interest for a new expedition. I read about lots of previous dives, starting as early as the 1600s. I'd have thought that anything of any worth would have been found by now."

"Aye, you're right, Edward – they've found guns and pewter plates, and a cannon that's at Inveraray Castle." Grant seemed to know a lot about the ship. "There were always rumours about chests of Spanish gold, but they haven't been forthcoming."

"Maybe that's what this dive will discover." Laura's eyes were gleaming.

"Aye, maybe. But I have my doubts," Grant declared.

"Still, it all sounds very romantic and exciting," Mum added.

I agreed that Laura certainly seemed to be infected by Spanish romance, but I kept quiet. Maybe something like this was just what she needed to help her forget her introspection and take an interest in the world again.

The next day I was up early to prepare a sustaining breakfast for my parents before they set out to catch the ferry. Helen was looking after the shop, so I was able to assist with the last-minute preparations. Dad and Grant had loaded up the van with the stock to be transferred south from the shop on Friday afternoon. But Mum was still rushing around gathering toiletries together, as my dad sat in the driver's seat, drumming his fingers on the wheel and repeatedly looking at his watch. Journeys to the mainland always relied on catching the ferry.

"Don't worry, Dad, you're booked on and you still have plenty of time," I reassured him as I brought a small holdall out to the vehicle.

"As long as we don't get stuck behind a tractor on the single-track road," he replied grumpily.

"Och, they always pull over to let you pass." Grant had come alongside, and he tried to calm the situation. "He'll be tooting the horn soon if she doesn't hurry up," he muttered to me as an aside.

Just then Mum and Laura emerged from the house into the yard, their arms full of jackets and waterproof gear. "Bye, Edward." Laura deposited her load of clothes onto the back seat of the van and approached the open driver's door, giving a playful finger-wave. Maybe she was trying to protect Mum, who was now hugging me tight. It seemed to work.

Dad smiled. "Goodbye, Laura. It was good to see you, and take care of yourself." Then he quickly grew impatient again. "Come on, Barbara, or we'll be swimming to Oban." He closed his door and started the engine.

Mum clambered up into the passenger seat and pulled her door shut. The van was moving off before she'd fastened her seat belt. She rushed to open her window so that she could stick out an arm to wave to us.

"Just as well that I opened the gate earlier, or their racing start would stutter to a halt gey soon," Grant commented. "I'll away down and shut it again. Seeing that your dad's in such a hurry, I think he might just forget. I'll do a wee bit in the office while I'm down there, but maybe come up for coffee in about an hour?"

"OK, see you then," I agreed, and turned back towards the kitchen. That would give me enough time to tidy up and put on a load of laundry. I also had to get round to some flute practice later in the day. I needed to go over the fingering in one of the reels where I felt I'd fumbled during our last gig, and Archie wanted me to play a classical piece for a performance that was coming up next month. I'd have to look through my music to find something suitable.

"Claire, when are you going across to Oban next?" Laura followed me into the kitchen.

"I don't have any plans right now, but is there something you want from there?"

"Well, I was thinking of maybe going to the hairdressers there. Isla recommended one on Albany Street. I don't want to be going to an island one."

"OK, well, why don't you phone to book an appointment? Then I can arrange my schedule around that."

"Right. And Dad will pay, won't he?"

"Of course, no problem," I promised.

I began to load the dirty breakfast dishes into the dishwasher as Laura went to find her mobile. Good for Isla; she'd obviously got a word in. But maybe Alejandro had something to do with it too, unknowingly. I was sure that Helen would swap if the appointment clashed with one of my shifts in the shop. Everyone had been so concerned about Laura, but there was little that they could do to help. So, I felt free to ask for a favour, knowing that it would be willingly granted.

I always got a flat feeling after my parents' visits were over. I missed them, only meeting up two or three times a year. Admittedly, we spoke several times a week by phone or Skype, but it wasn't the same as actually being together. I wiped down the kitchen table, gathering the toast crumbs in my hand. The best way to lift my mood was to concentrate on positive things. It was good that Laura seemed brighter; that was encouraging. Her eating was still slow and hard work, but perhaps it was getting slightly easier. And Mairi's visit later in the week was something to look forward to, although Laura hadn't seemed terribly enthusiastic about seeing her sister. Was there an issue there that I wasn't aware of? I must ask Grant. If there was a problem or an undercurrent, then it would be helpful to be forewarned.

"I think that Mairi was maybe critical of Laura, impatient," Grant explained when I asked him about the sisters over coffee.

"What do you mean?"

"Well, she kind of blamed Laura, saying that her illness was all self-inflicted and attention-seeking, and what did she think she was doing; that sort of thing."

"I suppose we all maybe thought those things, but didn't say them."

"Aye, well, Mairi's not the most tactful of characters, as you know."

"Yes, calls a spade an effing shovel."

"But I'm sure it'll all be fine now. These things usually blow over." Grant thought that I had an idealistic view of sibling relationships, being an only child. He said that I hadn't experienced the constant rivalry and squabbling that goes on throughout a lifetime together. But similarly, I didn't have the kind of bond that exists between brothers or sisters despite all of that. "I'll phone Mairi and have a chat with her before she visits. Explain the strategy. Will that help?"

"Yeah, hopefully. Surely they can get on together – after all, it's only for a few days."

Chapter 23

The sisters were sitting next to each other on the settee watching television when I arrived home from the shop on Saturday evening a week later. Seeing them there, side by side, brought back the first time I'd met them both together on that Easter visit to Iona. The difference in their colouring was still as striking: Laura dark like Grant and Mairi fair, more like Ruth. Laura and I had taken a trip to Oban during the week and her hair had been cut in a chin-length bob. Freed from its previous weight, it framed her face in loose ringlets, and the shorter style made it look much glossier and thicker. Her face was still relatively pale – she wasn't going outdoors much yet – but even so her skin was darker than Mairi's milky complexion. I knew that Mairi spent lots of time outdoors, with her horse and on the hockey field, but she never seemed to get a suntan. She'd have done well in the olden days when it was fashionable for women to be pale. Her hair was very long, drawn back in a ponytail that reached almost to her waist. Even tied back it had a tendency to frizz rather than curl, forming a cloud round her head and a mane down her back. I wondered what she would look like with a short haircut; maybe a bit like a dandelion clock, how Art Garfunkel used to look when he still had hair.

"Hi, Claire." Mairi rose, crossed the room and gave me a hug.

"Hello, how was your journey?" Grant had been down to the ferry terminal to pick Mairi up from the boat after her train journey from Glasgow to Oban.

"It was good, thanks. Plenty of time to catch up on some reading."

"What are you watching?"

"Oh, it's rubbish, really – *Don't Tell the Bride.*"

"Oi, I like it," Laura complained.

"Oh, sorry to insult your choice."

Laura stuck out her tongue at her sister.

"OK, I'm going to get changed, then I'll see what there is for dinner." I was quite happy to leave them to their bickering. Grant was right: I hadn't any practice at sibling relationships and tended to overreact to what he would describe as banter. So, making myself scarce seemed to be a good option.

"You don't need to worry; Dad's ordered takeaway from The Spice," Mairi informed me. "They said it'll be ready at seven and he's going to drive down and collect it."

"Oh, that's nice," I said. "In that case I'll have a gin and tonic once I've changed."

I exchanged my smart trousers and blouse for jeans and a sweatshirt and headed through to the kitchen to turn on the oven for heating plates and make myself that drink. Grant was sitting at the kitchen table reading a newspaper.

"Hi, are you avoiding the girly TV? I hear that we're having Indian tonight," I greeted him.

"Aye, I thought it would be a wee change."

"Want a drink?" I offered as I pushed ice cubes out of their tray into my glass.

"No, I'll wait and have a beer after I've collected the food. By the way, I spoke to Mairi about being tactful on our drive home. So, hopefully it'll be a peaceful visit."

The next morning Mairi and I set off up the hill track on a hike towards Glengorm. Laura stayed at home with Grant. She was still not allowed to come walking. She'd accompanied me to the shop twice in the previous week and seemed to enjoy getting out of the house. But her weight yesterday had been static, so there was to be no increase in her activities. It was sunny and warm, one of the first really springlike days that we'd had so far that year.

"How's it going with Laura?" Mairi asked me. "She still looks like a stick insect."

"Well, she's a lot better than when she arrived, but she still has a long way to go," I replied.

"It just seems like such a crazy thing to me, starving yourself almost to death. I can't get my head round it. But I promised Dad that I'll be good, and hold my tongue."

"You don't have any clues about why she developed anorexia, then?"

"I don't, really. It seemed to happen after I left for uni. Do you think that might have had something to do with it?"

"What do you mean?"

"Well, then she was on her own with Mum, the centre of attention. I know that Laura's always felt that she doesn't measure up to me academically. But I'm sure that Mum wouldn't put any extra pressure on her."

"Maybe not intentionally, but it could have been how Laura perceived it: that she couldn't live up to expectations. She's not exactly a dunce, though, is she?"

"No, she isn't, but I remember her commenting when I was leaving school that she hoped no one would expect her to be dux just because I was. She's taken a completely different syllabus from me anyway, so there's no direct comparison."

"Different subjects would certainly help to avoid that, but maybe that's part of why she wanted to come here. She could move to a different school where there's no association with you."

"Could be. A fresh start is probably a good thing for her anyway."

"She'll start to get some work sent out from school next week. I'm sure that'll be good for her; she must be getting bored. Although she does have a romantic interest." And I told Mairi about Alejandro and the guitar lessons as we walked along past the stream and through the woods.

We decided to make for the standing stones above Glengorm Castle. From there we had a view of what was called a castle, but was really a turreted Victorian country house, now an upmarket hotel. We could also see out over the Atlantic Ocean to the Ardnamurchan peninsula and the island of Coll. There were a few yachts in the channel making good progress with the breeze behind them.

"I love coming back to Mull, but I couldn't live here all the time. I'm surprised that you adapted so well after London," Mairi commented as we gazed out over the view.

"Well, I'd done city life for quite a while by the time I first came here. I think I was just ready for a change."

"Don't you miss London?"

"Not really. When I lived there my friends and I were all working and single. Now most of them have moved away from the city; settled down with families. I do miss my parents, but we keep in touch regularly. Sharing the business is a great bond." As I said this, I thought of the conversation that I'd overheard about my parents retiring. I realised now that when they withdrew from the business it would create quite a change. It was bound to alter our relationship; everything would be less intertwined. I couldn't imagine what they would do going forward. How would they fill their time without the shop? It had always been there; such a huge part of all of our lives.

"And you go down to Edinburgh from time to time for some culture." Mairi continued our conversation.

"Yes. That's a good point. It makes a huge difference to have the flat available and to know that I can be in the city in half a day."

"Yeah, I'm probably going to look for a position in a country vet's practice once I qualify, cause I'd like to work mainly with large animals and horses. But it would have to be reasonably close to Edinburgh or Glasgow."

"Or an English or Welsh city?"

"True, I hadn't thought of that. I should widen my outlook, eh? Not just be the wee provincial Scottish lassie."

"Do you mind if we go back a different way, over the hill? I want to look for some antlers." I explained about the lopsided stag that my dad had spotted.

"Yeah, we could take a look. He's probably shed the other one by now too."

We were quieter on the return; it was a hard climb and we had to save our breath. Once we were over the summit, we followed the course of a fast-flowing burn. I scanned the ground, left and right, as we made our way down, looking for any object that resembled a branch. There weren't any trees on this side of the hill; it was moorland with low-growing plants, mainly heather and bracken. We crossed the stream where it widened, stepping on some big stones to keep our feet dry.

As we jumped over the muddy bank to regain dry ground, Mairi exclaimed, "Look at that!"

"What?" I couldn't see anything of interest.

"That paw print in the mud. It's huge."

I crouched down beside her and followed her pointing finger. I could see what she meant: there was a clear paw print pressed into the mud, like a cat's or a dog's, and it looked bigger than the palm of my hand. "What kind of animal could have made that?" I asked.

"I'm not sure. I think it looks like a cat, but it's way too big. It would even be huge for a large dog."

"What about a wildcat?"

"I don't think they're that much bigger than a domestic cat; maybe slightly."

"Could Alasdair's story be true, then?"

"What story?"

I told her about the lambs and the possible sighting of a big cat. "I don't think that there have been any more taken this past week, though."

"It could be. I'll take a photo and see if anyone can identify what might have been passing by."

"Should we put something beside the print to show the scale?" I asked.

"Good idea – what do we have in our pockets?"

We both rummaged around and I came up with a fifty-pence coin.

"That should do – lay it down on the ground next to the print," Mairi directed me. She then took several shots of the paw print from various angles.

Meanwhile, I kept scanning our surroundings. "Do you know, I'm feeling a bit nervous now, thinking that there could be a large predator out here with us on the hill."

"Well, I'm sure that it would steer well away from us, but I know what you mean. Let's head for home."

And we set off briskly down the hill, all thoughts of the antlers forgotten.

Grant was working in the office as we passed the window. Mairi preceded me in through the door. "Dad, look what we found," she called as she approached him, pulling her mobile phone out of her pocket.

"What is it exactly?" he asked, squinting at the photograph on the screen.

Mairi flicked her thumb and forefinger over the image to

zoom in and pointed to the impression in the mud. "It's a paw print. Look, it's huge."

"We think that it might be a big cat. Maybe Alasdair was right," I added.

Grant gazed at the picture and rubbed his chin thoughtfully. "Aye, it looks big. Do you have more photos?"

Mairi handed him the phone and he scrolled through the images.

"I think maybe we should take a wee run over to see if we can find Alasdair this afternoon and have a proper chat with him," he said.

"I could ask around at the vet school to see if anyone can identify the track more positively. I'll try to find out who'd be best to give us advice," Mairi offered.

"Maybe the zoo would help," I suggested.

"Good ideas, girls. Let's go and have lunch and make our plans." Grant seemed very keen to take some immediate action. Of course, I knew that the dead lambs had been bothering him immensely.

We walked up the track to the house together. When we reached the yard, I commented on the unfamiliar car that was parked there.

"It's the Spanish lad, for Laura's guitar lesson," Grant explained. In the excitement of the paw-print discovery, I'd forgotten all about the lesson.

When we opened the door, I could hear a few fumbling notes, followed by a faster, more confident run of the same pattern.

"Hello, we're back," I called, stepping into the lounge. "How's it going?"

They were sitting across from each other, their guitars poised. Laura screwed up her face, but Alejandro smiled. "She is making progress, but will need to practise."

"Would you like to stay and join us for lunch?" I asked. "I'm just about to heat up some soup."

"I am sorry, but now I must go to play football. It is a five-in-a-team match against some men from Tobermory. My friend met them at the pub and arranged."

"Oh, are you good at football?" Laura asked.

"No. Some of my friends, they are good. I need for the numbers."

"They need you to make up the numbers," Mairi clarified. She'd come into the room behind me. "Hi, I'm Mairi, Laura's sister." She put out her hand. Alejandro stood to meet her, shook it, and then began to pack his guitar into its case.

"Maybe I could go to watch the football," Laura suggested.

"Not this week, Laura. Maybe another time." Grant had come into the room too. "Good luck in the game, lad. I'll come out and get the gate for you." And the two men left together.

"He's nice," Mairi commented. "When's the next lesson?"

"We're making it Sundays because he doesn't dive that day."

"Cool. Are you paying him?"

"No, it's just a friendly thing," Laura replied. Then, to me, "I could have gone to watch. He would have given me a lift and someone could have picked me up."

"Well, first you need to eat lunch, and second your dad said not this week," I replied. I knew that this was code for not having gained that privilege, and that Laura would understand that without me spelling it out. I felt a bit mean, because on the whole I thought that she had been trying to keep to her contract, and she hadn't given us too much trouble.

Luckily Mairi broke the tension, distracting her sister by showing her the photographs of our discovery and outlining our possible lines of enquiry.

"So, maybe I can come with you to hear what Alasdair says?" Laura tried again.

"Yes, I'm sure that will be fine. We're going after lunch," I confirmed.

Chapter 24

We set off to look for Alasdair after lunch. I was surprised that both girls joined us enthusiastically with no need for persuasion. Perhaps they were excited by the mystery and the idea of being detectives.

"It's not guaranteed that he'll be at home," Grant warned us.

"No, but I suppose that Sunday will be his day off, so he's less likely to be up on the hills," I added.

"Aye, I can't imagine that he's a regular churchgoer, and he's not the type to go to the pub until later in the day. I don't think that joining the Sunday lunch crowd would be quite his thing. So, he might be around."

Leaving our estate, we turned right onto the single-track road, following my old commuting route towards Dervaig. About half a mile after we crossed the bridge there, we made a left turn onto an even narrower road that went across country to Achleck.

"OK, we're looking for a track off to the left in about a mile," Grant said. "Then we need to go up past the farm and continue for as far as the track is made up to find Alasdair's cottage."

We found the farm track, and followed it uphill. I had to jump out for a gate, and then there was a cattle grid and we were out onto the open moor. In another mile we came to a lone cottage. There was no vehicle outside.

"Does he have a car?" Mairi asked.

"Don't know, but I doubt it," Grant replied.

We all climbed out from the Range Rover. The cottage looked exactly like a child's drawing: white walls, with a window on either side of a red-painted door. The roof was corrugated iron and the chimney was puffing lazily. Everything looked well kept: the walls were reasonably white, not stained or flaky, the paintwork on the windows and door was sound, and the roof didn't look rusty at all.

"The estate will be responsible for keeping the cottage weathertight," Grant commented, noticing my appraisal of the property.

"Yeah, I guess I was expecting something a bit more ramshackle," I admitted.

Grant strode up to the door and knocked firmly. We all waited. There was no response. He tried again and shouted, "Alasdair?" Still no response.

"You should try the door," Mairi recommended.

"Do you think so?" I was doubtful.

"Well, we've come all this way. He might just be asleep," Mairi suggested.

Grant knocked again, and this time he also turned the doorknob and pushed. The door opened and he stuck his head inside. "Alasdair?" he called again.

I thought that I could hear a faint response.

"It's Grant Maclean here. I've got the family with me; come for a visit."

There was another muttered response.

"Stay out here," Grant ordered, and he disappeared inside.

Mairi proceeded to walk round the outside of the cottage, and Laura parked herself on a large, flat boulder sitting in the sun. "It just looks the same at the back," Mairi reported on her return. "Two windows and a door. Nothing interesting."

"What were you expecting – a tiger in a cage?" Laura asked.

"Naw, just wondering—"

She was interrupted by Grant's reappearance with Alasdair at his shoulder. The old man looked as if he'd just been woken up, and was probably recovering from a heavy night's drinking. He screwed up his eyes against the daylight. I could see several days' growth of silvery stubble on his chin, standing out from his weathered face, and what looked like tracks of dried drool at the corners of his mouth. His grey hair was wild, like a bird's nest, and he was wearing stained fawn gaberdine trousers held up by braces over a yellowish, discoloured long-sleeved vest. His feet were bare, the toenails hornlike.

"Ach, man, I'm not in a state to be receiving lady visitors just now." Alasdair's voice was surprisingly gentle with a melodic Highland lilt.

"Don't worry, Alasdair. We'll wait until you smarten up," I tried to reassure him. Grant and I had agreed earlier that we'd suggest that Alasdair join us for afternoon tea at the Bellachroy Hotel. We didn't think that he'd be up to entertaining visitors in his cottage.

"Aye, get a quick wash and spruce up, and we'll treat you to tea and scones." Grant added his encouragement.

I thought that Alasdair looked tempted.

"We want to hear your story about the big cat," I added.

Alasdair nodded sagely. "Aye, well, I could do with a cup of tea; I have a fair thirst on me. If you can just give me ten minutes, I'll make myself respectable for your company." With that, he turned back inside his cottage, closing the door behind him.

"He was asleep, still in his armchair," Grant reported. "And I don't think he's had a window open in that front room for months; there's quite a fug."

"Anyway, mission accomplished, Dad. Well done." Mairi clapped Grant on the back.

When he reappeared, Alasdair's grooming was much improved. He was clean-shaven and his hair had been dampened and tamed, slicked back under a tweed cap. The trousers looked the same, but he now wore a shirt and a sports jacket with leather patches on the elbows. His boots had been recently polished.

"You jump up in the front with Grant, Alasdair. I'll squeeze in with the girls," I suggested. As he walked past me, I caught the scent of minty toothpaste, but that didn't entirely mask the miasma of stale alcohol.

"Well now, this is very kind of you," he commented as Grant turned the car and we began to retrace our journey down the track towards Dervaig. "What was it that you said was the reason for your visit?"

"Well, you know that there have been a lot more lambs than usual attacked this spring?" Grant began.

"Aye, it's been shocking, right enough," Alasdair agreed.

"And today Claire and Mairi found a very large paw print in the mud by the stream up the hill from us, towards Glengorm," Grant continued.

"I've got some photos of it that I can show you," Mairi interjected, waving her phone in the air. "When we get to the hotel."

"Oh, aye?" Alasdair nodded.

"Anyway, it put us in mind of the tale you were telling the other week about seeing a big cat. So, we wondered if we could ask you more about that," Grant explained.

"Of course, I'd be delighted to describe it to you."

"Well, here we are at the inn. Maybe we should get settled and order our tea before you begin," I suggested.

Grant parked in the car park and we all followed him into the hotel.

"Good afternoon, everyone. Is that you, Grant, and Alasdair?" the woman behind the bar greeted us.

"Aye, Sara. We're looking for tea and scones with cream and jam, please," Grant replied.

"Of course. Now, where would you like to sit? There's the bar, or the lounge might be more comfortable."

We opted for the lounge and settled ourselves around a table near the window while Sara went to prepare our order.

"I'll show you those photos now," Mairi offered. Perched beside Alasdair on the arm of his chair, she brought up the paw-print photos on her phone screen. She was very patient with the old man, enlarging the images and pointing out features to him, including the scale as demonstrated by the fifty-pence coin.

"Aye, that's certainly something out of the ordinary," he responded.

"So, when was it that you saw the cat?" Mairi asked him, returning to her own seat.

"It must have been nigh on three weeks past now." The skin on Alasdair's leathery brow wrinkled into deep corrugations as he calculated the timescale.

Meanwhile, Sara returned with a large tray which she deposited on the table. She set out cups, saucers and plates for everyone, and then cutlery and napkins. "I'll be back with the tea, just now," she promised as she left the lounge.

"And where exactly was it?" Grant asked.

"Well, it was late in the day; I was coming home, down off the hill. I'd been up above the river and I'd just crossed over when I looked back, up to the ridge behind."

Alasdair was interrupted by the reappearance of Sara with her tray. This time she brought two large pots of tea and a jug of milk. She was followed by a younger woman who was holding an old-fashioned cake stand with three layers, each one crammed with scones.

"Just put that down there, Fiona," Sara instructed, pointing to the table. "And I'll bring in the butter, jam and cream. Now, does anyone need sugar for their tea?"

Alasdair raised his hand.

"I'll get that too, then." She bustled away.

"So, this was just above the Bellart?" Grant clarified.

"Aye, on the ridge near the waterfalls," Alasdair responded.

The rest of our food arrived. "The jam is strawberry, home-made," Sara told us before she left.

We all began to help ourselves to scones: we spread them with the butter and strawberry jam, then dolloped a spoonful of clotted cream on top. Even Laura took a scone, although I noticed that she halved it, and applied a very thin scraping of butter and jam, and no cream. She took a tiny bite as I asked, "And what did it look like?"

"It was a stealthy creature, moving slowly and close to the ground, as if it was stalking something. It was broad at the shoulders, and I could see a long, thick tail."

"It couldn't have been a dog?" Grant asked.

"Naw, it didna move like a dog. Definitely a cat."

"What colour was it?" Laura asked.

"That's harder to say. It was coming on for dark and it was in the shadow; it looked gey dark-coloured. But that could have been the light. I dinna think it was black; maybe more a tan colour."

"What did it do next?" Mairi asked.

"I dinna know if it saw me, but it scrambled up past the edge of the ridge and I lost sight of it."

"And you've only seen it the once?" Grant asked.

"Aye."

"Have you noticed any paw marks or unusual droppings?" Mairi wanted to know.

"I havna, but then I wasna really looking closely. Maybe now, if I keep my eyes open, I'll come across a sign of it."

"If you do, can you let me know?" Grant asked.

"I will do that," Alasdair confirmed. "We've lost two lambs of our own here, so Mr McPherson would be interested too."

"What do you think it was, Alasdair?" Laura asked.

"I wonder if it wasna a puma," he replied. "You're all maybe a bit too young, but I can mind that there was a puma caught up by Inverness way, probably back in the 1980s. And I think that it had been on the loose for a good few year afore it was captured."

"Wow, that would be cool," Laura said.

"But where would it have come from?" I asked.

"Where indeed. A good question," Alasdair agreed.

"Have another scone, Alasdair," Grant said. "And you need to finish yours, Laura."

I could see Mairi rolling her eyes in response to her sister being told to eat. Luckily, Laura didn't notice. After we'd demolished the scone supply and finished the tea, we offered Alasdair a lift back to his cottage.

"Och, there's no need, thank you all the same. I'll maybe just bide here a wee while and have a dram or two," he replied.

As we left, he was making his way into the bar.

"That'll be him for the rest of the night," Grant commented as we made for the car.

"But he's sweet, Dad. A real gentle soul," Laura commented.

Mairi raised her eyebrows this time.

"So, what do you all think?" I asked once we were on our way back home.

"I believe it's a puma," Laura declared. "One hundred per cent."

"Well, I'm more inclined to believe it now that there's a bit of corroborating evidence," Grant admitted.

"I feel bad that I just automatically decided that it must be rubbish because it came from Alasdair," I confessed. "I even made a big joke of it to my mum, but I'm more convinced after finding the print this morning."

"Yeah, I'm with all of you guys." Mairi joined in. "But will we ever be able to prove it?"

Chapter 25

Over the course of the following week, I began to notice that the atmosphere in our house had lightened. On Monday morning Laura and I drove Mairi down to Craignure to catch the ferry; the first stage of her journey back to Glasgow.

"Good luck with your assignment," I said, hugging her goodbye.

"Remember to let us know about the paw print," Laura instructed.

"Sure, sis. And you make sure to put some more weight on before I see you again."

Laura scowled, but refrained from any riposte.

Back at the house, I shut myself away with my flute and music for some concentrated practice. The concert was on Friday evening and I had a lot of work to do in order to polish my playing. I'd decided on the piece – Debussy's 'Syrinx' – and I wanted to be able to perform it without reading the music. Although it was only three minutes long, it would still be a major challenge for me to get it right. Every now and then, when I broke to rest or to consider a phrase more closely, I could hear fumbling guitar notes coming from Laura's room. She was practising too.

I don't know if it was the effect of Mairi's visit, or the mystery of the paw print, or our shared musical endeavours, but suddenly we seemed to be more relaxed together. I even felt that I could leave Laura in charge of the shop on her own for a couple of hours on two afternoons, giving me the chance for more flute practice. When I arrived to collect her on Thursday afternoon, I found her chatting to Archie.

"Hello, there. Your glamorous assistant here tells me that your flute piece is going to be fantastic," he greeted me.

"Hi, Archie. I think I'm competent; I wouldn't say fantastic."

"She's too modest. I've been listening to her practising and it's really good." Laura surprised me with her praise.

"Well, thanks. Hopefully it'll be all right tomorrow night," I replied.

"Aye, I'm sure it will be. I called by to say that I'll pick you up, since I have to go past your road end anyway. We're to be there ready to play at seven. So, will I say six?"

"Yeah, that's great."

"Where's the concert?" Laura asked.

"Oh, did she not tell you? It's at the castle. Caisteal Glas," Archie announced.

"Wow, I hear it's a posh venue now," Laura said. "What are you going to wear, Claire?"

"She refuses to wear any tartan," Archie complained.

"Well, I'm not Scottish. It's all right for you to wear a kilt but I'd feel like an imposter."

"You're entitled to wear the Maclean tartan, since you're married to Dad," Laura reassured me.

"No, I'll stick to black. It's conventional for a concert and more my style."

"Let's not argue with her." Archie nudged Laura jokily. "We don't want to upset our prima donna."

On Friday evening I heard the gravel crunching in the yard, the dogs barking and, rather unnecessarily given the other warning noises, a car horn tooting. When I looked out from the window, I saw Archie's new van. He'd traded in his rusty Citroën a few years ago. The replacement, a Volkswagen Caddy, was a huge improvement: the paintwork was light blue and seemed to be intact. I opened the kitchen door and waved to him, then called goodbye to Grant and Laura.

"Good luck."

"Play well," they called in reply.

"Evening, Claire," Archie greeted me as I settled into the passenger seat. "We're meeting Willie down at the landing." Willie was an occasional member of Archie's group. He played keyboard or piano, and tonight it would be the baby grand at Caisteal Glas.

Archie had left the sheep gate open, and once he'd driven through, he hopped out of the driver's seat and ran back to close it, his kilt swinging.

Although I was feeling nervous about performing tonight, I was also very excited to be revisiting the castle. I hadn't been back there since I'd finished the valuation, more than ten years ago now. I knew that it had taken a number of years for all of the administration to be completed and for the castle to go on sale. I'd still been living in London when it eventually went on the market. Then there was a hiatus of two or three years until a serious buyer came forward; perhaps because the building was relatively small with very little scope for extension, and because it was quite difficult to get to. As Laura had said, it had subsequently been developed as a venue and was aimed at the exclusive end of the market. The gatherings held there tended to be small society weddings and celebrations, or corporate entertainment. I'd been told that the group we'd be playing for tonight were investment bankers from London and New York.

In the past few years, I'd occasionally caught sight of a sleek grey minibus with the castle's new logo driving around the island. When Archie and I pulled into the parking area at Croig, I spotted a new metal plaque with the same design. It was oval in shape and depicted a black silhouette of the castle on its rock, against a light blue background with a hint of fading orange sunlight creating a corona effect. The wording on the sign was, as before, 'Laimrig Glas'. When I stepped out of Archie's van, I noticed that the car park had been resurfaced; no more potholes and puddles. And it had a neat picket fence all around it, painted the same pale grey as the minibus, which I could see was parked at one end of the enclosed area. Archie crossed the road to the quayside to look for the launch. I heard him talking to someone, so assumed that the boat was waiting.

A few minutes later, Willie drove up in his red Mini Countryman and parked beside the van. "Evening, Claire," he greeted me as he closed his car door. Like Archie, he was wearing tartan, but he had opted for trews rather than a kilt.

"Hi, Willie," I replied. "Archie's talking to the boatman." I pointed across the road.

"I guess we're ready for sailing, then. Have you got everything you need?"

"I have, but Archie's fiddle's still here in the van."

"I'll take it over for him." Willie picked up the instrument case from the back seat; then we crossed over to the quayside.

Since I had to look smart, I was wearing high-heeled court shoes. The steep stone steps were shiny with moisture, making me worry about slipping in my impractical footwear. I clung to the metal rail with one hand, clutching my flute case in the other, and descended very cautiously. When I reached the bottom safely, I wasn't surprised to notice that the launch tied up there was pale grey with light blue lines and peachy-orange seats. Our captain was a young lad that I recognised from around Tobermory. He looked very capable dressed in a pale grey sailor's sweater with a castle badge sewn onto the left breast. He had darker grey trousers and rubber boots, all matching.

"This is Ewan." Archie introduced us. "He's a far cry from your previous skipper," he added to me, laughing.

"Yes, I was just thinking the same," I agreed.

We were all given life jackets to wear – yes, pale grey. Then Ewan gunned the engine and slipped the ropes and we were under way. It was a calm evening, so no huge waves or excessive bumping. But I still held on tightly to my seat edge. It was hard to believe that I'd made this trip every day for several months.

"So, what's the story about you and the castle?" Willie wanted to know.

I explained about being sent from London and meeting Archie, and the job of making an inventory of the castle's contents.

"I mind I felt a wee bit anxious, leaving you there on your own that first day," Archie confessed.

"And I felt pretty much abandoned as you sailed off," I admitted.

"So, you're going to notice if they've made any big changes," Willie commented.

"Yes, I went over every room with a fine-tooth comb. But it was ten years ago, so I'll have forgotten some of it. I'm quite excited about seeing it again."

"I suspect that it won't have retained the same atmosphere at all," Archie commented, showing his more soulful, artistic side.

"Yes, I remember that first day you really surprised me by saying it could be 'enchanting'. I didn't really know whether to take you seriously then. But I came to feel quite strongly about the place after a few weeks."

"Look, we can see the castle now." Archie pointed. It was half past six but still quite light; the clocks had changed over a month ago and the evenings were definitely stretching out. The castle looked almost like its picture on the badge, minus the orange sunset behind.

"I've never been over before, although I've lived in Tobermory all my life. I've sailed past a few times, but it was owned by the family; you couldn't visit without an invitation," said Willie.

"Prepare to be impressed," I advised him.

We arrived at the castle jetty and Archie helped me to clamber up out of the boat and onto the stone walkway. Ewan instructed us to make our way up to the front of the building, adding that he'd see us later for our return journey.

"Oh, we get to go in through the front door," I said. "I've only done that once before."

I felt that I was holding my breath as we made our way up the stone steps to the heavy oak door. There was a member of staff waiting to let us in. I guessed that Ewan had radioed ahead to warn him that we were approaching. When I stepped into the entrance hall, I wasn't disappointed. It was still just as impressive, if not more so. The display of armoury remained on the walls, but now it was incredibly shiny; polished and gleaming brightly in improved lighting. The chandelier was still a feature, buffed diamond-bright, but now there were also additional spotlights perfectly placed to highlight the wall displays. I suspected that the stags had been overhauled by a taxidermist since I'd last met them. They certainly looked less dusty. Tonight, this space was obviously in use as a lounge and gathering area. There were groups of armchairs and sofas, and a long sideboard was topped with a snowy white cloth and an arrangement of champagne glasses. The piano had been placed in one of the back corners in front of three of the Iona marble columns, so this was presumably where we were to play. I approached one of the great hall's entrance doors to have a look, and saw that it was set out with tables decked in brilliant white cloths, shiny cutlery and sparkling glassware. There were still tapestries and portraits on the walls, but it didn't look like a living space in its present garb. It was impressive, but could have been a formal dining room in many major function venues.

"Excuse me, madam, if you'd like to leave your coat in here…" The staff member who'd admitted us was beckoning me to the front of the building and indicating the room that had been Murdo's library-cum-study. This room was much less cluttered than before. It had been preserved as a library or small lounge, and probably about half of the original bookcases had been retained. Some of the ornithological artefacts had also been saved for display. I instantly recognised the watercolours that hung between the cabinets; they were Murdo's work and had originally graced the walls of the small lounge on the other side of the building.

"Come on, Claire, come away from those pictures. We need to tune up." Archie summoned me.

"It's really interesting to see how many of the original contents have been kept," I told him as I shed my coat.

"Aye, but you're not here to take a new inventory. They want us in place and playing as the guests gather before their dinner."

"OK, I'm coming." Suddenly I felt more cheerful and much less nervous, knowing that our music would be a background for the pre-dinner reception, rather than a formal concert. People wouldn't be listening so carefully, or looking at us so intently. I still wanted to play well, but a lot of the pressure was off. Why hadn't Archie told me this? Or maybe he had, but I'd been distracted by Laura's problems. Anyway, it was going to be less stressful now; I might even enjoy myself.

The programme of music that Archie had compiled was a mixture of popular classical pieces and a selection from our more contemplative folk repertoire. There would be an assortment of solos, duets and trios, so I wasn't involved in every piece. We'd decided just to run through the performance with slight gaps, with no introductions or commentary. When I wasn't playing, I observed our audience. There were probably around twenty people, more men than women. They were formally dressed, the men in dinner suits and the women in smart cocktail dresses.

Everyone looked to be at the more mature end of their career; quite a few of the men had grey or white hair. The women looked younger, probably with the aid of hair dye. They were chatting quietly and circulating around the hall, sipping at their champagne. But at the end of each piece there was a smattering of applause, so at least some of them were paying attention to the music. The Debussy went well, I was happy with my rendition, and Willie and Archie were both complimentary. We finished up with 'Ae Fond Kiss', and then there was a resounding boom from a dinner gong and the guests began to drift into the dining area.

One man made his way to our corner. "Thank you so much for the music," he said in a strong American accent. "It added wonderfully to the atmosphere of this magnificent building. What was the last piece you played? Was it traditional?"

"Aye, it's by Robert Burns," Archie told him.

"Even I have heard of that famous Scot." The man then proceeded to shake each of us by the hand before making his way to the dining room.

"Well, I think that went OK," Willie pronounced, as we made our way back to the library.

Archie and I began to pack our instruments away.

"Aye, I think so too. Hopefully we'll be asked back another time. The money's very good." Archie looked pleased.

"I wish I could have a wander upstairs to see how they've renovated the bedrooms," I said wistfully.

"I think you'd have to be a paying guest to do that, unless the manager would let you come by for a peek when he's not got a party in residence," Archie replied.

"Maybe you could ask him for me, since you know him now?" I suggested.

"Och, away with your wheedling, woman." Archie pooh-poohed my idea. But I knew that he was really a soft-hearted sweetie under his skin, so I guessed that there was a possibility that he'd ask for me.

It was getting dark as we returned to the island jetty, and I was hungry. I was sure that this had been accentuated by the delicious smells of food that had wafted our way as we played. We'd been positioned very close to the top of the stairs leading from the kitchen.

"Do you think we could get a fish supper when we get back?" I asked.

"Aye, I'm sure we can afford that," Archie joked.

"It's pretty dark now; I've never done the sailing in the dark before." I was beginning to feel uneasy.

"Well, as long as Ewan has, there's no need to worry. Anyhow, it's not pitch-dark yet. There's still a fair bit of visibility," Archie tried to reassure me.

"Our eyes are just used to being indoors; they'll acclimatise." Willie joined in.

We descended to the boat, and I thought that I could see slightly farther ahead.

"It'll be better once we're out from the shadow of the castle." Ewan had heard my concern. "And I've done this trip a good few times now; we'll no get lost."

I donned my life jacket and settled myself inside the cabin, gripping my seat edge once more.

"So, do you drive that minibus too, Ewan?" Willie asked. "I've seen it dotting about the island."

"Aye, sometimes. We collect some of our guests from the ferry or the airfield at Glenforsa. Then there are excursions to the tourist spots: Calgary Bay, the distillery, Duart, the Iona ferry."

"Is the one bus enough?" Archie asked.

"Not always. Sometimes with a bigger group we need to use taxis as well. But other times guests bring their own cars across on the ferry, so it varies. I dinna think it'd be worth having another bus."

"So who's the other driver, then, when you're not on duty?" Archie could be quite nosy.

"It's Kenneth McInnes from Aros."

"Aye, I know who you mean. And does he sail this boat too?"

"Aye, we share the driving and the sailing. It adds up to about a half time job because the castle isna always in use. I go with my dad on the fishing boat other times."

I was listening to their conversation, but looking around me too. Behind us there was still light in the western sky, and the castle, although dark against the horizon, had lights blazing from all of its windows. Some of the light caught our wake and the tops of the waves, turning dark water to silver. Looking ahead, it was really dark; I couldn't distinguish the land from the sea or sky. But I could make out a few scattered, twinkling lights that seemed to be getting closer. They must come from the cottages around Croig, so we'd almost reached the safety of the harbour.

Chapter 26

As May progressed, more tourists arrived and the island gradually began to get busier. Tobermory's streets were suddenly crowded when a coach tour dropped off its passengers for an hour of free time and exploration. It was a great boost for my shop. Apart from the lead-up to Christmas, I made most of my profit in the summer months. I had this in common with many of the island businesses; the five months from May to September comprised our season.

Laura continued to gain weight slowly but steadily, and she seemed to be happier. I thought that the introduction of structured schoolwork had played a part in lifting her spirits; she'd probably been bored. Now, between her studies and her guitar lessons with Alejandro, she was kept busy. It was good to see her taking an interest in things again. Grant and I had progressed to allowing her some time alone in the house. She didn't seem to be in any danger of further heart arrythmias, so wasn't likely to suffer another collapse. And as she gained weight, we were becoming more relaxed about occasional missed energy drinks and snacks, although her meals were still closely regulated.

However, one Wednesday afternoon, just after five o'clock, I was alarmed to arrive home to an empty house. The yard was quiet when I drove in – no dogs barking – so I knew that Grant must still be out on the estate somewhere. I called a greeting as I came in the back door, but got no response. I knew that Laura had intended to work on a French essay after lunch, as we'd discussed the theme of it over our meal. I knocked on her bedroom door and popped my head round. I could see a jotter open on her desk and her laptop screen was lit up, but there was no sign of her. She wasn't in the toilet or in any of the public rooms. Feeling slightly foolish, I crossed the courtyard and checked in all of the barns. Nothing. Where could she be? She had nowhere to go within walking distance and I would have seen her on my drive home if she'd taken one of the bikes down the farm road. Maybe Alejandro had come by and taken her out for a drive, but she should have known to leave me a note. I felt mildly anxious, and cross, as I began to prepare our evening meal. I was no good at this. I hadn't developed any parenting skills through having a child of my own to practise on. It was tricky to be suddenly responsible for a troubled teenager. I banged saucepans about on the stovetop with unnecessary vigour.

Grant appeared about twenty minutes later.

"Do you know where Laura is?" was the first thing I asked him, even before a 'hello' or a kiss.

"No. Isn't she here?"

"No. Nowhere to be found."

"Well, maybe she's gone for a walk or Alejandro has taken her for a spin." Grant repeated a couple of my own guesses.

"She's not gone out on her own before," I commented.

"No, but she has more energy now. No doubt she's beginning to get a bit restless stuck in the house most of the time. It's a lovely evening and it's light for a while yet. Let's not worry too much; I'm sure she'll be home by dinner time."

"She should really leave me a note if she goes out," I complained.

"Aye, but youngsters aren't always that tuned in to what would be polite. I'll raise it with her, OK?"

He came to stand behind me at the worktop, wrapped his arms round me and gave me a hug, kissing the back of my neck. I nodded, somewhat appeased and also reassured that Grant didn't seem too worried, unless his 'Mr Calm' was just an act. He'd had more time to learn the requisite parenting skills and instincts, so I was happy to follow his lead.

He was vindicated when the kitchen door opened at twenty past six to admit a smiling Laura, sensibly dressed in walking shoes, jeans and a down jacket, with her camera hanging round her neck. "Hope I'm not late for dinner?" she greeted me.

I was stirring cheese into a sauce for our pasta. "No. Five minutes to go," I informed her, and congratulated myself on my light tone.

"Hi, Laura, been for a walk?" Grant came through from the lounge.

"Yeah. It was so nice. I got fed up being stuck in the house so I decided to go for a stroll with my camera, see if there was anything photogenic."

"Any luck?" Grant asked.

"Well, I'll have to check them out on the bigger screen, but I found some primroses still flowering up by the wee burn. The light on them was perfect, so I hope some of the pics will be good."

"The burn up the hill? Were you not tired?"

"No, Dad. Chill. I was fine. It was great to be out."

"OK, but next time could you please leave us a note, just saying where you've gone and the time?"

Laura sighed. "You weren't seriously worried, were you? I mean, nothing ever happens up here."

"Even so, it's just good manners, pet."

Another sigh. "OK. Now can I go and wash my hands?"

"Of course. And I'd love to see the photos once you've selected the best and done the editing." Grant was obviously trying to stay on her good side.

"Yeah, no worries. Fraser said that he'd make frames for me if I get some good shots and print them up. Then I can maybe sell them in his studio, or Claire's shop."

"That would be great," I chipped in to encourage her. After all, despite my slight panic, it was encouraging that she had the energy and the interest to take up her hobby again.

Our routine continued unmarred for the next few days. But at the weekend I couldn't help but overhear Laura yelling.

"No, I'm not. I'm just not and you can't make me."

Her phone had rung as we were finishing Sunday lunch and she'd gone into her room to chat. Grant had gone out to the office and I was loading the dishwasher when I heard the shouting. I wasn't certain, but I thought that it was her mum on the phone. They spoke several times a week, but so far Laura hadn't been back to visit Ruth. I listened, but didn't hear Laura's voice again. She must have rung off. I wondered what they were arguing about.

I'd tidied the kitchen when the dogs began a volley of barking and Alejandro's white Honda Jazz pulled into the courtyard. I dried my hands and went to the door to let him in. "No need for a doorbell when the dogs are home," I said. "I'll call Laura for you; just go through to the lounge."

I was sure that Laura would also have heard the dogs, but as she hadn't appeared, I went along to her room and tapped on the door, which was closed. "That's Alejandro here, Laura," I called.

"I'll just be a moment," she replied.

"OK, well, he's waiting in the lounge."

I joined him there to keep him company and found him standing by the coffee table unpacking his guitar from its case.

"Have a seat," I offered. "How's the dive going?"

"Well, is slow. We know that there will be little as there have been the previous attempts. But we are hoping to still uncover some new materials."

"That's good. And you're here for another few weeks?"

"Yes, until the end of June, then we go home. Ah, here she is." He stood up to greet Laura, giving her the customary continental cheek kisses.

As I turned to leave the room, allowing their lesson to begin, I caught sight of Laura's face. Her eyes looked pinkish and a bit puffy. Had she been crying? I carried on without commenting as I felt that being with Alejandro was bound to cheer her up.

When Grant reappeared half an hour later, I mentioned the shouting and the possible crying.

"Aye, I've had Ruth on the phone. It seems that Laura is refusing to go home to Edinburgh. Ruth was wanting her to stay for part of the summer holidays."

"Oh. Did she say why she won't go?"

"No; Ruth wants me to try and find out."

"Hmm."

I prepared a tray with mugs of tea and a plate of assorted biscuits and, reckoning that forty minutes had been sufficient for the guitar lesson, we joined the youngsters in the lounge.

"Did Laura tell you that the school have put her in touch with a guitar teacher in Oban? So, she'll be able to keep on with her lessons once you go back to Spain," Grant told Alejandro.

"No. That is so great, Laura. You must continue; you are making very good progress." Alejandro smiled encouragingly at Laura.

"Well, we think that she'll probably just sign up for a lesson every other week, what with the travelling and starting school properly after the summer break," Grant explained.

"But that is OK; will give plenty of time for the practising in-between," Alejandro commented.

"Yeah, I think that will be enough once I'm back at school. There'll be a lot of other things going on," Laura agreed. She appeared to be quite happy now, smiling and sunny with no trace of tears. After our tea she persuaded Alejandro to play us another of his flamenco pieces. His playing was flamboyant and exciting.

"Alejandro's going to be playing over the summer in different tourist bars and restaurants," Laura told us.

"Yes, I earn my money that way. In the summer I stay at home in Malaga, so a lot of places want an entertainment. Once I go back to Barcelona in September, I can also find gigs there."

"You could be a professional musician," Laura suggested.

"Oh no – for that I am not good enough. Plus, I like to do it for the pleasure and the joy. I don't think it would be so much fun if it is my whole job for life."

"Dad, could we visit Alejandro in Barcelona sometime?" Laura asked.

"Wow. Well, I suppose that's a possibility. It's certainly an amazing city; Claire and I visited a few years ago and really liked it. I'm sure you'd love it, Laura; it would be a fantastic place for photography."

"Yes, that would be so great if you would all come to visit." Alejandro sounded keen. "I could show you some more local life, not only the tourist places."

"Well, something to think about." Grant wasn't going to commit himself straight away.

That evening he spoke to Laura about spending some time with her mum in Edinburgh. I had made myself scarce, but I could easily hear Laura's reaction. Grant's voice was reduced to a low rumble by the time it reached me in our bedroom. But Laura quickly became agitated, her voice strident.

"Dad, I just really don't want to go back to that house. Please don't gang up against me."

Another rumble, presumably asking for an explanation.

"It's not that I don't want to see Mum. But I'm seriously worried that being back there will make me ill again."

A couple of sentences from Grant which sounded soothing.

"Iain's OK. I don't mind him, but I don't love him either. Look, I know if I go there, Mum will expect me to meet up with people from my old school and there's no one that I want to see, but she won't get that or leave it alone. She thinks that mixing is 'good for me.'"

I didn't hear any more, and then there was the sound of music from the television. The Sunday night drama series was about to start and Grant called me through to watch it with them.

Later, in bed, he brought up the subject with me. "Do you think that she could have been bullied?" he asked. "She's not admitting to it, but she mentioned not wanting to see anyone from her old school, and it might explain why she wanted to move here and change school."

"Has it never come up in your psychiatry sessions?"

"No, not in the family ones. What she says in her personal counselling is obviously confidential. Although, I'd have thought that she'd have been encouraged to share anything like that with Ruth and me."

"Maybe you could bring it up at your next chat with the consultant."

"Aye, maybe. I think I'm going to suggest to Ruth that she takes Laura away somewhere for a week or two. Meet on neutral territory."

"That's a good idea; they could go for a summer holiday together."

"Aye, best to give the Edinburgh thing a rest. It might sort itself out with a bit of time and space."

"I agree; I could hear from her tone that Laura was genuinely stressed. You don't want to push her too hard. The last thing you need is to cause a relapse just when she's making good progress."

227

"I know, but we can't let her manipulate us on a whim either. That could give us problems in the future."

"It didn't sound like a whim; I think there's something significant at the bottom of it all."

On the following Friday, Laura had lost weight for the first week since coming to Mull. It was only two pounds and we all tried not to panic about it, or make too much of a fuss. She'd been attending the nurse appointments by herself for the past three weeks; she took a notebook with her which the nurse filled in. The nurse had written a comment about an increase in exercise and physical activity which might need a corresponding increase in calories. I realised that we'd possibly been too hasty in allowing Laura to cut back on her snacks and energy drinks. Partly, it had been for our own convenience; it was easier and more relaxed not to always be monitoring those and nagging. But Grant and I were also concerned that the discussions over the previous weekend had stressed Laura and sparked some kind of relapse. Thankfully, Ruth seemed to have adopted Grant's suggestion of going for a holiday and I'd seen Laura looking at some fantastic potential destinations on her laptop, so that was something positive to plan and look forward to.

That evening the three of us had a powwow which stuck firmly to physical matters: an increase in exercise requiring more calories. Between us we agreed to reinstate the snacks and drinks, and to increase a portion of protein or carbohydrate at each meal. Laura seemed to be surprisingly accepting of this, and I felt that I had to check with her.

"No, really, it's fine. I like having more energy. And I need to keep putting on weight if I want to go to Barcelona."

I wasn't sure that there had ever been a firm promise made about that trip, but she was probably right. I could predict that it would be added to her list of privileges. Grant was obviously correct that he needed to be wary of manipulation. At the moment, if we were keeping a score, it would be one-nil to Laura.

Chapter 27

I t was a warm, dry afternoon and I was pulling up wilted crocus and daffodil leaves, and weeds from between the rose bushes and shrubs. I wasn't a natural gardener. As a youngster my only interest in my parents' garden had been as a spot for sunbathing in the summer. Then I'd lived in a series of flats. Sheelagh had created this lovely garden; south-facing and in the shelter of the house and barns. Since moving to the island I'd been drawn to tend to it, to the best of my ability. When my weed container was full, I stood up, stretching and straightening my back, preparing to carry it along to the compost bin. Just then I saw Grant emerging from the French doors onto the patio.

"Hi there," I greeted him.

"I've just had an interesting phone call from Duncan, the ghillie down at Ardura." Grant sounded excited.

"Uh-huh?" I said enquiringly.

"He was on the lochan fishing last night when he saw the beast."

"The puma?" I asked. We'd had feedback from both Edinburgh Zoo and the Glasgow vet school, confirming that our paw print was likely to have been produced by a puma.

"Aye. He was in a rowing boat, out on the water, when it appeared. It came right down to the waterside and began to drink. He froze and it didn't seem to notice him, so he got a good look at it even though it was dusk."

"And did he think it was a puma?"

"Aye – well, not that he's seen one before. But he went online when he got home and he thinks that's the nearest match."

"Wow, so what do we do now?"

"I thought maybe I should phone the zoo again, see what they recommend. Maybe they can send someone to help us."

"Ardura's quite a long way from Bellart where Alasdair saw it," I commented.

"I'd guess that a large predator like that can range over a fair distance." Grant consulted his watch. "I'll go and phone now while it's still office hours. Do you want me to put the kettle on for some tea while I'm in the house?"

"Yeah, that would be good. And make some for Laura too; she's due her snack."

The evidence for the big cat was certainly growing now. Not long after our visit to Alasdair, he'd been back in contact with Grant. He'd found several large paw prints in the soil of the riverbank, close to the location of his previous sighting of the animal. Grant had gone with him to look, and taken more photographs.

The midges were beginning to bite, so I decided that my gardening was over for the day. I collected my tools together and returned them to the small barn, or 'the wee barn' as I was learning to call it. Then I dumped the weeds I'd collected into the compost bin. I entered the house through the utility room, where I removed my old boots and washed my muddy hands, scrubbing under my nails with a brush.

When I arrived in the kitchen Laura was pouring hot water from the kettle into the teapot. "Dad says someone else has seen the puma," she greeted me.

"Yes, he's gone to phone the zoo. I wonder what they'll suggest. What do you want to eat with your tea?" I asked her. "There are scones or chocolate biscuits."

Laura chose a biscuit and we took our drinks through to the lounge.

Grant appeared with his mug and sat on the sofa next to Laura. "Well, they're going to get in touch with the Highland Wildlife Park near Aviemore to see if they can accommodate our puma. Then they propose that we should try to catch it and transport it there."

"Catch it? How on earth can we do that?" Laura sounded dubious.

"They think that it might be relatively simple at this time of the year because it's light for so long. Apparently pumas hunt and are active mainly around dawn and dusk. The long daylight hours give us a much bigger chance to see it."

"Right enough – both of the sightings were at dusk," I realised.

"Aye, and both near to water, so the animal tends to come for a drink around then. The guy at the zoo thinks that we could maybe set some bait near to the water, then a marksman could dart it with a sedative."

"Who would that be? Do they have someone on hand at the zoo?" Laura asked.

"I suppose that we'll find out once the wildlife park call me back."

"They'd need to supply a big cage or a crate as well," I added.

"Aye, I suppose they could manage that."

"So, when will they let us know?" Laura asked.

"Probably tomorrow," Grant replied.

"Wow, wouldn't Mairi love to be in on it all? I'm going to send her a WhatsApp." Laura gulped down the last of her tea and got up, heading for her room.

"I think she'll be too wrapped up with studying for her exams to be able to come," I called after her.

"Still, she'll want to know what's happening."

"It's so good to see Laura animated again," I commented to Grant once she'd left the room.

"Aye. I should think that having a puma on the loose in your area would be enough to interest most people," he laughed.

Things began to gather pace. The next day we had a call from the big cat expert at the wildlife park. She was willing to come in person to assist with the capture and transport of the puma. She would bring all of the necessary equipment with her. Grant called Isla to book a room, and it was agreed that Kathy would arrive in two days' time. Meanwhile, she'd explained that the vet covering the wildlife park was on holiday and asked Grant if he could find a local vet willing to assist.

"She said that, ideally, we should be a party of three, as it could be hard work transporting the sedated animal down from the hills. Also, it might take a few nights to make the capture. Who do you think I should ask?"

"I know – what about that young vet. I can't remember his name. He joined the practice last summer. Remember he came up to see one of the ewes at lambing?"

"Aye, he came on a shoot too, not long after he arrived. Was it Hugh? Naw, but I'm sure it began with an 'H' – that's right, it's Hugo. Kathy's keen that we try to have a vet on hand in case of side effects from the drugs. I'll give him a call."

Apparently, Hugo had heard rumours about the big cat and, once he'd convinced himself that Grant's call wasn't a hoax, he was flattered to be asked to help with the capture.

"He wasn't sure if I was pulling his leg at first," Grant reported. "I suppose it does sound a bit far-fetched. He's going to give Kathy a call to discuss the drugs she'll be bringing and any equipment that we'll need. I think it's good that we'll have two experts in attendance."

Two days later, just before lunchtime, Isla called to let us know that Kathy had arrived at the guest house. Grant, Laura and I drove down to meet her and parked next to a Land Rover with a trailer attached. The trailer looked similar to a small horsebox, and had the Highland Wildlife Park logo on the sides. We walked round the house and in through the back door to the kitchen. Kathy was sitting at the kitchen table nursing a mug of tea and didn't look at all like I'd imagined a big cat keeper would. She was a slight, late-middle-aged woman with shoulder-length greying blonde hair tied back in a ponytail. She seemed very enthusiastic, though, and immediately asked Grant to take her to both of the places where the puma had been seen.

"Now, just wait and have a bite to eat before you set out," Isla insisted. "You can't work on an empty stomach."

So, we settled around Isla's table and tucked into a variety of sandwiches, home-baked scones and shortbread, all accompanied by mugs of tea.

"How do you think that a puma has ended up here on Mull?" I asked Kathy as I munched my salmon and cucumber sandwich.

"Well, there are no licensed wild animal holders in the vicinity," Kathy informed us. "I checked on that. So, the most likely thing is that someone smuggled the animal onto the island and let it go free."

"But why would they do that?" Laura asked.

"I don't know. Maybe they got it illegally as a cub and it got to be bigger and wilder than they'd anticipated."

"I'd guess that it's only been here within the past year," Grant said. "No one saw any signs of it before that. So, do you think it might be quite a young animal?"

"It's hard to say, but it seems that it only took newborn lambs. That could be because they were smaller and so easier prey for a young animal. Or maybe it was actively fed by an owner before, and therefore isn't an experienced hunter," Kathy said.

"Of course, at the time of year the lambs are born, other wildlife isn't so plentiful. Now there are more rabbits and ground birds that it can live off," Grant added.

"Talking of its food, what kind of bait do you think will tempt it?" I asked.

"Oh, just something like a chicken or a rabbit freshly killed should do the job," Kathy replied. She sounded very matter-of-fact.

"What other kinds of big cats do you look after at the park?" I asked.

"Lynx, snow leopards and tigers," Kathy listed. I reckoned that she should know how to tempt a puma, then.

After lunch she and Grant set out to tour the sighting spots, Isla stayed to prep the evening meal for her visitors, and I walked down to the harbour with Laura to my shop.

"I don't suppose we'll be allowed to go on the puma hunt." Laura sounded disappointed.

"Well, no. I think they'll just have three people. You could hardly invite a whole crowd. They don't want to scare it off."

"But Dad will go."

"Yes; he's been involved from the start."

"Then maybe he could phone us to come and see it once they've darted it. I'd really love to see it."

"Well, we can ask him. I don't see why that wouldn't work," I agreed.

That evening Grant set out with Kathy and Hugo. We'd arranged that he would call us if they bagged the puma, but he arrived home at breakfast time the next morning. "No luck, I'm afraid," he reported.

"How many nights will you try for?" Laura asked.

"I'm not sure. Let's just hope we catch it soon. I'm knackered." He downed some toast and tea and staggered off to bed.

That night the threesome went out again. They'd decided to stick to the Ardura lochan area where the most recent sighting had been, unless new information became available. Just after one o'clock in the morning my mobile rang, waking me.

"Hi," I croaked groggily.

"We got it." Grant sounded exuberant. "You and Laura should come up here."

"Where are you exactly?"

"By the time you get here we'll be down at the road end where the vehicles are; in the lay-by just after the road to Ardura. We've got a kind of stretcher thing to carry it down off the hill."

"OK, see you there."

I hurried through to wake Laura and we both dressed in record time, then jumped into the car. I reckoned that the road would be empty at this time of night, so the drive shouldn't take us any more than forty minutes. It was nearing the summer solstice and the night sky didn't really get fully dark. It was a kind of hazy navy-blue colour. We sped south, past the ferry port and the road end to Duart Castle. Then we saw a collection of vehicles pulled up in a lay-by on the right-hand side of the road. The Land Rover had its headlights on and there was a spotlight set up on a stand. It illuminated a huddle of people. I pulled in and parked beyond the farthest vehicle and Laura and I ran back to see what was happening.

Grant and Kathy were standing at either end of a canvas stretcher that was laid on the ground, and Hugo was crouched over with a stethoscope in his ears. He was pressing the other end of the instrument to the underside of a large tawny-coloured animal which lay sprawled on its right side. I guessed that it must measure about six feet in length, including its tail. I came to a halt at the bottom of the stretcher, close to the end of the puma's tail, which was tipped with black. Its eyes were closed and I could see that it was breathing evenly.

"Is it OK?" Laura asked.

"Aye," Grant replied. "Hugo's just checking her heart rate. We might need to top up the sedative to get her into the cage."

"It's a female, then?" I checked.

"Yes; probably around five or six years old. Though I'll be able to learn more once I get her back to Kingussie," Kathy told us.

235

"She's beautiful," Laura breathed.

"You can see that she's healthy, in very good condition," Kathy informed us in a low voice. "She's well nourished with good muscle mass, and her coat looks sleek. She's obviously been able to hunt successfully and feed herself."

"Can I touch her?" Laura asked.

"Just wait a minute until Hugo's done," Grant advised.

A moment later, Hugo straightened. "OK, I think we're good to move her."

When he and Grant moved over to the Land Rover to unlock the trailer, Laura and I moved closer to the puma. Laura laid her hand on the cat's flank and stroked gently; then she dug her fingers in deeper.

"Wow, her coat is really thick, and quite coarse," she commented. "Come on, Claire, give her a stroke. You'll never get the chance again."

She was right, but I was nervous. The puma's mouth was slightly open and I could see an array of very sharp-looking teeth.

"Look at the size of those paws." Laura was touching one of the puma's legs now; then she moved closer to its head. "And what amazing whiskers!"

I mustered my courage, squatted down and ran my hand along the length of the animal's back. It was very warm and the fur was dense.

"Cool, isn't it?" Laura asked, her eyes shining. "Wait till I tell Mairi."

"Right, girls, stand aside." Grant and Hugo were getting ready to transfer the stretcher into the trailer.

Kathy sprang into action. "I think it'll be easiest if we put her in on the stretcher, then we can just remove the poles and shut up the door. The canvas will help to protect her if she starts to rouse and gets restless."

The transfer to the cage was uneventful and the animal didn't stir.

"How long will it take you to drive back to Kingussie?" I asked.

"The drive's about two and a half hours from Oban. I hope I'll get onto the first ferry."

"There shouldn't be a problem. You can wait down at the terminal; that way you'll be first in line," Grant reckoned.

"What time does it leave?" Kathy asked.

"7.15."

"You didn't tell us what happened. How you caught her," Laura complained.

"Oh, well, we'd laid the bait down by the lochan shore and hidden ourselves behind some bushes a way up the hillside," Grant began. "Then, about eleven, we saw the animal approaching from the west, coming down from the hills. She came down to the water and drank. Then she seemed to get the scent of the meat."

"But we weren't sure that she was going to stay and look for it; she seemed nervous. Maybe she could sense that there were humans nearby too," Hugo added.

"And we needed her to stay put to get a good shot at her," Grant continued.

"Anyway, she must have been hungry, because she tracked down the food and began to eat it on the spot, allowing me to dart her. I was edgy, though; if I'd missed, who knows when we'd have had another chance?" Kathy sounded relieved.

"Did she fall immediately after the shot?" Laura asked.

"Pretty quickly; she did run for a good few metres before the drugs kicked in," Hugo told us.

"It was ideal terrain, though – just grass and heather. So, no rocks that would hurt her or trees to make her hard to track down," Grant added.

"You'll have quite a tale to tell everyone." I grinned at the men.

"Aye, but now I'd quite like to get to my bed," Grant admitted. "If there's nothing else that you need help with, Kathy?"

"No, I'm fine. I'll head along to Craignure. How long do you think she'll be out for, Hugo?"

"She should be OK for at least a couple of hours, and you've got a top-up of the sedative if she starts to get distressed."

"Yeah, cool. It's best to keep her tranquil until we're back at Kingussie. She might hurt herself if she starts to thrash about in the cage. I'll try to grab a couple of hours' sleep before the ferry. I can stretch out on the back seat. Thank you all for your assistance."

"Will you let us know how she's getting on at the wildlife park?" Laura asked.

"Of course. And why don't you come and visit her later in the summer once she's settled in?"

"That would be great. Can we?" Laura asked Grant.

"Aye, I'm sure that we can fit that in. Goodbye then, Kathy."

We all shook hands with the big cat keeper, then watched and waved as she turned her vehicle in the road and headed north towards the ferry terminal.

"Dad, I know that it wasn't possible for her to stay here as a wild predator, but I can't help feeling sorry for her. She wasn't designed to be a captive; she should be allowed to run free." Laura sounded wistful.

"Aye, you're right. But, circumstances being as they are, the wildlife park is the best option. They'll look after her well; the enclosures there are quite large." Grant put his arm around Laura's shoulders and hugged her in close to his side.

"We'll make a definite plan to go and visit," I promised.

Chapter 28

There was huge local excitement over the capture of the puma. Grant was interviewed by journalists from the island and from Oban. The story found its way into the national press and was even covered on radio and television news. We saw TV footage of the cat, now named Pearl, being released into her enclosure at the Highland Wildlife Park. So, for a few weeks Grant and Hugo were celebrities. Most people admired the puma capture, but there were one or two who thought that the animal should have been shot. In their opinion it was a pest that had killed livestock. I overheard one woman's comments, as she'd intended, when I was queuing in the baker's shop: "After all, you'd shoot a dog if it killed your animals. Tch, incomers and Sassenachs with their sentimental ways."

I buttoned my lip and pretended that I hadn't heard; I wasn't going to give her the satisfaction of a response. But she could hardly fit my husband into either of those categories. When I'd first arrived to live on Mull, people on the island had generally been friendly and welcoming, but this particular woman seemed to have resented me from the outset. I'd never known why, nor what her grudge was, so I just tried to ignore her.

Gradually, other news began to take over and the attention died down. At the beginning of July, Grant drove Laura down to Glasgow airport to meet her mum. The school where Ruth taught had broken up for the summer holidays and she and Laura had finally agreed on a destination for their holiday. They were bound for Turkey, to a beach resort with water sports, but also with archaeological sites to visit nearby.

I was spending most of my days at the shop, helping to cope with the summer rush. But when I was at home the house seemed incredibly quiet. July was also a busy month for Grant. It was the beginning of the stag shooting season. He had a lot of parties booked and needed to be on hand to help out as it was too much work for Jamie to cope with on his own. Grant was often out long into the evening and I was home on my own. That's when I began to realise how much I'd got used to having Laura's company over the past six months. Recently, she'd been much livelier, and had become quite a chatterbox again. She'd been helping me out at the shop too, so I missed her there as well as at home. Still, it was good for her to get away and to spend time with her mum. I couldn't help worrying slightly about her diet, hoping that she'd maintain her weight without my supervision. But her consultant had reassured us that she was past the stage where we needed to be so anxious. Her weight was approaching seven stone, which was still classed as underweight, but not severely so. He felt that now we needed to readjust our priorities; boosting Laura's psychological well-being was becoming just as important as counting calories. A holiday and a change of scene would benefit her, and a few lost pounds could be regained.

Predictably, the departure of Alejandro and the other Spanish divers the previous week had upset Laura. She'd spent a lot of time with Alejandro. In addition to teaching her guitar, he'd called in at the shop or the house two or three times a week to chat with her. I knew that Laura had a huge crush on the Spaniard. But he was either unaware of this, or chose to ignore it and was simply friendly and charming. Because of Alejandro's open manner, Grant hadn't worried about the friendship. The Spanish dive hadn't uncovered any new major treasure: a few coins, a pewter bowl, and some horn discs that had possibly been used as buttons, or counters for some kind of game. But the team didn't seem to be disappointed, and were in good spirits when they turned up for the farewell party that Isla and I organised. We held the event at the Mishnish and it turned into a very long, but wonderful, night. There was a mixture of Spanish and Scottish music and dancing, with performances from Archie and our group, and from Alejandro backed up by a friend on drums and castanets. Isla prepared some Spanish tapas dishes which were delicious, and our patron had found a recipe for sangria. It was a great send-off, but I knew that, on her return from Turkey, Laura would really miss her friend. I hoped that she'd soon make some new friends of her own age once she started school, but there would be another month to fill before the beginning of term.

With that in mind, I swiped my phone to see if I'd had a reply from Mairi. Grant had suggested that, while Laura was still free, we make a 'girls' trip' to Aviemore. The plan was to include Mairi. We'd stay in a luxury hotel where we could pamper ourselves, and also go to visit Pearl the puma at the wildlife park, which was nearby. It would give Laura something to look forward to. Currently I was trying to get Mairi to commit to a date for our trip. I found a new message:

Hi, Claire. I could make the last week in July – might be best to avoid weekends if quieter. Is it OK if my friend Fiona comes (she'd pay her way)? M x

Well, I guessed that would be fine. I didn't think that Laura would mind, and it was never good value to stay at a hotel as a singleton.

All fine. I'll check availability. C x

So, on the last Tuesday in July, Laura and I were driving up the A82 towards Fort William, on our way to meet Mairi and her friend at Aviemore. I'd left Helen in charge of the shop. She'd be assisted by Kirsten, a university student who was home for the summer break. I felt exhilarated as we bowled along beside the sparkling lochside, and realised that I'd needed a break. Apart from attending a few house sales and auctions for work, I hadn't been off the island since arriving back from Edinburgh in the spring. That meant that Grant hadn't had a break either. We really must get something organised; maybe the October school holiday week would work.

Laura had chosen our soundtrack and was singing along to a Taylor Swift song. She was very tanned after her trip to Turkey and her hair had grown a lot. She now had curls and ringlets reaching down to her shoulder blades. "Do you know anything about Mairi's friend Fiona?" she asked me.

"I think she's a vet student too, and plays hockey. That's it," I replied.

"Oh, I forgot to tell you; I got an email from Kathy this morning before we left. She says that tomorrow would be good for a visit to see Pearl. She's tied up with some sort of training day on Thursday."

"That's fine; we can plan around that, then." I knew that Laura was very keen to see the puma again, so had suggested that she contact the keeper. That way we were likely to get VIP treatment.

"It looks like the weather will be good until the end of the week. What else will we do?"

"Well, there are all the facilities at the hotel. Then there are plenty of walks and the tennis courts. You can hire bikes or canoes nearby, and there's a quad bike trail just down the road. We won't be bored," I promised.

We arrived at our hotel at lunchtime. Our room wasn't ready yet, so we left our bags in the car and headed for the brasserie for something to eat.

We'd just been served with our paninis when Mairi appeared beside our table. "Hi, you guys. Oh, look at the colour of you, Laura. Did you have a good time in Turkey, then?"

We half-stood and exchanged hugs and kisses.

"Where's Fiona?" I asked as I sat back down.

"She had to go to the loo. She'll be along in a minute. Can we join you?"

"Of course." I moved my handbag, which I'd put on the spare seat beside me, and Mairi sat down there. She reached across for a menu from the end of the table and began to scan it.

"Wow, I'm starving. Those look good," she commented, and proceeded to steal one of Laura's chips.

Laura made a half-hearted attempt to fend her off.

"Here's Fi. Come and sit next to my sister, Laura. And this is Claire."

"Hi, nice to meet you. Thank you for letting me tag along." Fiona was small, about five foot two, but looked sturdy and muscular. She had blonde hair cut short in a pixie style, and multiple piercings, with various silver earrings inserted, on the rims of both of her ears.

"Here, Fi, grab a menu. I'm going to have a panini; they look great."

"So, how's your summer going so far?" I asked Mairi after the girls had placed their orders.

"Good, thanks. The vets' practice in Dumfries is great. It has a good mixture of pets and farm animals, and quite a lot of horses."

"Yeah, I think that Mairi landed on her feet with that placement," Fiona added.

"What about you? Where are you working?" I asked her.

"I'm in a Glasgow city practice, which suits me, cause I'm more into the small animals."

"Suits a small girl," Mairi said, grinning. It seemed like an in-joke.

"What do you think of our puma capture?" Laura asked. "Did you see her on TV? And Dad in the papers?"

"You guys were really famous. Mairi kept telling everyone, 'That's my dad' and 'That's where I come from,'" Fiona told us.

"Yeah, it was so cool. I wish I could have been there." Mairi sounded wistful.

"Well, it was you that found the original paw print," I reminded her.

"The spoor," Fiona laughed. "Mairi the big game hunter."

"We've arranged a visit to the wildlife park to see her tomorrow," Laura informed them. "We know her keeper, so hopefully we should get up close. Maybe I'll be able to take some photos."

"Dad was telling me that you've got back into your photography. That's good." Mairi sounded encouraging.

"Yeah, I've even sold some. Fraser made the frames for me and we put a wee display up in his workshop, some at the Mishnish, and more in Claire's shop."

"Quite the young businesswoman," Mairi commented.

"And I got some brilliant shots in Turkey, at the ruins. I'll show you later."

"But it's your nature shots and local scenes that are selling. I suppose that the puma might fit both descriptions," I added.

"I don't suppose I'll get anything that's good enough to sell."

The next day we were all standing, spellbound, at the puma enclosure. After we'd introduced ourselves to the attendant at the gate, Kathy had come to meet us at the park entrance. She explained that she'd held back from feeding Pearl so that the cat would be more active. "She normally just goes off to sleep after she's eaten, so she could be hard to spot."

As it was, Pearl was pacing around the perimeter of her enclosure. She ducked out of our sight when she reached the back of her territory, where there were rocks and bushes, but we got a fantastic view of her as she crossed the front area. She was sleek and healthy-looking. Her stride was loose and graceful, just like a prowling house cat, but multiplied by ten. On one of her laps, she seemed to glance sideways at us, but otherwise she kept her gaze fixed forwards. After just gazing at the puma for a few circuits, Laura was now clicking fast on her camera whenever Pearl came into view.

"I'll go and get her food now," Kathy said. She'd been watching with us, and had given us an update on Pearl's health.

A few minutes later the puma froze mid-stride with her ears pricked forwards. She seemed to be sniffing the air.

"I think she's heard movement by the gate where her food arrives," Mairi whispered.

Suddenly Pearl broke from her circuit lapping and sprang diagonally across her area towards the front left, where, if we stretched, we could see a small gate. A lump of meat was on the ground. The puma leapt at it, picked it up in her mouth and jumped up onto a low-hanging tree branch. There she proceeded to devour her meal, ripping and tearing at it with very sharp teeth.

"That was scarily cool," Laura pronounced.

"Yeah, but I'm glad that I saw it after she'd been caught. It's a bit unnerving to think that she was wandering around freely on our estate while we were out and about," I agreed.

"But you're too big to be her prey. She'd have steered well clear of you." Kathy had reappeared and overheard me. She tried to reassure us.

"Well, she's in the best place now. And thank you so much for taking the time to meet with us." I shook Kathy's hand.

"Not at all, you're welcome. Come back any time, and do stay and look round the rest of our collection."

It was a warm day, so we voted for refreshments and headed for the ice-cream stall. Then we agreed to look round at our own pace and meet back in an hour. I knew that Laura would be slow, stopping to take photographs, and I had an intuition that Mairi and Fiona would rather be on their own. So I set off ambling, under the shade of some trees, to look at the wolves and the reindeer. As I strolled along, licking my ninety-nine cone, I wondered if I should say anything to Mairi. Yesterday I had sensed, from their body language and closeness, that she and Fiona were more than just friends. Today, I was sure. They hadn't been embracing or holding hands, but there were glances, and small, almost accidental touches. I realised that I wasn't really surprised. I hadn't thought about it before, but Mairi had never mentioned any boyfriends. If it had crossed my mind, I'd probably have put it down to her hectic lifestyle: studying, hockey and horse riding all took up a lot of her time. But I'd been a student; I knew that being busy didn't exclude a romantic interest. Somehow that could always be fitted in. So, in Mairi's case, it now seemed clear that no mention of boys hadn't added up to no romance. I watched the reindeer nuzzling each other. One had a young calf that was suckling lustily. I decided not to say anything. Mairi would raise the subject if she wanted to; maybe she was testing the waters first.

We'd reserved one of the hotel's tennis courts for five o'clock. So, on our return we all had a short rest, then reassembled courtside. We had a casual doubles knock-up for about fifteen minutes, then I decided that it was time for me to sit out. Laura and Fiona elected to play each other, with the winner scheduled to play Mairi. There was a convenient bench overlooking the courts where we could sit to watch the others playing. I gulped down a slug from my water bottle, feeling out of condition, and outrun by the younger women.

"Phew, that was enough running around for me; I need a rest," I gasped.

"Laura's doing OK, though," Mairi commented. "It's great to see how much healthier she looks."

"Yes, you must see a big difference. I just hope that she'll be happy once she starts school; that she'll fit in OK. If that all works out, I feel that we'll be through the worst."

"Yeah. And I don't want to add to any worries, but I think you'll have guessed that Fiona and I are a couple?"

I glanced at Mairi and noticed that her face was flushed, and she was rotating her tennis racquet on the ground between her legs in a nervous fashion.

"Yes, I had noticed, but it's fine with me. Fiona seems to be a lovely person."

"Well, I thought that you'd be cool with everything. After all, you've lived in London; you've got a broader outlook."

It occurred to me that I also had less of an emotional investment, but I kept quiet and Mairi continued.

"We've been together for over a year now, and we're totally out when we're in Glasgow. But we both feel that it's time to let our families know, and it's a bit scary."

"Your mum doesn't know either?"

"No."

"Presumably you've had a few other girlfriends before Fiona?"

"Yeah, three or four, but no one serious or lasting. The first one was while I was still at school."

"And you're concerned that Grant and Ruth will react badly?"

"I guess I'm hoping that they'll be accepting, if not approving. With all of the worry they've had this year with Laura, I don't want to burden them further. On the other hand, though, I'd like Fiona to be recognised as an important part of my life."

"Seriously, I'm not sure what Grant's initial reaction will be. But I know that he loves you and wants you to be happy. I'm sure that he'll welcome Fiona, and once he gets to know her it'll be no big deal."

"You don't think he'll be disappointed?"

"Well, maybe at first, because it's not what he'll have expected. But I'm sure he'll adapt. What about Fiona's family?"

"She hasn't come out to them yet either. They're quite religious, so she thinks it'll be a big drama."

"Does she have any brothers or sisters?"

"Yeah, her big brother's a lawyer in Edinburgh, and her sister is coming to Glasgow to uni in September. That's one of the reasons we have to tell everyone. It wouldn't be fair to let her sister just discover everything once she arrives and then not know whether to talk about it."

"Maybe Fiona should chat to her first, then tell her parents later."

I could see Laura approaching us, and Fiona waving from the court.

"Looks like your turn to play again, Mairi. But please, don't worry too much. It'll all work out."

She stood up, ready to play, but leant down and gave me a hug before jogging down the steps to the court. Laura gave her sister a high five as she passed on her way up to the bench.

"What was the score?" I asked.

"Oh, don't ask. Fiona's seriously fit; she beat me easily. It was fun, though. I haven't played tennis for ages." She took a swig from her juice bottle, then looked at me. "You two seemed to be having a very serious conversation. Coming out, was she?"

"You guessed."

"Seemed obvious to me. But I've suspected for a while that she was into women."

"OK. How do you think your mum and dad will be? Mairi's quite worried."

"Don't know. I think Mum might be more put out than Dad, but they'll come around."

"That's what I said. Maybe you should chat to Mairi about it; you could help to reassure her."

"Yeah, sure. But really she just needs to get on with it."

Chapter 29

"Bloody hell," Grant exclaimed. "Can't one of my daughters just be normal?!"

His outburst came once we were alone. He'd been very quiet, then left the lounge almost immediately after Mairi, on her next visit to Mull, had told him about Fiona. We heard the kitchen door bang shut as he went outside.

Mairi broke down in tears. "I knew it. I knew he'd hate me," she sobbed.

I went to put my arms around her. "Don't be overdramatic, Mairi. There is no way that he hates you. He's just had a shock, and he doesn't know the right thing to say because he doesn't want to hurt you. You need to give him some time."

"I guess."

"He'll go for a walk and be able to talk to you about it when he comes back."

My prediction was correct. Grant arrived back at the house at quarter past six, just before our evening meal. He apologised to Mairi for storming off, explaining that he'd not known what to say and didn't want to say the wrong thing. "Tell me about Fiona," he invited her as we settled down to eat.

That was a good strategy, as Mairi was happy to chat at length about her girlfriend, so Grant didn't have to contribute very much. He confined himself to asking for a few more details here and there, managing to sound interested rather than interrogative. By the end of our meal, they seemed to have made peace with each other.

"I'm going down to town for a drink," Mairi announced after coffee. "Anyone want to come?"

We declined, but I asked Mairi if she'd mind picking Laura up. She'd arranged to have tea with a new school friend, Joanne, before we'd known that Mairi was coming to visit. "It would save me having to drive down to collect her, if that's OK."

"Yeah, that's fine. I'm meeting Eilidh at the Mishnish. I'll text Laura to come and meet us there."

"Maybe Joanne would want to come too."

"Not a problem; the more the merrier. See you guys later."

"You knew, didn't you?" Grant asked, after his initial outburst.

"Yes." I explained that Mairi had told me in Aviemore but requested me to keep quiet, as she knew that she ought to tell her parents herself, face to face.

"And Laura?"

"Yes, she knows too. But actually, she'd guessed. We both asked Mairi to try and come to see you quickly. It hasn't been easy to say nothing, knowing that a bombshell was about to be dropped."

"Aye, I'm sure," he acknowledged. "Well, it's not the end of the world, but she's not making life easy for herself with this choice."

"I'm not sure that it's a choice," I responded. "I think it's how she is."

"So, you don't think that it's any reflection on me? That I've been a bad father, a poor role model of a male?"

"No, there's no way I'd think that."

"And then there's the divorce. Has that affected both of the girls in different ways?" He ran his fingers through his hair as he spoke.

"Grant, I get the impression that it's just Mairi's make-up. And we don't know about Laura, but lots of children have parents who divorce, and they don't all turn out to be gay or anorexic." I'd come to the conclusion, over the few weeks since we'd been in Aviemore, that Mairi was likely to find that her announcement would cause a lot less of a reaction in the aftermath of Laura's illness. I didn't think that being gay really compared with almost dying, and I was sure that both of her parents would be a lot less stressed by her news now than they would have been prior to Laura's admission to the intensive care unit.

"And what about having a family?" Grant suddenly asked.

"Lots of gay couples have babies. I knew a few families like that down in London."

"Artificial insemination; I suppose I should know all about that as a stock breeder myself," he sighed. "Although I like to use the rams where I can. Sometimes I think that the males of the species will become redundant."

"Hey, you're not redundant to me." I crossed over to sit on his lap to give him a hug.

He pulled me in close and nuzzled my hair. "Aye, I think I'm in need of a lot of reassurance on that front," he joked, kissing me. And we soon retired to the bedroom.

I offered to drive Mairi down to Craignure to catch the Sunday afternoon ferry. She had a busy week ahead – the beginning of a new term – and the following weekend she was planning to visit her mum.

"So, was it as bad as you expected, telling Dad?" Laura had accompanied us.

251

"I don't know. I guess I'd steeled myself for a big outburst. But he just kind of froze; went pale and silent. And then he walked out. That was quite bad."

"But he's cool with it all now, isn't he? And you're to bring Fiona to visit us soon; he's bound to like her, she's the best." Laura had taken quite a shine to Fiona while we were at Aviemore, and had hinted several times recently that she'd like to get some more ear piercings. At the moment she had the standard one on each earlobe. Her other current favourite topics were driving lessons for her upcoming seventeenth birthday present, and nagging us about setting a date to visit Barcelona.

I smiled – we hadn't been happy before, when she was too quiet and the only thoughts on all of our minds were of food and calories. Now, thankfully, we had a whole range of subjects to discuss, and food only came up when we were planning weekly menus.

"Yeah, we'll try to arrange something. But it gets hard once the hockey season starts. We're playing most weekends; sometimes both days. And I need to put in my hours at the stables too."

"Well, maybe we'll just have to come down to Glasgow to visit you," I suggested.

"Yeah. That's a great idea. We could go shopping." Laura sounded very enthusiastic.

When we dropped Mairi off the ferry was already unloading its incoming passengers. She gave us a quick wave, shouldered her backpack and strode off to the ticket office. I turned the car and we headed back up north.

"I wish we saw Mairi more often," Laura complained.

"We might now, you know. She's probably been staying away because she's felt awkward."

"Mm, maybe. She was brave, though, wasn't she? It makes me feel a bit bad by comparison, cause there's a thing I've not mentioned."

"Oh?" I kept still and quiet, eyes on the road ahead, to see if she might continue.

"Maybe I could try to tell you first, like Mairi did."

"Well, that's OK with me. You know that you can tell me anything, Laura."

"I know, but it's hard." She sighed. "Right, well, this all started about three years ago when I was in second year. I was fourteen. I went to a gathering one weekend; it was at a girl from school's house and I knew most of the people there. Her parents were out and there was some cider and vodka. That's one of the reasons I couldn't tell Mum or Dad: because I knew that I shouldn't have been drinking and that they'd freak out at me."

"Mm." I wasn't sure what was coming, but tried to sound encouraging and non-judgemental.

"Anyway, then someone suggested we play strip poker. It was all girls, and I'd had a few drinks, so I was happy to go along with it. It didn't seem like a big deal. I didn't score too well, though, and was eventually down to just my pants. I didn't notice, but someone took a photo of me. Then the next week I discovered that it was all over social media and everyone was looking at it, including boys. I was mortified, and people were being catty, saying that I was fat or well endowed. I knew that my boobs were a lot bigger than most of the other girls' but it had never bothered me before. I tried to think that maybe some of them were a wee bit jealous. But it was embarrassing and I felt bad. Next, they started to post doctored pictures of Page Three girls, and women from porno magazines, with my head on top. That really got to me, and I decided that I had to lose some weight."

"So that was why you started dieting?"

"Yes, and then I suppose it all just got out of hand. I still felt so bad all the time. I couldn't get away from those people; they were at school and at all of the activity clubs I went to. And I thought that if I was thinner, and my boobs were smaller, they would stop. I wanted to be a different person."

"And did you ever know who it was? Who'd posted the original photo?"

"No, not definitely, but I have my suspicions. And then later I think it was a whole group of them."

"Haven't you even told your doctors about this?"

"No, I was too ashamed, and it was too late to do anything about it anyway. The damage was done."

I felt really sad for Laura. What a horrible thing to have happened. I could understand how it must have eroded her confidence. It was doubly sad that she'd been unable to confide in anyone; that she'd felt so alone. "Well, thank you for telling me," I said. "I don't think that anything you did was so very terrible. You're right, you know. Those other girls were probably jealous of you."

"Yeah, that's what I believe now. And obviously I've had a lot of time to think things through."

"Do you think that it would help to tell your doctor or your parents?"

"I don't know. I'll wait for a bit; see how I feel after telling you. But I think it's been good to share it with at least one person."

"Well, I won't say anything," I reassured her.

"No, I know that. And I definitely feel better being here, and at a new school where I don't have those pictures hanging over me."

"Yes, I can imagine," I agreed.

"But I caused a lot of worry and trouble, with the anorexia."

"That wasn't your fault, Laura. You were ill; no one blames you." The last thing I wanted was for her to start feeling guilty about her illness next.

"Yeah, that's what my doctor says. I try to believe him."

When we got home, Laura hurried off to her room, telling me that she had homework to complete for the next day. It was still sunny with no wind, so I gathered up some sections of the Sunday paper and went out to sit on the bench by the

French windows overlooking the garden. Before I unfolded the newspaper, I surveyed the garden and congratulated myself; my work had paid off and the flowers were making a good show. The roses were on to a second bloom, thanks to my deadheading, and the Japanese anemones and Michaelmas daisies were in full flower.

I couldn't really settle to reading; Laura's story was disturbing me. It had obviously been a terrible ordeal for her. I recalled some details from the reading on anorexia that I'd done when we were stuck in Edinburgh and I'd been trying to understand Laura's condition. There had been several references which described how anorexia was often about a girl 'taking control' and 'being in control'. That made a lot of sense now. In Laura's case, she hadn't been able to control the emergence of the images on social media, or people's reactions to them. But she could control her diet. I was flattered that she had trusted me enough to confide in me, as had Mairi before her. But I wished that I could share her story with Grant. I knew that he felt partly to blame for her illness. Some of the comments that he'd made about Mairi applied to Laura too. In particular, he thought that his divorce had had a damaging effect on his daughters. What Laura had told me would help him to understand that his guilt was unfounded. Unless she'd have been more likely to confide in her parents if they'd been together. But who could be sure about that?

I decided to go and speak to Grant. I thought that he was down in his office, so I dumped the paper, unread, on the bench and walked down the track to the bungalow. I could see him through the window. His dark curls were bent over the computer keyboard; he was typing. I tapped on the window and waved, then walked round to the door and let myself in.

"Hi. Number one daughter is delivered to the ferry, then?" he greeted me.

"Yes. And I was thinking; if we want to see her, and Fiona, any time soon we'd be best to go to Glasgow. Mairi was saying how hectic their weekends are with sports fixtures and her riding. Laura would be keen to visit too."

"Aye, I think you're right. I've been thinking too."

"Oh?"

"Aye, you're not the only one. I think that we should book a trip to Barcelona in the October school holiday. You and I both need a holiday."

"Won't Ruth expect to have Laura for the October week?"

"Well, I've checked that, and they don't actually get the same week off. Different areas take different weeks."

"So, it would work out. I love Barcelona, and Laura would be so pleased to meet up with Alejandro again. So would I, actually. That would be great. How about if we fly from Glasgow? We could spend a couple of nights there first, then go to Spain. We don't need to be there for a whole week."

"You're a genius. Let me just finish these figures, then we can have a look at what's available. Bring a chair over."

"I'll put the kettle on. Do you want a cup of tea?"

"Sure. Laura's going to be so excited about this. I can't wait to tell her."

I smiled; I'd put something positive in motion. I couldn't change the past, but at least I could try hard to make things work for Laura now, and in the future.

Chapter 30

"Hello, madam. Are you ready to order?"

I looked up from the meze menu that I was studying. The waiter had dark hair, and his arms looked very tanned next to his white shirt.

"My friend hasn't arrived yet. Could I have a glass of the Pinot Grigio and some bread and olives while I'm waiting, please?"

"Of course. I'll bring that straight away."

He hurried off and I checked my phone to see if there was any message from Jess. We'd arranged to meet for lunch on the South Bank, but she was obviously running late. I'd just seen that there was no message when she rushed up to the table.

"Whoops, sorry I'm a bit late," she greeted me, breathing hard.

I rose to hug her. "No worries. How are you?"

It was over a year since we'd last managed to meet up and Jess looked very well, but she was no longer the slave to fashion that she used to be. While still not fat, she'd gained at least a stone in weight and now seemed to dress mainly for comfort. Today she wore flat ballet-style pumps, coral-coloured cropped chinos, and a white peasant-style blouse with three-quarter length sleeves and white embroidered detail around the neck. Her dark hair was cut short, and she wore no jewellery and minimal make-up. I was sure that I'd also changed in the past twelve years, and I didn't have the excuse of having three children for any lowering of standards. But living in the country meant that my wardrobe was definitely more casual than it had been when I was working here in London.

"I'm well," Jess replied. Then, as the waiter brought my wine, bread and olives, "Oh, I'll have a glass of the same wine, please. It's so great to see you, Claire. I wish that you didn't live so far away."

"I've missed you too. How are the kids? And Chris?"

"They're all fine. Should we choose what we're going to order before the waiter comes back? Then we can chat uninterrupted."

We agreed to share a variety of dishes, and settled on our six favourites. After we'd given our order, Jess filled me in on her family news. She and Chris had two sons and a daughter and had moved out from the city to Sevenoaks in suburban Kent. Two of the children were now at school and the youngest was at nursery. Jess had left the high-powered world of advertising and retrained as a classroom assistant. She now worked part time at the local primary school.

"It's really handy: no commute, and the same holidays as the children."

"And do you enjoy it?" I asked. I found it hard to envisage Jess, who had led life at a frenetic pace, having much patience with slow learners, or children with difficulties.

"OK, some days are boring, but it can be exciting when one of the kids makes a real breakthrough. And I think that I'm finding my creative side with all of the arts and crafts projects."

I must have looked doubtful.

"Seriously, I'm thinking of taking art classes at night school."

"Good for you, Jess." Then I brought her up to date with our news: Laura's recovery, Mairi's coming out, and the puma.

"Well, you've certainly not been having a quiet life, despite living in the sticks," she commented.

"No, it doesn't seem to work that way," I agreed.

"And are you OK now with Laura in permanent residence? I seem to remember that you were a bit doubtful about how that would work out."

"It was incredibly stressful when she first arrived. She was so frail, and we had to watch over her at every meal to make sure that she ate, but at the same time we weren't meant to make a big thing about eating. I felt that I was walking on eggshells the whole time. But now that she's better, it's fine. She's made friends at school and she's good company."

"And what about the Ruth thing? You were really freaked out about that. What did Grant say?"

I realised that I must have phoned Jess when I was staying in Edinburgh during the time that Laura was in hospital. I'd spent a lot of that time on my own while Grant was visiting her, and must have spoken to Jess when I was particularly stressed out. "I think that I probably overreacted. In the end, I didn't even say anything to Grant. I spoke to Isla about it, and she thought, from my description, that Ruth must have changed quite a bit. But she still didn't think that we were very alike, so I felt better about it after that. I'm sorry; I must have offloaded on you when I was having a bad day."

"That's OK – it's what friends are for, isn't it? I'm glad to hear that it's all worked out. But remind me: why have we been graced with a visit from the far north?"

"Well, my parents want to retire and we need to agree on what to do with their side of the business," I explained. After the busy summer months, my dad had eventually raised this subject with me. I hadn't confessed to him about overhearing their discussion earlier in the year, but I was glad that I'd had some warning. It had given me time to think about the future of the business, and to talk things through with Grant. "We're hoping to find someone who'll take on the Tunbridge Wells shop and be interested in maintaining a partnership with me. I've thought it all through and I don't think that it would work for me to be responsible for Dad's shop at a distance, even if we could find a good manager. And I think my shop is a bit small to be able to go it alone."

"So, have you found someone who's interested?"

"We hope so; I'm going to meet him tomorrow. He's already got his own place locally, but is apparently looking to expand."

"Sounds promising."

"Well, Dad's met up with him a few times and they seem to get on. But I need to get to know him myself to see if we hit it off and can agree terms."

"Good luck with all of that, then. Do you think you'll be down to visit more often in the future?"

"I don't know, but I don't see myself ever living in London again. I've decided to put my flat on the market. I hope it'll make me enough money to buy half of Dad's business. It should definitely go a long way towards it."

"That's really burning your bridges."

"It's hardly impetuous, though, Jess. I've lived with Grant for ten years and we've been married for nine of those. I'm not really a city type anymore."

"No, I don't suppose that I am either. Chris and I are content to live the suburban life."

"But you must come up to Mull with the kids for a visit soon. Maybe next Easter or summer? Say you will."

"I promise to think about it. But it's quite a journey; a very long drive with three restless kids."

"Oh, we never drive. I've left the car at Glasgow airport. Or, if you don't want to fly, you can do most of the journey by train, right to Oban. The kids would think it was an adventure, and they'd love the ferry. There's lots to do on the island: castles to explore, animals to see, boat excursions."

"You should get a job with the tourist board."

"I'll take that as a compliment, coming from an ex-advertising whizz. But I'm going to have to run now. I've got an appointment with the estate agent about selling the flat."

When we parted, I thought that I might have persuaded Jess that a Scottish holiday would be fun. I could keep up the pressure via email and texts.

The next day I walked with Dad across Tunbridge Wells to the shop. My potential new business partner was meeting us there at ten o'clock. The bell on the shop door pinged at five to ten. I looked up to see a slim man of medium height entering. He was neatly dressed in light grey chinos and a navy guernsey sweater with a pale blue shirt showing at the collar. His hair was dark blond, straight, and cut short at the sides but longer and floppy on top. He had grey-blue eyes and a small moustache.

"Hello, I'm Max Kiszka. I'm guessing that you're Claire Ford." He approached with his right hand stretched out. We shook hands.

"Hi, yes, I'm Claire. My married name is Maclean, but I keep Ford for work since it fits in with the business. Dad's in the back. Would you like a coffee?"

"Yes, that would be great. Black, no sugar," he replied.

I called through to Dad and he offered to make the drinks while Max and I began to get acquainted. We sat on high stools behind the main counter.

"Edward has been kind enough to show me round here. It's a superb location, isn't it?" Max looked around as he spoke, and he sounded enthusiastic.

"Yes, we get a good footfall, being right in the old town. Where's your shop?"

"It's in Crowborough; on Crowborough Hill, quite near to the crossroads with the A26. So, I get a fair bit of passing trade, but it's much smaller than these premises; not really in the same league. I'm really keen to step up a few rungs on the ladder."

Dad appeared with a tray holding three coffee mugs and a plate of biscuits. "I gave Max the accounts from both of our shops, and some photos of the Tobermory premises," he told me. "What did you think, Max?"

"Things look very healthy. I see that you're just renting the shop on Mull. Would you consider buying?" Max asked me.

"It's never come up so far. But maybe in the future if the owner wanted to sell. The location is brilliant; right by the harbour. I don't think I could be better situated."

"And the craft workshop next door is quite a draw," Dad added.

"You should come up for a visit," I suggested.

"Yes, I think that Max should certainly do that before making any firm agreement," Dad advised.

"And, Claire, you should come to see my place. It will give you an idea of my interests and current stock," Max said.

"Well, my flight back isn't until Friday, so I could drive down if Mum lends me her car."

"I'm sure that won't be a problem." Dad smiled.

"Do you want to know a bit about my background?" Max offered.

I nodded.

"So, I'm second-generation Polish. My grandparents on my father's side moved to England during the war; my father was just a small boy. He met my mother at a Polish social centre in London. In those days it was a tight community; most families seemed to interact only with other Polish people. But my sister and I, we're British. We mixed more at school and made wider friendships."

"How did you get into the antiques business?" I asked.

"Funnily, it started out as a Saturday job when I was a teenager. A Polish friend of my dad's had a shop close to our house in Ealing. He probably gave me the job as a favour to my dad. But I was intrigued by the objects and the business, and I spent a lot of my free time and holidays there. Then Lukasz began to coach me; he took me to sales and gave me reading materials. I've just gone from there."

We'd finished our coffee, so I suggested that I check with Mum that I could have the car, and then let Max know when I could visit.

"If you plan to come late afternoon you could have dinner with us. My wife would love to meet you."

"OK, I'll try to come tomorrow at about half past four if the car's available. I'll send you a text to confirm once I've spoken to Mum."

We shook hands all round and Max departed.

"Well, what do you think?" Dad asked.

"He seems perfectly nice, and very enthusiastic," I replied. "But I think it's a good idea to meet a few times and get to know each other better. Do you have his accounts for me to look over?"

"Yes, they're through the back, I'll get them. He's making a respectable profit."

That sounded encouraging. I had a good feeling about Max, but I didn't want to rush into anything.

On Friday morning I had a leisurely breakfast with Mum as my flight wasn't until mid-afternoon.

"So, do you think it'll work out with Max?" she asked me.

"Yes, I think so. Dinner with his family was nice; I had a good time. His wife is really friendly and they have such adorable twin daughters. Max is planning to come up to Mull for a visit after we get home from our Barcelona trip."

"Oh yes, the Spanish excursion. Is Laura still sweet on that student?"

"Yes, but I think she's also realistic – she understands that although Alejandro is friendly, that's as far as it goes."

"She'll be meeting more boys of her own age now that she's at school."

"Yes, not that I've heard her mention anyone. But what about you and Dad? What are you going to do with yourselves once you don't have a shop to run?"

"Well, we've got a few travel plans. I've always wanted to visit my cousin, Christine, in New Zealand. And your dad wants to go to California, to drive the Pacific Coast Highway and see the giant sequoia. We're thinking of taking bridge lessons, and maybe joining the bowling club. I don't think we'll be bored. There are a lot of things that we've put off doing because we were too busy, so now we'll do them."

"And you'll still come up to visit me?"

"Of course we will. It'll be funny, though. The shop will still be there, but it won't be any of our concern. I should think that you'll even change the name."

"Max and I talked about that a bit. We didn't think that any combination of Ford and Kiszka, or Kiszka and Maclean, went very well together. Currently, Tunbridge & Tobermory Antiques is our working brand name."

"Mm, that might work." I thought that Mum sounded wistful.

"You don't mind, do you?" I asked, suddenly concerned.

She smiled. "No, not at all. We're looking forward to the freedom."

That conversation came back to me later that afternoon as I was driving. My parents must have mixed feelings. They would appreciate a more relaxed lifestyle with time for travel and hobbies. But it must be difficult to hand over your life's work to someone else, and to be aware that any new owner is going to make changes, do things differently.

I'd driven over the Erskine Bridge and Loch Lomond was on my right side, sparkling in the late afternoon sunshine. I wasn't in a rush; I was booked onto the last ferry crossing and had plenty of time to get there. So, I could take my time and enjoy the views as I travelled the now-familiar road which meandered along the western lochside.

I sighed and felt a release of tension from my shoulders. I'd had a productive week. The two meetings with Max had gone well, I'd put my flat on the market, and I'd convinced myself that my parents would be contented in their retirement.

When I drove this road on my own, I often thought back to my first journey here. Today it made me wonder about fate; how my life could have taken a completely different course. If Murdo Maclean hadn't died and left his castle to be valued, there would have been no assignment to take me to Mull. And if Miles White's mother hadn't died, he would have made the trip instead of me. I might still be preparing to take over the Tunbridge Wells business from my parents, but it was most unlikely that Grant and I would ever have met. My old lifestyle wouldn't have overlapped with Grant's at all. That was a scary thought – how could the things that were most precious to me now have relied on such flimsy chance occurrences?

I gave myself a shake and decided to stop the philosophical worrying; my mum always said that worrying was a waste of energy, because it didn't have the power to change anything. And all these things were in the past now anyway. Perhaps everything in my life wasn't perfect, but I enjoyed living as I did. And I was very happy to be travelling home.

Author's Note

This book is a work of fiction. None of the characters are
real people, and although they visit some real locations,
the houses and businesses belonging to the characters do
not exist.

The *San Juan de Sicilia* did sink in Tobermory Bay on 5th
November 1588 following an explosion. There were rumours of
Spanish gold, and there have been numerous diving expeditions:
but no 2017 Spanish expedition took place.

There has never, to my knowledge, been a wild puma on
the loose on the island of Mull. Pearl's story is inspired by that
of 'the Puma of the Glen'. That animal was captured in 1980 by
farmer Ted Noble at Cannich, near Drumnadrochit. Sightings
had dated back to 1976. The puma, thereafter known as Felicity,
lived in the Highland Wildlife Park at Kingussie until her death
in 1985. She was then preserved by a taxidermist and is now on
display in the Inverness Museum.

Acknowledgements

'd like to thank Dave Hill for another great cover design. I love the result; a classic Scottish castle.

Thanks to David Miller for his inspired thinking when a book title is required; and for all of his support for my writing projects. Thankfully, he thoroughly enjoyed our research trip to Mull.

The team members at Matador have been approachable, easy to work with and efficient. In particular I'm grateful to my editor, Faye Booth. In addition to her eagle eye for dodgy spelling, grammar and punctuation, she provided comments which were helpful and thought-provoking.

The following two books provided me with additional insight and information about the condition of anorexia nervosa:

How to Disappear Completely by Kelsey Osgood
Brave Girl Eating by Harriet Brown

 Matador

For exclusive discounts on Matador titles,
sign up to our occasional newsletter at
troubador.co.uk/bookshop